OUR

Tantoo Cardinal

Tomson Highway

Basil Johnston

Thomas King

Brian Maracle

Lee Maracle

Jovette Marchessault

Rachel A. Qitsualik

Drew Hayden Taylor

ABORIGINAL VOICES
ON CANADA'S PAST

STORY

Preface by RUDYARD GRIFFITHS

Foreword by ADRIENNE CLARKSON

ANCHOR CANADA

With support from:

Where Energy Meets People
www.enbridge.com

Enbridge, the Enbridge logo, and Enbridge Energy Spiral are trademarks or registered
trademarks of Enbridge Inc. in Canada and other countries.
Anchor Canada and colophon are trademarks.

LIBRARY AND ARCHIVES CANADA CATALOGUING IN PUBLICATION

Our story : Aboriginal voices on Canada's past / Tantoo
Cardinal . . . [et al.]; foreword by Adrienne Clarkson.

ISBN 0-385-66076-6

1. Short stories, Canadian (English). 2. Canadian fiction (English)—Native authors.
3. Native peoples—Canada—History—Fiction. 4. Canada—History—Fiction.
5. Historical fiction, Canadian (English). 6. Canadian fiction (English)—21st century.
I. Cardinal, Tantoo

PS8235.I6O97 2005   C813'.010806   C2005-903306-1

Cover image: Hans Neleman/Getty Images
Cover design: Leah Springate
Printed and bound in the USA

Published in Canada by
Anchor Canada, a division of
Random House of Canada Limited

Visit Random House of Canada Limited's website: www.randomhouse.ca

BVG   10   9   8   7

Contents

THE STANDARD TEXTBOOK HISTORY of Aboriginal peoples begins twelve millennia ago as the world was coming out of an Ice Age. The ancestors of Canada's Aboriginal peoples crossed the Bering Strait from Siberia to North America. Moving steadily south and east, over the course of hundreds of generations, the descedants of this original group of explorers won for themselves a continent. In the path of their migration, up and down the face of North and South America, they created a quilt-work of civilizations, each with its own history and values. Over the millennia these nations rose, fell, and evolved in concert with the larger rhythms of nature.

Flash forward to the early 1500s when our conventional narrative gathers steam. Along the eastern shore of North America the first European explorers make their landfalls and experience the 'first contact' that gave Canada its name. The arc of history moves through the early wars of conquest to the establishment of the first permanent European settlements in the 16th and 17th centuries. To Canadians, the signposts in this historical journey are a series of familiar dates strung out in succession: Jacques Cartier landing at Chaleur Bay in 1534, Champlain's voyage up the St. Lawrence in 1603, and the creation of the Hudson Bay Company in 1670.

Having witnessed the European migration to their land, Aboriginal peoples are moved figuratively to the sidelines of history. The standard history of Canada from the 17th century onward is the story of European colonial wars, the introduction and impact of Western technology and industry, and the deepening of a North American political culture based on the ideas of the Enlightenment. Increasingly strangers in their own lands, Aboriginal peoples come to be perceived, more and more, as an administrative challenge as opposed to a dynamic force in the unfolding of the country's identity. The combined effects of the treaty and reserve systems, the failed Rebellions of 1885 and subsequent Indian Acts all conspire to render Canada's Aboriginal peoples an historical anachronism in the eyes of the dominant culture. This sentiment, in various forms, has continued up to the present-day despite a decades-long revival of Aboriginal culture, industry, and government.

Even this most cursory look at the traditional narrative of the history of Aboriginal peoples confirms that we read their story through our systems of understanding. It is difficult, if not impossible, for one culture to capture the historical reality of another culture that it has displaced. As hard as non-Aboriginals might try to correct for biases, our history and traditions are different. European culture sees the passage of time as a chronology of events as opposed to cycle of being and becoming. It embraces scientific criteria to determine what is an historical fact and looks askance at myth and oral history. And ultimately, it stresses the very process of historical inquiry as a hallmark of civilization. All of these attitudes not only set Western culture apart from an Aboriginal world view, they determine the very way history is recorded, created, and conveyed to future generations.

This is not to say that Aboriginal and non-Aboriginal cultures are incapable of creating common understandings and mutual respect. What we need to work on is finding new ways—after more than four hundred years of living together—to hear each others' stories anew, to step out of preconceived notions of not only what constitutes our history but how our history is constituted. *Our Story* is an important contribution to moving dialogue in this direction.

The nine works of fiction contained in this volume tell the story of Aboriginal peoples in Canada not as a string of facts laid bare in chronological order. Instead, each of the Aboriginal authors has chosen an historical event and through the act of storytelling, turned it into a work of fiction. In each of these fictionalized accounts we are exposed to the Aboriginal sense of place, the passage of time, and the complex relationship of myth and truth. The result is a new vantage point not just on how Aboriginals perceive their place in Canadian history but a different approach to recounting the past and making it come alive in the present.

As a fusion of Aboriginal and non-Aboriginal notions of storytelling and history, *Our Story* contains, at its heart, the basis for the two cultures not only to better understand and appreciate each other, but also to move forward together.

Rudyard Griffiths

FOREWORD

As the years go by, the circle of the Ojibway gets bigger and bigger. Canadians of all colours and religions are entering that circle. You might feel that you have roots somewhere else, but in reality, you are right here with us.

IN MY INSTALLATION ADDRESS as Governor General, I cited these words of Chief John Kelly as a meaningful expression of the Aboriginal peoples' regard for all those who came later, for those who dispossessed them. Consider the baleful history that they have had to live; consider the almost total ignorance in Canada about that history and about their present situation. It is astonishing, then, the extent to which Aboriginal peoples still engage in intercultural dialogue with generosity, understanding and goodwill. When there is so much room and reason for misunderstanding, for bitterness and frustration, I have always marvelled at how measured, wise, yet impassioned *their* statement of their being is—the manner in which they tell their stories, the way in which they want to include the rest of us, although they still struggle to know what is theirs and to make it ever more deeply theirs.

A collection like *Our Story*—permeated with pain, struck by joy and veined with personal experience—is not only about what historical events can mean to different people, but also about how the threads of this collective narrative make a cloth that is strong and beautiful.

Just to look at the lives and work of these authors is to realize how our cultural life, and therefore our life as a nation, has been enriched by Aboriginal artists like these: Tantoo Cardinal, Tomson Highway, Basil Johnston, Thomas King, Brian Maracle, Lee Maracle, Jovette Marchessault, Rachel A. Qitsualik, and Drew Hayden Taylor. They speak not only as Aboriginal people but also as fine writers, who do everything that writers are supposed to do: create characters, engage emotions, dispel despair.

"A Blurry Image on the 6 O'Clock News" is a story set against the backdrop of an event not far in our past, the so-called Oka Crisis. Drew Hayden Taylor takes us there again—or more precisely, to Kanesatake—through the eyes of a white woman watching for the appearances of her ex-husband among the Mohawk protesters. The story of their love and of their breakup, of a mixed couple's struggle to find love and harmony, is a potent symbol of what we are still not quite able to do right—to live together.

This collection also reaches back for the deep background to the encounter between Aboriginal and non-Aboriginal. Brian Maracle's "The First Words" represents the drama of creation as *the* defining moment in the history of his people. As he notes, pivotal events with white people "have helped determine where and how we live, but they have not determined how we think or what we believe." His retelling of the Iroquois Creation Story evokes a world in which everything is held together in a loving tension, but also one in which things can fall off the edge. In the languages of the Six Nations confederacy, there are many ways to say "we," which can include not only the people speaking but those being spoken to. What a profound reverence for harmony, a concern for people and relationships that is built right into the creation tale *and* into the languages in which it has traditionally been told.

This myth provides the underpinning of the rest of *Our Story,* including Basil Johnston's "The Wampum Belt Tells Us." It emphasizes the importance of story and of the generosity of the land, as the *mazhinawae* recites the history of the Anishinaubae people and their encounters with whites. Their land and their story are gradually taken away and turned inside out. In spite of all this, dreams remain as "the unfulfilled desires of the spirit," but the recitation of the wampum sash ends with sadness and disillusion:

> Within a few years . . . the Indians were no longer free to come
> and go as they were once accustomed to do, for they no longer
> had anywhere to go. They now had Indian agents as masters.
> Missionaries came among them to tell them what was right
> and what was not. They were now no better off than the
> Pequots or the Narragansetts. In fighting for the White man's
> freedom, the Indians lost theirs.

Another history, retold and reclaimed, is found in "Skraeling" by Rachel A. Qitsualik, the story of the coming of white men—the "giant men [who] had killed without purpose," with ice-blue eyes and monstrous boats. All this is seen from the fascinating perspective of an Inuit man (the word Inuit means "those living here now") who encounters his "now-extinct cousins," the Tunit, just as they meet the Vikings. Qitsualik's beautiful description allows us to feel the eternity of the land and the shock that anything could happen to it or its age-old custodians, that anything or anyone could deny their fundamentally right place in the universe.

The image of the dream ending and the awakening to an unpleasant and unsought reality permeates the stories in this collection. As Lee Maracle writes in "Good-Bye Snauq," "I need to know what is ending so I can appreciate and identify with the beginning." There is a deep sense that the loss of property—in this case, a once-strong stream that was homeland and supermarket and sacred ground—is not just a transaction, as the negotiators might see it, but rather a loss of the limitless freedom and generous behaviour that comes from living in harmony with nature.

These stories look at the society and culture that have been created here, north of the 49th parallel, in a significantly different way than we generally do. Property is not simply to be possessed by someone who pays the most or cuts the best deal. When one character says, "no one in this country has to deal with ancestry in quite the way we must," it is a very poignant statement about possession and dispossession and the maintenance of Aboriginal identity.

For identity is essential to these stories. Métis life in the early 20th century, plagued by despair in the face of a proud history ignored, is seen through the eyes of Francis in Tantoo Cardinal's "There Is a Place.""I was lost, lost for a long while there," he says as he struggles to overcome grief and separation. Flashes of joy and hope lie in the closeness of forgiving relationships and the kind of history that is written from parent to child, or grandchild. "The Moon of the Dancing Suns" is by Jovette Marchessault, a Montagnais writer, and it finds hope in similar places as it explores the role of Aboriginals in two world wars. We should all know and be ashamed that they did not get the same financial and educational opportunities that our other veterans did after fighting for their country. In her tale, "while death galloped rapidly around the world," there is acceptance and a sort of redemption in the vision of children, even though their fathers, "like so many other Natives, were buried in the lovely Canadian military cemeteries somewhere in Europe. 'Kahgee pohn noten took,' the Crees say. This means, 'the battle is over.'" The gentle irony, the dance of hope and despair in these two stories, is heartbreaking.

In "Coyote and the Enemy Aliens" and "Hearts and Flowers," Thomas King and Tomson Highway deal with identity and the question at the very heart of racism: is the Other a human being? Even though our laws did not explicitly state that Aboriginal people were not human, they were routinely excluded from society. They were separated because they were Aboriginal, and this comes forward very clearly in King's sly and darkly humorous story of the connection between Aboriginal people and the Japanese

Canadians who were imprisoned and dispossessed during the Second World War. The trickster Coyote is again at work here, and the loss and humiliation of these two marginalized peoples is shown to be fundamentally inhuman and rather ridiculous. In Highway's telling, the long-withheld conferring of the vote to Aboriginals—in 1960!—preoccupies a young boy whose musical talent does not obscure his awareness that people like him, in the eyes of many, are not worth consideration. Appreciating and creating beauty make us truly human, yet there exist hideous structures and attitudes which reject this and cause the boy to suffer and wonder what it means to be a human being.

When we read a work of literary art, it should never be a purely didactic exercise, a moralizing lesson. It is something that pleases us and helps us to understand what we haven't experienced, what we might not have known that we didn't know. That's what *Our Story* does. That's why these stories are important. These are voices which we must all listen to, for they form a part of all that we are. And they tell an amazing tale.

Adrienne Clarkson

BRIAN MARACLE

The First Words

CONTRIBUTOR'S NOTE

WHEN I WAS INVITED to write about a "defining moment" in our people's history, I considered and immediately rejected obvious dates of great historical significance like 1492, when Columbus was discovered. And 1527, when Pizarro unleashed the holocaust of epidemics that eventually wiped out fifty million people. I rejected recent Canadian dates like 1982, when "aboriginal and treaty rights" were enshrined in the Constitution.

I also rejected significant events in the history of my own people, the Rotinonhsyón:ni—the people of the Six Nations Iroquois Confederacy. The people here in my home community of Grand River have long memories and a strong sense of history, and many would nominate 1779 as a defining moment. That's when George Washington burned our villages to the ground, thus earning him the Iroquois name that he and all the subsequent presidents of the United States are known by: Ranatakáryas, the Town Destroyer. Many would say a defining moment was 1784, when we were forced to move from New York State to the Grand River Territory. Others would say one was 1799, when the Seneca chief Skanyatarí:yo had a vision that led to the establishment of the longhouse "religion" that has kept our language and culture alive in the face of five hundred years of pressure to assimilate. And still others would choose 1924, when the Canadian government outlawed the traditional chiefs and—at gunpoint—installed an elected band council, creating a rift that has plagued our community to this day.

All of these were pivotal moments in our history, it's true. But all of them involve our interactions with so-called "white people." They were not about *us*. Most of them involve things that happened *to* us. They have helped determine where and how we live but they have not determined how we think or what we believe. The event that determined those things, that determined our true nature, the event that defined us as a people without reference to others, occurred a very long time ago.

But it wasn't, as some might think, the founding of the Iroquois Confederacy. Even though that event predates European contact and certainly was a defining moment in our history, it is not about our true self. We created the Confederacy as a reaction to a crisis we were facing. At that time the nations of the Iroquois were warring with one another in an endless and devastating cycle of blood feuds. So, we are told, the Creator sent a messenger to the earth who persuaded our ancestors to stop all the killing and accept a life of peace. This man, known in English as the Peacemaker, also brought with him a set of laws that laid out how the nations would work together in a confederacy based on consensus. When he had finished, the Peacemaker had restored the world to a life of peace and harmony, the way it was at the time of Creation.

And it was *that* time—the moment of Creation—that was *the* defining moment in our history. That was when our character as a people was determined. That was when we were given the gift of speech and, with it, a unique way of looking at and understanding the world. That was when we were given the sacred responsibilities that shape our lives. That was the moment that shaped how we think and what we believe.

The First Words

The woman took a quick breath, opened her eyes, sat up, and looked around. She was sitting on a riverbank, surrounded by flowers and an abundance of plant life. Every variety of bird and animal stood, perched, or floated nearby, watching her. She was young, she was beautiful, and she was naked.

Hundreds of pairs of eyes silently watched her as she struggled to absorb everything in sight. Everything—*everything*—was entirely new to her and she was overwhelmed by the beauty and the wonder of it all. Every one of the creatures and plant forms, she noticed, was so different from every other and, as she looked down at herself, so different from her as well.

And then she noticed that one pair of eyes watched her with greater interest and intensity than all the others. They belonged to a creature whose life form was much like her own. She sensed a kinship with this being whose body glowed softly from within.

"Ónhka ní:se?" she asked at last. "Who are you?"

"Konya'tíson ní:'i," the being replied. "I am the one who made you."

"Ónhka ní:'i?" she asked. "Who am I?"

"Sónkwe ní:se," came the reply. "You are a human being."

"Oh ní:yoht takya'tíson?" she asked. "How did you make me?"

"Enkonna'tónhahse," the being replied. "I'll show you."

With a few quick movements, the glowing being reached down, scooped up a handful of clay from the riverbank, and shaped it into the doll-like form of a man. The being then laid the doll-like figure on the riverbank next to the woman and gently blew into its mouth. Instantly, the clay doll was transformed into a human being. Hair grew out of its head, skin covered its body, and facial features appeared. The man took a quick breath, opened his eyes, sat up, and looked around.

Like the woman, the man sat silently at first, awestruck and struggling to comprehend everything before him. The woman and the glowing being waited, saying nothing. Finally, the man began focusing his attention on the woman. He noticed that he did not have the breasts or the shape of the woman. Instead, he had the same muscles and form as the glowing figure. In spite of his physical resemblance to the glowing man he felt a greater kinship with the woman. And it was to her he spoke.

"Ónhka ní:se?" he asked. "Who are you?"

"Kónkwe . . . tenon . . . tenónkwe," she replied hesitantly. "I . . . we . . . we're human beings."

"Ónhka ne raónha?" the man asked. "Who is he?"

"Shonkwaya'tíson," she answered. "He is the one who made us."

"Ka' nítewe's?" he then asked. "Where are we? What is this place?"

The woman, not knowing what to say, looked to the glowing being.

"*Tsyatahonhsí:yohst, keniyén:'a,*" he said. "Listen well, my children." He then settled himself on the ground before them and continued. "Enkenikaratónhahse. I will now tell you the story of this place and how you've come to be here. It's a long story and you must listen well."

The man and woman quickly nodded agreement and the glowing man began.

"É:neken tsyatkáhtho," he said. "Look up, into the sky."

The man and woman then tilted their heads back and scanned the sky.

"You see the flying creatures, the clouds and the sun, do you not?" he asked.

"Hén:'en," the humans responded. "Yes. We see all those things and it is all so beautiful."

"It is not within your power to see beyond the deepest part of the sky," the glowing man continued, "but I want you to know there is another world above this one, a sky-world. It is a special and beautiful place, just like here. And there are beings who live in the sky-world. They look much like you and me. And one day you and I, and many others, will all live together there."

The human beings did not know how to respond and sat there, silent, and the glowing manlike being continued.

"In the sky-world, there are manlike beings and womanlike beings. After they live together for a time, the womanlike being will bear a child. This, too, will happen to you one day."

The man and the woman looked at each other, bewildered, but said nothing.

"Many, many days ago, there was a womanlike being in the sky-world whose stomach grew bigger and bigger, a sign that she would soon bear a child.

"But one day the woman became sick. She was barely able to walk. She said to her elder brother, 'We must go to the shining tree. It is there I will find the medicine I need to make myself well again.' So the two of them journeyed to the centre of the sky-world where the shining tree stood.

"This tree is a giant tree," the glowing man-being said. "Its limbs are heavy with blossoms, fruit, and nuts of every kind. It glows from within with the light of a sun that never sets.

"At the base of the tree grow the medicine plants that the beings of the sky-world use to make themselves well. When the woman and her brother arrived at the shining tree, the brother began digging the medicine roots and the woman began gathering the medicine leaves and flowers. Soon the woman had made and taken her medicine and was resting by the edge of the hole that her brother had dug.

"She looked into the hole but could not see its bottom. So she leaned over further and fell into the hole. She grabbed at the plants and roots at the edge of the hole but she could not stop her fall. She fell through the hole in the sky-world.

"Her brother reached out for her when he saw her begin to fall. He tried but he could not catch her. He looked down into the hole and saw her falling away into the blackness. He then went to the shining tree. He ate the fruit that hung from its limbs, and he began to glow from inside his body, just like the tree. He went back, lay down, and looked down into the hole, and his glowing face lit up the sky with the brightest of all light. He saw his sister falling further and further away.

"When his sister looked down, she saw nothing but water—water everywhere—as far as the eye could see. She fell and she fell."

The human beings, even though they had no knowledge of falling or death, grew fearful. Shonkwaya'tíson then stopped his storytelling and pointed with his chin to the birds that were flying overhead. "Shé:ken ken ne thí:ken?" he asked. "Do you see them?"

"Hén:'en. Otsi'ten'okón:'a nen né:'e," the human beings replied. "Yes. They are flying beings."

"Well," Shonkwaya'tíson continued, "the flying beings were there at that time, and they saw the woman falling and went to help her. A great flock of many different flying beings flew very close together and made a bed with their wings. They caught her and stopped her fall. But they soon grew tired. They wanted to rest but there was no place to put her down, so they called to the water creatures for help.

"All the creatures that inhabit the waters came to the surface to help the woman who had fallen out of the sky. One of them, A'nó:wara—the shell creature—rose from the waters and told the woman that she could rest on its shell. So the flying creatures placed the woman on A'nó:wara's back.

"The woman looked all around and saw only the hard, bare shell, the water, the sky, the flying beings, and the water creatures. She looked at her hands and noticed that many seeds and roots had stuck to her fingers when she fell through the hole in the sky-world. This made her think of her family and her home in the sky-world, and she became sad and lonely. She knew that the flying beings could not carry her back to the sky-world. They were too small, she was too big, and it was too far away. She knew she would have to live here, on the hard, bare shell of A'nó:wara.

"But, the woman thought, if only she had some earth, she could plant the seeds and roots that had stuck to her fingers and she could create a new life for herself on the shell creature's back. So she called the flying beings and the water creatures together. She asked them if they knew where to find some earth. 'There is earth at the bottom of the water,' they said."

Shonkwaya'tíson then told the humans to look at one of the water creatures floating nearby, a fat and furry one with a broad flat tail and long front teeth. "Tsyanì:to was the first to try. It dove for the bottom, and the woman and the other creatures waited and waited but Tsyanì:to never returned."

Shonkwaya'tíson then pointed to a long-bodied, short-limbed creature floating on its back nearby. "Tawí:ne was the next to try. It dove for the bottom and, like before, the woman and the other creatures waited a very long time but Tawí:ne never returned.

"The next creature to try," Shonkwaya'tíson said, "was that one— Anókyen," pointing to a round, brown furry creature that had burrowed into the riverbank. Its long, thin tail had no hair and it was the smallest of all the water creatures.

"Anókyen dove for the bottom, and the woman and the others waited. And waited. After a very long time, Anókyen finally rose to the surface. It was dead but it had a small piece of earth in its paws.

"The woman took the earth and placed it on the middle of the shell creature's back. After she planted the seeds and roots she had brought from the sky-world, she began to walk around the edge of the shell creature's back. As she walked, the earth on the shell began to grow. The more she walked, the more the earth grew. Soon the earth had completely covered over the shell creature's back. Finally, the time came when the woman gave birth to the child she was carrying, a daughter. The daughter grew up quickly, and she and her mother continued to walk around the edge of the earth and make it grow even more.

"One day, after she was fully grown, the daughter was lying down, asleep. As she slept, the wind from the west blew over her body. The west wind left two arrows resting on her stomach, one of them straight and sharp, the other bent and blunt. Her mother soon came and found her, woke her up, and showed her the two arrows. 'This is a sign,' the mother told her, 'that soon you will have children—twins.'

"Time passed and the daughter's stomach grew bigger and bigger. She was carrying twin boys. One was right-handed and had a good mind. The other was left-handed and had an evil mind. When the time came for them to be born, they began to argue about how they should leave her body.

"They could feel their mother's body pushing them outside. But the left-handed twin wanted to go out through his mother's side. The right-handed twin argued with his brother, trying to get him to follow him as he left. But the left-handed twin wouldn't listen and he tore his way out through his mother's side, and this killed her.

"So then the woman who fell from the sky buried her daughter and her body became one with the earth. From the head of her grave grew Ó:nenhste, Ohsahè:ta, and Onon'òn:sera."

Shonkwaya'tíson pointed at the plant life growing nearby. "There they are," he said. He pointed to the thin stalk that was taller than the human beings, its long leaves filled with tender kernels. He pointed as well to the vine of pointed leaves that twined up around the tall stalk bearing long, thin pods filled with seeds. He then pointed to the big-leafed vine that surrounded the stalk, shading its large gourds.

"These three sister beings are the foods you will use above all others to keep you alive. And those there," he said, pointing to a cluster of many different green growing things, "are Onónhkwa. They carry the medicines that you can use to make yourself well when you are sick, just as the sky-woman did before she entered this world.

"And one of the medicines," he added, "is that one, Niyohontéhsha, the one with a heart-shaped red fruit. It is sweet to eat and its juice is sweet to drink. Remember it well because a time will come when the plant life you see around you will stop growing and the earth will be covered by a cold white blanket for a long time. A wind from the south will bring warmth back to the land and the plant beings will grow again. Remember Niyohontéhsha, because it will be the first of the life-sustainers to appear when the cold time is over, and it will be a sign that more foods will come.

"And that there," Shonkwaya'tíson said, pointing to a broad-leafed plant with many small seed pods, "is Oyèn:kwa. It grew from where the heart of the daughter was buried. Its leaves are a messenger. You will need them one day to send your messages to me, because soon I will journey to the sky-world. You will put your thoughts into the dried leaves and put the leaves into a fire, and the smoke from the fire will carry your words to me."

The human beings sat there trying to absorb and understand it all, still saying nothing, so Shonkwaya'tíson continued.

"The woman who fell from the sky was sad and angry over her daughter's death and she called her grandsons to her. She named the right-handed twin Tharonhyawá:kon. She named the left-handed twin Thawíhskaron."

"The grandmother then asked the twins which one had killed her daughter. The left-handed one lied and said it was Tharonhyawá:kon who had killed their mother. He tricked his grandmother into believing him, so he became the twin she liked best. The grandmother then became angry with the right-handed twin, and she made him leave their lodge and live in the forest."

The thought of the woman sending her grandson away shocked the human beings.

"A great wrong was done to that boy that day," the glowing man-being said. Pausing slightly, he added, "And that boy was me."

The man and the woman were stunned. They looked at each other and looked at the glowing man-being, blinking, mouths open, struggling to comprehend everything that they had been told. Finally the woman said, "So you are the right-handed twin. You are Tharonhyawá:kon."

"Yes," he replied, "I am the right-handed twin. I am Tharonhyawá:kon. It was my grandmother who made me live in the forest. She was the one who fell out of the hole in the sky-world. It is her elder brother who brightens the sky during the day. It is my twin brother who ripped his way out of my mother's side and killed her. And it is my mother whose flesh we are resting on."

The man and woman were still speechless, so Shonkwaya'tíson—Tharonhyawá:kon—continued.

"When my grandmother pushed me out of her lodge and into the forest that day, the same wind that had blown over my mother's body—the west wind—my father—came up and swirled around me. He protected me from harm and whispered instructions that helped me find shelter in the forest. He helped me live and be strong. When I was fully grown, my father told me that I must make the earth ready for human beings—for you.

"And so then I began my work of creation."

Pointing to the long-legged, antlered animals standing nearby, he said, "I went across the earth and made Ohskennón:ton and Ska'nyónhsa." Pointing to the long-eared animals hopping nearby he said, "And I made Tehahonhtané:ken and Kwayén:'a. I made all these creatures so that their flesh will give you strength and their skins and fur will keep you warm.

"But when I had finished, my twin brother, Thawíhskaron, came along behind me and made other creatures to eat the creatures I had made." And here Shonkwaya'tíson pointed to Okwáho and Kén:reks—large, snarling, long-tailed creatures with big teeth and long claws that crouched nearby.

"I went across the land," Shonkwaya'tíson continued, "and laid down the waters. These are the waters you will use to sustain yourselves when you are thirsty. These are the waters you will use to travel about on this earth. I made these waters flow in two directions so that it would be easy for you to make your way.

"But again," he said, "my twin brother came along behind me and worked to undo what I had made. He spoiled some of the waters, making them undrinkable. He placed rocks in some of the waterways and made them flow in just one direction so that it will be hard and dangerous for you to travel.

"I then went to the waters and made Kéntsyonk." Pointing to the swimming creatures drifting in the river, Shonkwaya'tíson said, "I filled the waters with Kéntsyonk so that you could use their flesh to make you strong.

"And again," he said, "my twin brother came along after and undid what I had done. He made more creatures to eat the Kéntsyonk I made for you.

"I made many more foods grow from the earth. I made small crawling and flying creatures to help them grow. And again my brother came along after and spoiled what I had made. He made more crawling creatures to eat the foods I had made. He made growing things that will sicken you if you eat them. He made growing things that sicken the foods I had made. He made crawling creatures to eat the foods I had made. And he made crawling, flying, biting creatures to sicken you and all the creatures I had made.

"Everything I tried to make, he tried to spoil. Even those things I had no hand in doing, he tried to undo." Looking up at the sun, which was now approaching the horizon, Shonkwaya'tíson said, "With some of his power he made the sun fall from the sky every day.

"Thawíhskaron then told me that since he had the power to move the sun, he would be the master of everything on earth. He demanded that I go to the underworld while the sun was in the sky but I refused. We argued for a long time, and finally we decided to settle it with a contest. Whoever won the contest would go to the underworld.

"We began by playing Kayentowá:nen." The man and woman exchanged quizzical glances and Shonkwaya'tíson explained. "It is a game played with a large wooden bowl holding stones that are blackened on one side. I tossed the bowl and tried to get all the dark sides of the stones to land face up but I couldn't. Then my brother tried and he couldn't. We played the game for many days but no one won.

"So then we played Tehonttsihkwá:'eks." Again the man and woman looked confused and Shonkwaya'tíson explained. "We each took a long stick, bent the end and laced it back together so that it would hold a small round stone. We then used these sticks and the stone and struggled against each other. I tried to move the stone past my brother and couldn't. He tried to move the stone past me and he couldn't. We battled for many days but no one won.

"And then we began to fight. I grabbed my brother and pushed him to the ground. He grabbed me and pulled me down. He tried to hold me down but I broke free. I tried to hold him down but he broke free. Neither one of us was stronger than the other. One moment I was on top, the next moment he was. We fought for many days.

"All the creatures that Thawíhskaron and I had created had long stopped what they were doing and had come to watch us fight. After we had been fighting for many days I saw one of them, Ohskennón:ton, the long-legged, sharp-antlered one, lower its head to the ground and drop its antlers. I picked them up and used them to push my brother back. Their power helped me pushed my brother over the edge of the earth."

At this, Tharonhyawá:kon sat quietly for several moments before continuing. "My brother still lives in the underworld. He is there right now and he wants to come back and spoil more things on earth. But now that I have created you," he said, looking squarely at the man and woman, "he wants to come back and create mischief and trouble for you."

The human beings exchanged worried glances.

"Do not be afraid," he said, "I will watch over you and protect you. I have asked my grandfather—the husband of the woman who fell from the sky—to come down from his home in the sky-world to help you. He is Rawé:ras and he lives with the west wind. From time to time he will come with the west wind and bring the rains that will replenish the waters on earth that will sustain you. He will use his loud voice and his bright fire spears to keep my brother in the underworld. So now the only time my brother can leave the world below is at night. And because the sun is no longer in the sky, he has no power when he is here on earth. He can only prowl about."

"When I pushed my brother over the edge of the world, my grandmother became very sad. She liked my brother very much, she missed him greatly, and she died soon after. So I put her head in the sky so that she

24

would watch over the earth during the night and watch over her grandson when he comes up from the world below to move about.

"There was still one more thing that happened here on earth before I created you," Shonkwaya'tíson added. "I was walking through the forest one day when I met a manlike being. He said he was very powerful and could do many special things. He said that he had created all the swimming creatures, walking creatures, foods, and rivers on earth. I told him that it was not true, that I had created those things. So he challenged me to see who had the greater power. 'The one whose power is greater is the one who is telling the truth,' he said. I then told him to look in the distance, for there, far away, stood a great mountain. I challenged this being to use his power to move the mountain as far as he could. He stood there looking at the mountain, gathered all of his powers, and made the mountain move closer. He turned to me, smiled and said, 'It's true, you see. I have great power for I have moved a mountain.'

"'It's my turn,' I told him. And I looked at the mountain, I looked *hard* at the mountain, and made it fly to where we were standing. It flew across the valley with a great roar and a rush of wind. This startled the being and he turned to see what had caused it. He turned so fast that he smashed his face on the side of the flying mountain just as it came to rest at his feet. When he turned back around, his face had been pushed to the side; his nose was bent and his lips were twisted.

"The deformed being then said to me, 'Truly, it is you who has the greater power and it was you who created all the good things on earth.' I then told him of my plan to create you, the human beings, and he agreed to use his powers to help you. So if a time comes when you become sick, you may burn the dried leaves of Oyèn:kwa and call on him for help. He will come to you and you will know him by his twisted mouth and broken nose. He will help you and make you well again.

"And then everything was in place for me to make you."

"Oh ní:yoht takya'tíson?" the man asked. "How did you make me?"

"Enyesahró:ri," he answered. "She will tell you. And together you will tell your children everything I have told you."

The man and woman looked at each other and nodded.

"Yes, you will have children. Many children. And," he said, nodding at the sun which was now settling into the horizon, "you will have much to tell them because there is still more I must tell you before I leave.

"You now know how you've come to be here and how this earth and everything on it was created. You should know that this land and all of its wonders I made just for you. I have given you the knowledge of how to use all the many forms of life on earth to sustain yourselves. I have given you the knowledge of how to build your lodges, where to find and how to make the things you will need. Everything you will need to know is already within you.

"Before I leave this earth I will make more human beings. You will meet them. In time you and they will have children. Together your children and their children will have more children. And it is my wish that you will all live together and love one another. It is also my wish that you respect the earth and all the blessings that I have laid before you.

"Now consider this. I have given you life, this land, the knowledge of survival, and the ability to speak with one another, with the medicine beings, and with me. It is my wish that you will be grateful for all of these things; that you will give me your thanks every day; that you will celebrate the earth's blessings at mid-winter, at harvest time, and at other times throughout the year; and lastly, that you will pass on my words to your children and their children until the end of time. This is what I ask of you."

The first human beings sat silent for several moments as they considered the burden to be borne for the magnitude of Creation. Finally, they spoke together. "Tó:kenhske ki wáhi, eh nenyakení:yere tsi niyenhén:we." "Truly, we will do these things of which you spoke forever."

Their promise made, Shonkwaya'tíson stood up and gathered himself to leave. It was dark now. His body, which had softly glimmered during the day, was now glowing warmly and lighting everything around him.

"My work here on earth is nearly complete. I will soon journey to the sky-world."

The humans looked dismayed but Shonkwaya'tíson went on. "Your days here on earth are numbered and when you have reached their end, you will do as I do. You will walk the path of stars that lead to the sky-world, where we will meet one another again."

The man and woman stood holding each other as the Creator moved away, his glow fading into the distance, his grandmother's face shining brightly in the southern sky.

To most people, the story I have just told is just that—a story. Quaint and colourful, yes, but just a story. But it is far more than that to the people who have been telling it since Shonkwaya'tíson told it to the first human beings.

For starters, when Shonkwaya'tíson told the first human beings the story of their creation, it wasn't in English. He told it to them in *His* language—the language He gave them when He gave them the gift of speech. And beginning with the first human beings, our people have handed down the story of our creation in the Creator's language ever since. Only in the most recent generation has the story been widely shared in English.

And when Shonkwaya'tíson gave us our language, He gave us a unique way of looking at the world around us—*His* way. He made it clumsy for us to express things that involve negative concepts. For example, we don't have a word in our language for "zero," "empty," or "failure." We *can* say them but only by saying, "It isn't something," "It doesn't have something in it," or "Something did not succeed."

He did not make us obsessed with objects. If He had, He would have given us the need and the ability to separate, categorize, and classify everything on earth by giving them all different names, just as Western society through the English language does. He could have given us this obsession, but He didn't.

One thing He did give us through our language, though, is an obsession with people. We have many more ways of describing exactly who is doing what than English has. For example, although there is only one word for "we" in English, there are four in our language, depending on the number of people involved in the "we" and whether "we" includes the person being spoken to. As a result, we are much more precise and much less ambiguous than we are in English when we are talking about people—which is to say, nearly all the time.

From these few observations about our language, outsiders can gain a few insights into our traditional values and way of thinking—the way our Creator wants us to think. We know from the language that our Creator has given us that we should not think "negatively"; that we should not be obsessed with objects; and that we should be more concerned with people and relationships. Pretty good advice, don't you think?

One telling aspect of the Creation Story is that all the nations of the Iroquois tell the story the same way. Many details vary from one version to another but the major elements are all the same: a woman fell through a hole in the sky-world and came to rest on a turtle's back. She gave birth to a daughter, who died giving birth to twin boys. After creating the features of the earth, the twins battled for control. The right-handed twin won and created the first human beings with a handful of clay.

Those first human beings we call *onkwehón:we*, the real, first, original persons. Today we say that an *onkwehón:we* is someone who speaks the language of the Creator, who still carries the unique way of thinking and looking at life that stems from our language. More important, an *onkwehón:we* is someone who still honours the instructions of the Creator—who loves people and respects the earth and who gives thanks to Him.

The Creation Story gives all *onkwehón:we* a shared way of thinking and looking at the world. But it does even more than that.

It specifically tells us that the *onkwehón:we* did not arrive here on what we now call Turtle Island by walking over some land bridge from Asia.

It explains why we call the earth our mother, the moon our grandmother, the sun our elder brother, and the thunder our grandfather.

It explains why we spend so much time giving thanks in our longhouses and in our daily get-togethers.

It gives us comfort, security, and a sense of purpose.

It tells us that the only things we were given were the knowledge of how to survive on this land, the gift of speech, and the responsibility to give thanks, and that therefore things like aboriginal rights, tax exemptions, college tuition, and free prescriptions did not come from the Creator.

It tells us that the many social, economic, and political problems we now face are a distant second in importance to the overriding imperative that we honour our obligations stemming from the time of Creation.

Clearly, the Creation Story is more than just a story. We take its teachings to be the guiding light in how we conduct our lives. We honour our obligations, every day, all across Iroquoia, from Quebec to Wisconsin. In most of our schools and in every gathering of *onkwehón:we*, someone will stand and recite, in the Creator's language, the Ohén:ton Karihwatéhkwen—the words that come before all others. Known as the Opening Address or the Thanksgiving Address, this ritual gives thanks for all the blessings of Creation.

A short version may be just a few dozen words. A long, formal version may last forty-five minutes. But no matter who recites it and which language he uses (the speaker is traditionally a man), all of the speeches follow the same general pattern.

"Ó:nen sewatahonhsí:yohst kentyóhkwa," the speaker will begin. "Listen well, everyone who is now here assembled.

"It is my duty to recite the words of thanksgiving that come before all others. It is Shonkwaya'tíson's intention that whenever we gather together, we give thanks for all the blessings of Creation as our first order of business.

"So first of all, let us put our minds together as one and give greetings to all the peoples of the earth. And let us give thanks for all the peoples here gathered, that we have all arrived here safely, that we are all at peace and of a good mind. Let us remember those who could not be here because they are sick, and let us pray that they quickly regain their health. Let us remember as well and thank those who help us to keep our language and traditions alive.

"E'tho niyohtónhak nonkwa'nikòn:ra," the speaker will then say. "So let all of our minds come together as one on this matter." When the speaker finishes expressing this hope, the men in the crowd will respond on cue with a chorus of "Nyeah!" signifying that they are in agreement with what has just been said.

"And now let us give thanks to our mother the earth," the speaker will continue, "for all the blessings that she continues to provide for us. And let us give thanks to her for supporting our feet so lovingly as we walk about on the earth.

"E'tho niyohtónhak nonkwa'nikòn:ra," the speaker will add. "Nyeah!" the men will respond.

The speaker will then give similarly detailed thanks to all the elements of creation, beginning with the earth and reaching to the stars. He will give thanks to all the waters of the earth; the fish life that inhabits them; the insects; the medicine plants; the fruits, especially the strawberries; the food plants, especially corn, beans, and squash; the animals, especially the deer; the trees, especially the maple; the birds, especially the eagle; the four winds; the thunderers that bring the rains; the sun; the moon; the stars; Handsome Lake; and four special sky-beings who watch over human beings on earth.

Lastly, the speaker will tell the people to turn their faces to the sky-world where the Creator resides. "Let us put together our kindest and most loving words," he will say, "and throw them skyward to give Him our thanks for everything He has provided for us on this earth.

"E'tho niyohtónhak nonkwa'nikòn:ra," he will add. "Nyeah!" the men will respond.

Only when this sometimes lengthy ritual is finished can a meeting, or anything else, be started. And at the end of the meeting, before everyone goes home, a man will stand up and once again recite the verses of the Ohén:ton Karihwatéhkwen; the speaker reciting the reasons for being grateful and urging everyone to come to one mind, the men chorusing agreement.

The Thanksgiving Address, which constitutes the first words and the last words spoken at all of our gatherings, is a beautiful and impressive reminder of the abiding and loving relationship we are to have with one another and with all the works of Creation, and it reminds us that our relationship with the earth and our obligations to the Creator are more important than the day-to-day affairs of human beings.

"Nyeah!"

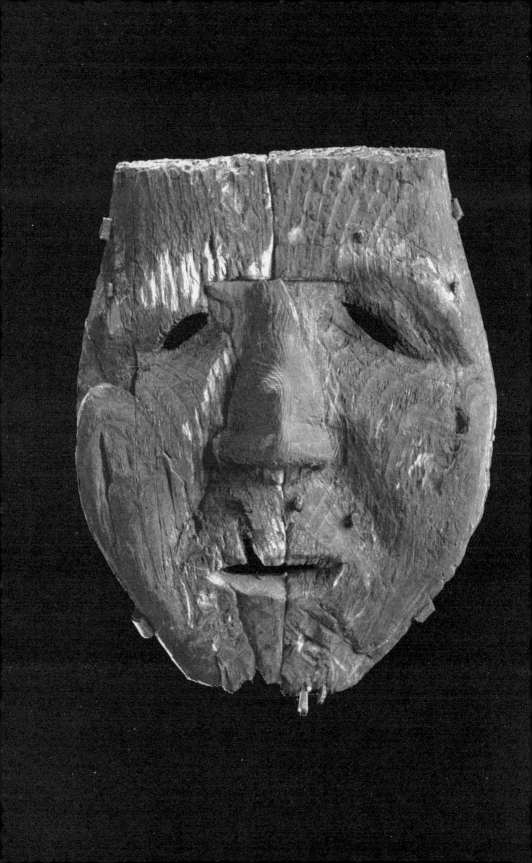

RACHEL A. QITSUALIK

Skraeling

CONTRIBUTOR'S NOTE

I ASSUMED, IN SETTING OUT to write this story, that I would require some psychological time travel. I should have known better. One forces nothing upon the Arctic, it seems—not even in fiction.

It was an understandable error. After all, from 800 to 1200 AD, the world was warmer, drawing the dogsledding progenitors of Inuit ("Thule") culture out of Alaska, overlapping the ancient habitations of their now-extinct cousins, the Tunit ("Dorset"). This story explores a possible meeting between these peoples, and one other, along Baffin Island's eastern edge.

When I step out in early summer, however, I still step onto the same land. I walk in the same hills that newly arrived Inuit walked in. I see the same orange lichens, the same spectacular purple of flowers in bloom, the same fat black spiders racing through the moss. The persistence of this land forbids true time travel. Instead, I can only drift, ghostlike, between the worlds of then and now, whose differences lie far more in people than in the land itself. For if the Arctic regarded itself, it would recognize no change, and the peoples that have settled or passed over time would be no more noteworthy than the spiders in the moss.

This leaves only a familiar challenge, that of dealing with culture. You see, I'm already a bit of a time traveller, old enough to remember a crazy shaman who used to get stuck in trances (needing my dad to snap her out of it) and young enough to remain sore about my mother smashing my Rolling Stones records. I've never had trouble reconciling "then" and "now," so I've been happy to explain my culture—whether through fiction or exposition—to others.

Which is exactly why I'm *avoiding* doing so in this story.

Some of the characters in this tale are bound to be doing and believing things that are puzzling to non-Inuit readers. Good. We live in a time when critical thinking is not "hip," when we demand a thorough explanation of everything presented to us, preferably in easy-to-read, brochure form. While this facilitates speed, it is also the cognitive equivalent of living on marshmallows.

I could go into great, galloping detail on how Inuit hold individual freedom to be sacred, about how open displays of violence are forbidden, or how confrontation is traditionally avoided. I could include an "inside" look at shamanism, making it accessible. But is this truly charitable? No, my feeling is that if the reader wants to understand a people, he or she has to live with those people for a while. And a story is the ultimate magic by which this may occur. Let the reader puzzle out those alien behaviours, as children might among adults. Let the reader feel the uncertainty of living in a little-understood land, as newly arrived Inuit might. Let the reader not feel comfortable with unseen powers seething in the very air, but instead feel the trepidation, uncertainty, and outright horror that early peoples knew.

Welcome to the land before it was named.

Skraeling

Kannujaq stood atop a ridge, while ravens wheeled and cursed from violet slopes.

He was soaked with sweat, but a chill nevertheless ran through him. It was unusually cold for spring, true, but no cold could so disquiet him. It was what lay among the shallow, winding valleys. Upon the hills.

All around him were *inuksuit*—structures of rock, in the image of men. Kannujaq recalled his grandfather's tales of how these were made by the Tunit, the elusive people who had occupied the land long before Kannujaq's people arrived. This was the way in which the Tunit hunted. Every year, the caribou would take paths that avoided the *inuksuit*. And every year, the Tunit herded them into kill zones. Kannujaq's grandfather had seen one such site: there the Tunit had left piles of bones, piles that could have accumulated only after generations.

Who would live like this? Kannujaq thought.

Being unmarried, Kannujaq travelled alone. He had almost become complacent over this last winter, used to being in one place. It had been a sweet, rich autumn of good fishing, better seal hunting. He had lived under a shelter of interlocking whale ribs, found all over the rocky shores of this area. There he had practised patience while living alongside the family of his hunting partner. Elders had spent all season telling him about the much harsher winters in the times of their forefathers. He had managed to escape around the time the ravens, those first nest builders of spring, began their nuptial dances in the sky. It had been a long winter.

(But, oh, how he and the others had brought in *tuugaaliit*, those small, dark whales with the spiralled tusks!)

For it was whales that drew Kannujaq, like everyone else, to this place, and ever eastward, deeper into the unknown lands, just as whales and walrus had lured his father, and his father before him. Kannujaq's father had not been much of a storyteller, but his grandfather had been an endless source of tales, most often of the lands their family and others had passed through, of how there probably was land and islands and hunting forever ahead.

Kannujaq could never know that his grandfather was wrong. What lay east of them was mostly a vast ocean. On its opposite side, there stood the Byzantine Empire at its strongest, the envy of lands Kannujaq would never know, places steeped in centuries of iron and bloodshed.

Kannujaq's grandfather also told of the trees back west, supposedly thicker and higher as one moved southward. Among these lived the Iqqiliit, tall and painted and fearsome. The old man could never have imagined that, even as he spoke his words to young Kannujaq, a Mayan king stood atop a pyramid temple engineered with advanced mathematics, sacrificing his sacred blood to bring victory in war.

Kannujaq would never know that, even as he recalled his grandfather's tales, another man, named Alhazen, who had been studying lenses in a land called Egypt, was pondering his findings on the nature of rainbows. Alhazen's young religion, called Islam, was only now losing momentum after sweeping across a world that, strangely, subsisted almost entirely upon grains.

In fact, if Kannujaq had known even one hundredth of what was occurring while he was staring across the amber hills, he would have been immensely grateful for his relative isolation.

He was spared the knowledge, for example, that the great lust of many peoples was for a substance called gold, which had just brought African Ghana to its peak. He had no idea that the world could hold so many people who would demand such trivialities. In a place eventually known as China, commerce was flourishing under the nascent Sung Dynasty, ruling over sixty million souls. Its emperor was even now troubled by distant, distant relations of both Kannujaq and the Tunit— called Mongols.

Kannujaq might have been even more confused by the place called Europe. There, the empire of Charlemagne had finally fragmented, its western portion becoming young France. France had been having a difficult time, having had to placate a force of Scandinavians, called Norsemen, by handing over Normandy to them.

These Scandinavians were not only a problem for France. Over the last few generations, Danes had taken over more than half of an island called England.

If Kannujaq had known anything at all about these Scandinavians, he would have been as terrified of them as the Europeans were. A tribe of them had already founded Russia. The Nordic kingdoms of Denmark and Norway were vying for supremacy. Scandinavians had already discovered Iceland, and completely dominated the Irish coastline. An exile called Eric had recently used Iceland to hop all the way across the ocean, founding a colony in a place he liked to think of as "Greenland."

Kannujaq would have been most startled to learn that these were the End Times. A Catholic church was telling all of its flock to expect judgment; for, by their calendar, it was 1000 AD.

And their world was in the grip of the Viking.

Kannujaq was regretting having taken this detour. It had led him away from the coast, and his dog team was having a rough time among the rocks.

He sighed and started back down to his sled as a low howl began to make its way over the wind. In a moment, it was joined by another, then several more, until there was a mad cacophony rising and falling among the hills.

Not wolves, he thought. *Tunit. Driving the caribou by imitating wolves.*

The Tunit were hunting here. He tried to suppress the creeping nausea that ran through him at their howls, comforting himself with the thought that the Tunit—while immensely strong—were supposedly cowards, running whenever they saw real people. They might resemble humans, albeit shorter, more squat, but they were little more than beasts.

Kannujaq decided not to bother them, slipping and sliding his way back down to where his dogs awaited.

Soon the sled was again making its tortuous way back toward the coast, rushing ahead on the occasional patch of snow, sticking, rushing ahead, sticking again.

Despite the tongues lolling from their heads with overexertion, Kannujaq began to notice that his dogs were growing excited, and it took him a moment to realize that this meant they were smelling a community ahead—a potential source of food. Kannujaq was fond of the idea as well.

The timing was perfect, for a storm was moving in and the light snowfall interfered with his distance vision. Fortunately, the days were growing long, so there was still enough light for Kannujaq to spot twisting lines of smoke in the distance, where the ground levelled out.

Kannujaq grinned as several figures came into sight. Camp dwellers. He began to urge his dogs forward, but paused. Something bothered him about this place.

Where are the dogs? he wondered.

Then he spotted one loose dog out of the corner of his eye, and felt a bit better.

Where is that thing running to? he thought. It disappeared into the haze of thickening snowfall.

He was startled by an odd noise, a thin cry. He turned back toward the approaching figures and realized they were running at him.

There was no time to reach his bow. He could think only to fumble about for his spear. But the figures did not attack. Instead, they turned out to be a mixed group of Tunit men, women, and children, dark faces twisted up in fear. Some were carrying babies, awkwardly, in their arms. The men and women among them were marked by odd hairstyles. Both had great lengths of it twisted up tightly, but the men wore theirs in a peculiar ball atop their heads, while the women wore clusters over each temple. All they shared was their shabby, sooty tops, their bear-fur pants, and their short, squat frames.

No wonder there are so few dogs here, Kannujaq thought. *I've stumbled into a Tunit camp.* He, like his dogs, no doubt, had assumed that this was a human encampment. What a mistake. Now he would be ripped apart by Tunit.

Yet the Tunit did not attack. They caught sight of Kannujaq and ground to a halt. Then they turned and ran in a different direction.

Not attacking. Running. From what?

Only a single boy, hooded and not quite of proper hunting age, did not run. Instead, he paused, seemingly mesmerized by Kannujaq's dog team. Kannujaq went forward with raised arms, to show that he meant no harm.

The boy began to speak excitedly, but Kannujaq had some difficulty understanding the words. It was almost normal language, but different—a Tunit dialect. Strangely, the boy was grinning from the depths of his vast hood, which mostly concealed a sooty face.

The boy kept pointing at him. In a few moments, Kannujaq seemed to grasp what he was saying: he was glad Kannujaq had come, and . . . he was late? The boy had expected him? Also . . . *they* were here. Them. They had come. There were other words as well, words Kannujaq couldn't quite make out. And there was one word that the boy kept repeating, but it was no use—Kannujaq simply couldn't penetrate the weird dialect.

He did, however, realize that the boy was not pointing at him. He was rambling on about the necklace around Kannujaq's neck. Upon it were strung claws from Kannujaq's first bear, along with a special bauble his grandfather had given him. There a tiny piece of his namesake was strung, a reddish loop of *kannujaq*. It was all that remained of his grandmother's awl acquired back in the west, where people sometimes melted the stuff from rocks. It was hard and cold and pretty; but, annoyingly, if not constantly polished, the reddish *kannujaq* turned green.

The boy seemed fixated upon it.

With gentle touches at his arm, the boy began to lead Kannujaq into the Tunit camp. There was something desperate about the boy, something that compelled Kannujaq to indulge him. As they went, the boy's grin faded, and his pronunciations became impossible to understand. Increasingly, his voice became wrung by emotion. Stiffly, Kannujaq forced one foot in front of the other, somehow feeling more childlike than the one he followed.

I am in a dream, he thought. *Yes, that's it. These are not real Tunit. I'm asleep.*

Yet the weather would not let him remain convinced that this was fantasy. It was worsening, and quick, sharp gusts were whipping crystalline particles about like sand. Whenever they relented for a moment, Kannujaq could see a squat figure or two in frantic flight, as before. Sometimes he stiffened upon hearing a scream.

In a few moments, he spotted a row of seven glowing fires—the peculiar way in which Tunit kept their cook-fires—lined up outside an enclosure of flat rocks, about waist-high. The boy led him around it, slightly downhill, toward the shore. When the snow was not stinging his eyes, he could see the corners and walls of other stone dwellings, as well as . . .

Bodies?

Upon the ground lay several dark heaps. The boy led Kannujaq, stumbling, past the dead, who lay like so many seals dragged up from the shore. The Tunit site was all bare stones, devoid of old snow or ice, but wherever Kannujaq's eyes were allowed to rest for longer than a heartbeat, he could see new, wind-driven particles becoming caught upon rocks, sticky with dark vital fluid already freezing. The boy began to lead him quickly. Other details were lost to him, but he had spotted enough for his brain to begin whispering: *This is a place of murder . . .*

No! He should have turned back as soon as he saw that this was a Tunit encampment. If they were involved in a feud with another community, he wanted no part in it. He wheeled, looking for his dogs.

The boy's hand clamped down upon his wrist. Kannujaq froze in shock, momentarily forgetting his panic. No one had ever dared behave so aggressively toward him. Among his own kind, physical aggression occurred only between the most dire enemies—and never openly. Otherwise, it was a symptom of madness.

Yet these are not people, but Tunit, he thought.

He could hear shouting near the beach, much of it the unintelligible roars of men. Kannujaq realized that living Tunit were now passing him and the boy. Some were staggering about dazedly, barely noticing them. Most were kneeling on the ground, weeping over the dead.

As though suddenly realizing how aggressive he was being, the boy released Kannujaq. Then he spoke that odd word again, the one Kannujaq had had trouble understanding before.

He's saying "Help," Kannujaq suddenly realized. *It's "Help."*

The boy repeated "Help" one more time, pointed toward the beach, then raced to the side of a staggering Tunik.

Kannujaq was alone now. He could easily disappear, forget about this place. But he had been jarred out of his panic; it had been replaced with a kind of . . . curiosity.

So the boy wants my help, he thought. *Against what?*

He approached the shore.

In moments, he could almost see the beach past the snow. There were fires down there, figures moving about. Perhaps two or three? He realized that they were running toward the water. In a moment, he realized that they were not Tunit.

Giants. There were giants down there. Manlike. Hulking. Monstrous. Giants.

Then the snowfall somewhat abated, and Kannujaq almost fell back at the colossal thing revealed by the water's edge. The giants were nothing in comparison.

Impossible, he thought. *A bird. A loon. No . . . not a loon. Not truly.*

It was akin to a loon, a great, dark, majestic shape, larger than any creature or structure that Kannujaq could conceive of, larger than his sled, larger than any *iglu* he had seen before. Upon its back danced several swirling flames, and among these fires there strode a single, manlike being: the master of the giants. As the giants scrambled up onto the back of the loon-thing, this being turned toward Kannujaq, revealing a face that shone like the sun. Its flat features glowed like daylight upon waves.

One of the giants approached this Shining One, and an argument ensued. The giant pointed to the sky, saying something like "Elulang" or "Helulan." A word for weather?

The Shining One began to holler at the giant, pointing to the sky. Then he shoved him backward, as one who cannot control his temper might kick a dog. The other giants had clambered onto the loon—which was looking less like a loon and more like a boat with each passing moment. They were using long oars to push off from the beach.

The realization that he was looking at a kind of boat snapped Kannujaq's mind out of its terrified fugue. This was a boat, after all. Just a boat, although it was the largest he had ever seen, great enough to hold several torches along its gunwales. It was long and streamlined, with an overextended, stylized prow that had given it a loon-like appearance. In fact, Kannujaq could now see that the prow was not bird-like at all but had been deliberately fashioned to resemble some kind of beast, perhaps a wolf.

Nor were its crew truly giants, but simply large men, given the appearance of even greater size by ambiguous layers of fur and tools strapped to every part of their bodies. Even so, they were peculiar men. What little of their skin that could be seen seemed pale, cadaverous. At first, Kannujaq had assumed that the lower halves of their faces sported coverings of dog fur. He could now see that these were beards of surreal proportions, the colour of Kannujaq's dogs.

With fear overpowered by amazement, Kannujaq stepped closer as the boat left the shore, the men at the oars turning it about as though they were used to commanding the water. Kannujaq studied the Shining One, who did not row like the others but stood over them like a man over his dogs. Before that monstrous boat was at last obscured by the haze of snowfall, the shining face once more turned back toward Kannujaq. And while he thought it unlikely that the master of the boat could see him, Kannujaq could not help feeling as though the wide, dark eyes within that visage were fixed upon his own. It dawned on him then that this, too, was simply another man, one whose head was covered in *kannujaq* fashioned to look like a face.

A mask, he thought. *A leader who wears a mask.*

The realization did little to comfort him. The owl-like appearance of that mask was raising the hair on the back of his neck. The ptarmigan was Kannujaq's animal; but the owl was his traditional enemy.

The boy had misplaced his faith, Kannujaq realized. He was unsure of what, or who, these men were, but he had a feeling there was no helping anyone against them. Unless it was to advise flight.

Where is that boy?

Kannujaq found him nearby, weeping over a fallen Tunik, a youngster who had perhaps been a friend. A dead person was not very much like a seal, after all. The blood was much darker, blending with the colour of the stones beneath. Somewhat nauseated, refusing to look toward the sounds of other Tunit weeping around him, Kannujaq stood over the boy, who no longer seemed to register his presence. None of the other Tunit even seemed to realize that Kannujaq was there. Respectfully, he tried to keep his eyes averted from the dead.

Instead, he regarded the weeping boy for some time, watching soot-laden tears dropping steadily from his chin. He was seeing the boy in a new light. The boy was somehow more real, not at all a sort of character from a dream, as he had at first seemed. Kannujaq's eyes followed sooty trails of tears down the sides of the boy's neck, where lay a partially covered necklace of raven skulls. Among his own kind, it was something an *angakoq*—a master of the Hidden world—might wear; but here, it might simply be a boy's eccentric ornamentation. After all, the Tunit were strange.

45

But they are human, after all, he thought. *They are.*

He hunkered down next to the lad, and as he watched this mourning boy, who had so vainly hoped for his help against the Shining One, he felt tears well in his own eyes. He had not even bothered to ask the boy's name.

Who would murder like this? he thought. *Who would do this to these people?*

"What is your name?" he asked.

Instead of answering, the lad wiped his face against the back of his sleeve and turned to Kannujaq as though noticing him for the first time. He removed his hood.

A chill ran through Kannujaq.

Blue. They're blue . . .

The boy's eyes were like twin shards of ice, the coldest blue of frigid depths.

Kannujaq understood then. The raven skulls. The obsession with his grandfather's *kannujaq*. Those unearthly eyes, one of any number of unusual features that mark the Half Hidden. This boy was an *angakoq*.

A shaman.

Unsurprisingly, the boy's name turned out to be Siku ("ice"), and he was indeed the resident *angakoq* in this camp. The boy himself didn't seem to make much of this but simply walked Kannujaq to a nearby shelter. Kannujaq had heard that an *angakoq* was an *angakoq*, that his kind and the Tunit were the same in this respect. If so, was he endangering himself by openly befriending the boy? It would depend entirely upon the boy's personal reputation. All the Half Hidden were feared. Some, however, were able to make their powers of use to the community. Others were so terrible or mad as to warrant exile, perhaps even death. Every *angakoq* was eccentric, without exception, and the community was lucky if its *angakoq* was content to hunt and rear a family in peace. Fortunately, it was a good bet that there was only Siku here—the Half Hidden were jealous and did not like to share territory with one another. Siku was probably powerful. It was rare to find a child *angakoq*, and his eyes were a very strong sign. Who had tutored him?

The Shining One and his men had left quite a mess. There were bodies to gather up, homes to restore, people to comfort. Kannujaq was led past an old man who knelt alongside one of the rectangular Tunit homes. He was piling the stones of its low walls back together, but doing so dazedly, haphazardly. When Kannujaq saw his face, it was carved with agony, glistening with rheum. The eyes were wide and mad, as though gazing off at nothing in particular. Kannujaq barely tore his gaze away from the old creature in time to avoid stepping over two women who were literally lying atop a dead man, their hands clawing and gripping spastically. Their faces were hidden, but their long, despairing wails seemed to merge into a single voice.

The Shining One's giant men had killed without purpose, seemingly laying into whoever had made themselves most available. It was an angry, insane sort of thing, and even accounts Kannujaq had heard of vendetta attacks between families had not seemed as awful as this. Where people had not been available for murder, the giants had scattered cook-fires and kicked in the feeble little walls that made up the Tunit homes.

Kannujaq felt awkward as Tunit grieved and pitifully restored order all around him, and he began to stare downward, not wanting to take in any more of it. He passed only one person who seemed to notice that he was not a Tunik, a young mother who clutched her baby tighter at the sight of him. But Siku led Kannujaq along even faster, quickly bringing him to his own little Tunit-style place: a sunken, square-walled hovel strewn with odd carvings, bones, and bags stuffed with undisclosed materials—probably shamanic bric-a-brac. Kannujaq wasn't sure whether he was witnessing an *angakoq* lifestyle or simply a boy's tendency to collect things.

While Kannujaq picked up and chewed some dried meat, as was any guest's right, the boy stuffed fistfuls of heather into a near-dead fire. This place was a miniature version of the typical Tunit home. The flagstone floor was a shallow pit, given the illusion of greater height by the rectangle of short stone walls around them. The ceiling was tent-like. Kannujaq didn't have time to study it closely, since he was nearly overwhelmed by smoke billowing from the fire. He began to cough, but Siku just grinned at him from a cloud of fumes, seemingly unbothered.

I can see why the Tunit are all sooty, he thought. It was as he had heard. The Tunit did not use lamps.

There was a peculiar smell that accompanied the smoke, acrid but not entirely unpleasant. Soon Kannujaq began to relax, and he very much felt like talking.

"Perhaps you should tell me, now, why I am here," he said. "Did you think I could do something against those giants?"

So, as winds rasped at the outside world, the two of them talked. For how long, Kannujaq wasn't sure. But he quickly learned that this was not the first time the "sea monsters," as Siku often called them, had attacked. Further, there had been rumours going around that other Tunit camps had been attacked. It was said that they wiped out whole communities, always attacking men and women first. Some Tunit escaped them by fleeing inland. More died under their gigantic, whirling knives. Always, they laughed and shouted "Siaraili!" as they killed. In fact, that was a common name for them: the Siaraili.

There was peace over this past winter, during which time they heard nothing of the Siaraili. But just last month, the monsters appeared at the shore, savagely assaulting this camp.

Because the ice is breaking up, Kannujaq thought. *Their boat couldn't get through over the winter. The Tunit probably haven't realized that this means they travel only by water.*

Siku's belief was that the Siaraili had followed Angula, the camp's current boss, to this place. He claimed, with a scowl, that Angula was the cause of all this. Angula was a Tunik who had bought himself into power here by lending tools to others. Not just any tools, but special ones. Angula possessed a fabulous, secret store of tools, and it was this, the boy claimed, that helped him buy his way to power.

48

Kannujaq then learned why the boy had so fixated upon his *kannujaq* necklace. Every one of these "special tools" that Angula held so dear was made of *kannujaq*. Further, it was Siku's belief that Angula had somehow stolen these *kannujaq* things from the Shining One himself, who was now seeking vengeance and the return of his property.

Angula, however, had an altogether insane take on things. Increasingly, he claimed that spirits were giving him his *kannujaq* implements. He had begun to claim that he had special powers.

Madness, Kannujaq thought. *Weird tools can't give one powers.*

It was Siku's thought that Angula wanted to think of himself as an *angakoq*, perhaps even as something beyond an *angakoq*. And these were strange times. With raids by the Siaraili, people weren't sure what to believe. Many Tunit simply wanted to leave, despite the love of their homes, but Angula would not let anyone go.

Love of home? Kannujaq wondered at the foreign concept. *Home is but a place where one stops moving for a while.*

Angula's latest absurdity had been to tell the community that the Siaraili were under his direction. Their attacks, he claimed, were punishment for the people disobeying him. According to him, the Siaraili attacks would stop as soon as people stopped trying to leave and demonstrated complete submission to his will.

Kannujaq was scandalized. No mind, no *isuma*, must ever force anything upon another! But, he supposed, the Tunit were a shy people. Perhaps they were scared of this Angula.

Kannujaq's reverie was broken as Siku tossed something. It landed with a heavy clunk upon one of the flagstones.

He noted the weight of the peculiar object as soon as he picked it up. Heavier than it ought to be. Obviously some kind of knife.

Tunit could not have made this thing. Their craftsmanship was said to be ridiculously poor. And while Siku's clothes were well made, the rest of these people were dressed in what to Kannujaq's kind might have been rags. The few tools Kannujaq had seen here were no better. Not even any lamps. No dogsleds, either. Kannujaq wasn't sure how the Tunit managed to survive.

Yet this knife was of excellent make. What really caught his attention was the colour, the dark red of a *kannujaq* blade, which was cold, like stone. It was almost as long as his forearm, having only a single, straight edge. The dull side was oddly curved, and along it ran mysterious etchings.

Kannujaq scratched at it with his fingernail. Rust, as found on rocks, came away. Under it was a grey, cold, hard stuff like *kannujaq*, but more dense. Rock could leave scratches on his own sample of *kannujaq*, but when he tried scraping a piece of flint on this, there was no scoring. He clamped his teeth upon it, but knew that it would break his teeth before it gave way.

His heart began to beat faster. The boy had made a mistake. This was not *kannujaq* but something far better. The things one could do with a good supply of this stuff . . .

The boy explained that this knife was one that Angula was lending him in return for various services. His face, however, betrayed the fact that he had stolen it.

Kannujaq sat up, opening his mouth to tell the boy that the Tunit must leave this place, must get away from this Angula and from the shore . . .

He didn't get a chance. A voice, deep, as though from a chest more bear than man, suddenly called from outside,

"I wonder why the *angakoq* hides a dogsledder in our camp!"

Siku went rigid, and one look from him told Kannujaq that this voice belonged to Angula.

"I wonder," bellowed Angula again, "what a dogsledder wants from us Tunit!"

Kannujaq stepped outside to face the owner of that voice. There he saw before him the fattest imaginable Tunit man, chest adorned with set upon set of clumsily arranged bear-tooth amulets. Rather than dangle, they seemed to rest upon his middle-aged paunch. As a Tunik, he was already rather short and squat. The added weight simply enhanced the boulder-like appearance that all Tunit men possessed.

So this is the great Angula.

Angula stood flanked by three younger men, who eyed Kannujaq uneasily. Cronies, no doubt, their allegiance bought with Angula's treasures. Fortunately, there were no weapons being brandished at the moment. Kannujaq could see several other Tunit men, women, and children milling around behind Angula. Nervous glances everywhere.

And then Kannujaq saw the first beautiful thing that he had seen since coming here. It was a woman, one with eyes like dark stones beneath sunlit water. But the lines of her face bespoke frowning more than smiling. Her hair was worn in normal braids, rather than in the crazy Tunit way, and her clothes were of unusually high quality . . .

This was no Tunik! This was a woman of his own kind.

Kannujaq greeted Angula in a friendly manner, but the creature only made a *chuff* noise, like a bear. Again he began to wonder aloud why there was a stranger hiding in his camp. While he did so, his cronies snickered next to him, but their eyes—like those of the other Tunit here—betrayed the fact that they were uncomfortable with Angula's behaviour.

Angula obviously had a problem with Kannujaq's kind. He spoke more as a show of dominance, for the sake of the onlookers, rather than directly to Kannujaq. He constantly looked Kannujaq up and down, sometimes pursing his lips in disgust.

"It is obvious," Angula said, "that this is why the Siaraili have attacked yet again! This is a camp full of disobedience. I have been defied once more, for now someone has tried to hide one of the foreign dog-sledders among us."

Then he saw the knife, still in Kannujaq's hand.

"What is this?" he exploded, coming eye to eye with some of the people. They seemed to wither before him.

"A dogsledder comes among us to steal!" he railed. "It is bad enough that their dogsledding kind ever soil our traditional lands! But now the trespassers steal from us!"

Kannujaq noticed that Angula liked the term "dogsledder." It seemed to epitomize his detestation of Kannujaq's people.

Then Angula wheeled and pointed at Kannujaq, saying, "You are jealous! That's why you have come to steal! You dogsledding foreigners always think you have better things than Tunit! But now a Tunik has better things than you, and you can't stand it, can you?"

Kannujaq remained shocked into silence throughout the tirade. But Angula's shameful spectacle was not allowed to continue. A youthful voice suddenly barked at Angula from Kannujaq's rear.

"Angula!"

Siku had emerged. His blue eyes had paled even further with rage, blazing out at Angula. While all stood, dumbstruck, he uncurled the fingers of one hand to reveal his helper.

Kannujaq had one glimpse at a tiny, skeletal figure in the boy's palm—a carved figurine that symbolized the helper—before he looked away in horror. There were gasps all around, and the boy began to speak at Angula in an oddly spidery voice.

Kannujaq quickly realized that it was the helper, who announced himself as He Who Carries Beneath, speaking through the boy. An *angakoq* could have many helpers, whether monstrous spirits ritually tethered or the souls of animals or ancestors. No one would see He Who Carries Beneath, but the boy was revealing him through the figurine he had carved, a representation of the helper. If necessary, he could also arm him with invisible weapons, similar carvings of little knives or spears.

Yet it seemed that, for now, the helper was messenger only. Speaking through Siku, He Who Carries Beneath told Angula, "You are no longer leader of this camp. It is the dogsledder who must become the camp's headman for a time. It is the *kannujaq* he wears about his neck that is a sign of this. He will drive away the Siaraili."

The helper then addressed the people, saying, "It is Angula's sins that have brought the Siaraili among you. You will all perish if you continue to have Angula as leader. This I know by Hidden knowledge. If you doubt, simply look at the dogsledder's necklace to see that his people have power to match that of the Siaraili."

But they don't, Kannujaq thought. *I don't.* It made Kannujaq wonder if it was really the helper or Siku doing the talking here.

One way or another, the helper did not finish the message. There was a roar, and Angula rushed forward, knocking the boy down.

All the onlookers, including Kannujaq, stood paralyzed with shock. It was not that Angula had attacked an *angakoq.* It was not even that he had attacked a boy. It was that he had done it *openly,* in front of everyone. Open violence was forbidden.

Mad . . . thought Kannujaq. *He's mad . . .*

The mysterious, non-Tunit woman was by Siku's side in an instant, but the young *angakoq* was already up again. His gaze was fixed upon Angula. Kannujaq had never seen such sheer murder in a boy's eyes before.

Angula was panting, more with stress than with exertion, and he quickly whirled about, pointing at Kannujaq.

"This is exactly what I was afraid of!" he bellowed. "Look what you made me do! You are obviously a powerful *angakoq,* manipulating us all!"

But his eyes shifted about furtively, uncertain.

"I will forgive Siku!" Angula huffed. "He is merely under your control! But you will leave now! Try to stay, and you die!"

Angula glanced at his cronies, but they looked uncertain.

"No one," Angula yelled at the onlookers, "is to follow this dogsledder or listen to his lies! Anyone who does will die!"

For a time, the only motion was windblown snow. The only sound was the mourning of distant dogs.

At last, Kannujaq threw down Angula's knife and walked away. His eyes met the boy's, fleetingly. The pale blue shards held mingled confusion and despair at Kannujaq's flight.

Kannujaq went to his dogs. There were sounds behind him as he left— Angula making more proclamations, no doubt—but he ignored them. In a short time, he left the sounds and the Tunit madness behind him, and there were his dogs. He had never realized before how much he loved these mutts. He had never realized what a treasure he possessed in his simple sled.

He only had scraps of dried meat to throw for the dogs, but it would keep them going. The storm had pretty much passed, leaving a bit of snow behind, and it was an ideal time for departure. He went to see if everything was lashed down properly, then he went to relieve himself.

A footstep, and there was the sudden flutter of wings. White appeared out of nowhere: a male ptarmigan hidden in an old snow patch. The potential food item nearly flew straight over his head, and Kannujaq desperately looked around for a rock to wing it with.

Then he saw them.

There were four, one of them grossly fat. Kannujaq knew that one was Angula. So he had decided not to let Kannujaq live, after all. They were coming on fast, carrying obscenely long knives, much larger than the one Siku had shown him.

Angula has dipped into his treasures, Kannujaq thought.

And bows. This was not about fighting, but straight-out murder. They would cripple him with arrows, finish him with blades.

Kannujaq raced to the sled and frantically pulled away lashing, retrieving his own bow. His heart was pounding by the time he found arrows and stepped away from the dogs. He wanted no stray shots falling among them.

The Tunit saw this and froze. He could see the cronies darting questioning looks at Angula, probably trying to convince him that this was a bad idea. Angula only nocked an arrow and drew, aiming high for a good arc.

Kannujaq backed up and the arrow fell short.

Angula tried again. This time, his cronies joined in. Several arrows came at Kannujaq, but again he backed up, and they fell short. This happened twice more, and with every failed volley, Kannujaq's smile grew broader.

Kannujaq had realized something: his was not a Tunit bow. It was made from composite pieces of whalebone, with a stronger recurve than the Tunit style, and better lashing. Its range was greater.

Kannujaq carefully nocked his arrow and took his time in the draw. Breath suspended, he made sure of his stance and loosed.

There was dread elegance in the arrow's flight. Then it came down, finding a home in Angula's chest. There it quivered, before Angula fell to one knee. His cry was long, a wail more of despair than of pain. He fell and lay still.

Kannujaq was nocking another arrow when the cronies at last tore their eyes away and fled like rabbits.

Kannujaq walked over to the dead Angula, frowning, more angry at Angula's corpse than he had been at the living man.

The fool, he thought. *Making me kill him. The damn fool.*

He put his bow away and began to leave, but paused.

He actually found himself concerned about the Tunit. How would they fare once the Siaraili returned? Perhaps better, with Angula gone. But now they had no one to lead them. Would they have the wits to flee, or would they sit confused, waiting to be slaughtered? And where would they go? As long as they lived by a coast, that Siaraili vessel could find them.

It could find his own people, too.

He looked back toward the Tunit camp, now leaderless. The ptarmigan. His animal. If it had not taken flight, Angula and his cronies would have ambushed him. A sign?

"Probably not," he grumbled.

Well, there was no point in making away so quickly. He might as well tell Siku what had happened. Siku, young as he was, was somewhat respected. He might point the Tunit to a new leader.

As long as it wasn't Kannujaq.

He gave the dogs the rest of his dried meat reserves.

As Kannujaq had anticipated, the boy was overjoyed at his return. In his *angakoq* way, he saw Angula's death as assurance of exactly what Kannujaq refused to accept: that he was here to save the Tunit.

At least Angula's tether on the community had been cut. People actually smiled, however shyly, at Kannujaq. Enough people offered him food that he had to start refusing it.

One of the first things Siku did was to introduce him to his mother, Siaq, who greeted him coolly. This was the lovely woman whom Kannujaq had spotted earlier. He was still certain that she was not Tunit. What was she doing here, then? There was no chance to ask, since Siku had something of great importance to show him.

The only other person in the community who had ever lived like Siku—alone, that is—was Angula. Siaq had served him, but not as wife. Angula had taken many wives, never keeping any. Siaq, however, had always been only one thing: Angula's slave.

Angula's empty home was left untouched, as though it were a haunted place. So there was no one there to greet them as Siku led Kannujaq into it. It was large, not as big as most communal Tunit dwellings, but large enough for a family. There was something grave-like about it, now that it was abandoned.

The fire, Kannujaq thought. *It's dead, like Angula.*

Siku did not pause for a moment, leading Kannujaq to the rear of the place, where there was a kind of adjoining chamber meant for storage. There was nothing of value in here, merely old, ragged caribou hides, but Kannujaq already suspected what he was about to see.

Sure enough, Siku pulled the garbage aside to reveal overly large flagstones. With some effort, he heaved one aside.

Here were Angula's treasures, the things the Shining One so desperately sought. Kannujaq had felt that nothing could further impress him, but he was quite wrong.

The pit was crammed with treasures.

These were nothing like Siku's rusted knife. Here was a polished blade as long as his leg, shining like a fish belly, handle decorated with yellow-hued kannujaq. Its home was a sheath of fine leather, wood, and wolf fur.

Kannujaq was even more impressed with the other tools. The majority of them were great, curving crescents—like a woman's *ulu*, but over a handspan in length—attached to the sturdiest wooden hafts that Kannujaq had ever felt.

These, he thought, *could hack through anything.*

There were other things as well, spearheads and knives, everything of enormous proportions. It took Kannujaq some time to figure out that some items were belts. Other things he recognized as the bowls worn on the heads of the giants. There was cloth made out of tiny, tiny rings. There were curved plates with no apparent function, and some items that were obviously jewellery.

Kannujaq was excited, but saddened. This was further evidence that Angula had been mad. A sane man would have shared these with friends and family, making life easier for all.

Mostly, he felt panic. He understood why the Shining One wanted all of this back. How had Angula managed to steal it?

They replaced the items, and Siku took Kannujaq back to his dwelling. Siaq was already there, but as Kannujaq sat down, Siku departed, leaving the two of them alone.

A planned meeting, Kannujaq thought.

There was silence for a time. Finally, when Kannujaq could stand it no more, he asked Siaq why she lived among Tunit—especially as a slave.

She sighed, as though having dreaded the possibility of discussing such things. Then she placed something in the fire. There was thick smoke, the acrid smell Kannujaq now recognized. He began to relax. He realized, then, that she was burning something that had a calming effect on people, made them want to talk, and that she also possessed some *angakoq* knowledge.

"I had a husband once," she said.

It was so good to hear his own dialect again!

"But a time came," Siaq continued, "when he did not come home. I was alone, and I began to starve, eating my clothing in order to survive.

"In this state was I found by the Tunit. The Tunit were led by Angula. He took me in as a slave, since I could do waterproof stitching. The Tunit cannot. The Tunit do not like slaves, but Angula always had his way through bullying. And a slave's life among Tunit is better than death."

Barely, Kannujaq thought, but he did not speak. One must not interrupt a story.

"Angula attracts strange beings," Siaq sighed. "One spring, the Tunit discovered a great boat, wood instead of skin, lying gutted along the shore. There were beast-men there, Siaraili, covered in furs and hard shells. They had got wet. They lay frozen, dead, stuck to the ground. Only one among them had not quite died."

The Shining One?

"Angula dragged him to camp," Siaq said. "I was made to care for him. He was huge. Hair like a dog's. Pale, pale skin. He recovered quickly.

"This one was the Shining One, the one who hates us now. But back then, he was grateful only to Angula. He repaid Angula by intimidating others in the camp for him. Angula enjoyed it. It was like having a bear as a pet. In time, Angula made me teach the Shining One some of the way Tunit speak.

"More than anything else, Angula's pet wanted to get home, which he said was across the sea. What he could not know was that great boats were spotted now and again, probably searching for him. Cunning Angula always found ways to keep the Shining One out of sight of these boats, unaware of their presence. He kept him distracted with . . . games, and hunting. With me.

"Eventually, I was given to the Shining One, like a gift, and the stranger accepted readily. The giving over of slaves, I later learned, was common where he came from, a place called Gronland. His kind called the worthless Tunit lands Heluland, or Place of Flat Stones."

She broke off to wipe at her eyes, which were tearing. Kannujaq remained respectfully silent.

"But I was laughing at him inside, all the time," Siaq said, "because I knew that he was just Angula's slave, like me. Seasons went by, and I became sickened with it all. I started to tease Angula. I told him, sometimes, that I would tell the Shining One how Angula was keeping him from being rescued. Angula beat me terribly for this, threatened to kill me.

He was scared. Not only was he keeping the Shining One captive, but he had also stripped the bodies of the Shining One's dead companions. He had told the Shining One that they and their *kannujaq* implements had been lost to the sea. But he had actually kept the *kannujaq* tools, hiding them away safely.

"In time, the Shining One grew into the Tunit community. He even began to treat me kindly. But I was always tempted to tell him the truth about Angula.

"Then a night came when the Shining One and I were quarrelling. All of my hate came out somehow, made my mouth move on its own. I told him the truth. I told him everything. Everything."

Siaq went silent for some time.

"He never spoke after that," she said. "He never looked at me. Not at Angula. Not at the Tunit. Angula became scared. But he was relieved when the Shining One slipped away one day. No one saw him go. Maybe he sighted one of the ships of his people.

"It wasn't long before Angula started showing his *kannujaq* treasures around, claiming that spirits had given them to him, that he had special powers. He had learned that wealth can buy people. He began to lend his treasures out, in return for loyalty. In this way did he enslave everyone.

"But Angula had made a mistake, for the Shining One was no normal man. He was a leader among his own kind. Angula had only a few years to enjoy his power before the Shining One returned. And he brought the Siaraili. He sent out his giants to punish the Tunit shore encampments, laughing, killing, always searching for Angula and his stolen artifacts. Others died, but Angula escaped every time. Angula became mad, paranoid, trying to hold onto his waning power. He claimed that the sea raiders were punishing the community for disobeying him.

"In time, every Tunik in that camp was killed or scattered. Angula survived, fleeing to a new Tunit community—this one. I and Siku, who was smaller then, came with him. Here, over the next few years, it was easy for Angula to buy himself authority with his stolen artifacts. And the whole thing started again."

Siaq was weeping openly by the time she finished her tale; what from, exactly, Kannujaq could not tell. But there was lots to weep about. He suddenly understood how little her son truly knew of his mother. She had told Siku bits and pieces of truth, but he had interpreted everything through the eye of an *angakoq* (as well as that of a boy). To Siku, as to the other Tunit here, this was a battle against sea monsters. The Siaraili were *tuurngait*—evil spirits. In Siku's world, there were signs and portents all around him, but his mother's burden was truth. Only she and Angula had known what the Siaraili really were.

Kannujaq returned truth with truth.

"If all of us do not leave this place," he said, "we die."

Siaq sniffed and agreed.

"I can't leave the Tunit, though," she said. "I've been with them too long. They are friends, family. Life has more meaning among them, now, than it does among your . . . I mean, our kind."

She has become a Tunik, Kannujaq thought.

"And the Tunit are not like our people," she said, "always travelling, always sledding. The Tunit like their homes. Their homes are part of them."

Kannujaq could not understand why anyone would be attached to a home, but he said, "No time for this, Siaq. No time. The Siaraili left last time only because they were worried about the storm. But once they feel safe again, they'll finish this camp. If the Tunit do not move, because of love of their homes, then there is only one other thing they can do. They must fight."

He was surprised to find her laughing, a dry, mirthless, bitter sort of laughter.

"I told you how I taught the Shining One our language," she said. "But I learned some of his, too. The Tunit call the giants Siaraili because that is what they shout as they attack. The Tunit think that this is what the giants call themselves. But shall I tell you what they are really shouting? They shout 'Skraeling!' because they are calling to the Tunit, in mockery. It is their word for 'weakling.' They call the Tunit Skraelings, because they never fight, but simply run, and run, and run. As well they should. For the Shining One's people have spent generations at war. They have grown fond of it. How could a community of Tunit contend with even a few of those born of conflict, armed with materials harder than stone? This is why the giants run through the camp playfully, kicking walls in, slashing at everything blades can reach. This is fun for them. Afterward, they gorge themselves on whatever they find in camp, washing it down with a harsh tea they are fond of."

Kannujaq was silent. Siaq was right. There would be no standing against the giants, not even with their own artifacts. These were the men whose ship prow was carved like a beast, like a wolf. And that was how they attacked. The Tunit were like caribou. They were all caribou. And the sea raiders were wolves.

Wolves. Siaq was stuffing more heather into the fire when Kannujaq asked her, "How does a Tunik hunt a wolf?"

"They don't," she said. "Wolf pelts, among the Tunit, are rare and valuable, because it is almost impossible to get near enough to a wolf to kill it."

But Kannujaq knew how his own people hunted them.

You did not catch a wolf by running it down, nor by ambushing it. The creatures were too wily. They could sense humans, evading them every time. Instead, you used a wolf's habits against it. The wolf was like a dog. If it found food lying about, it would stuff itself with as much as its gut could carry, eating faster than it could think. So what Kannujaq's people did was this: Soften some sharpened antler. Bend and tie it. Freeze it into the centre of a piece of meat or fat. Invariably, the wolf would swallow it down. The meat and ties would melt and digest inside the wolf. The sharpened antler would spring open. Dead wolf.

Siku walked in while Kannujaq was trying to explain this to Siaq. He seemed to grasp immediately what Kannujaq was implying and began to rummage through his bags. In a few moments, he had retrieved a handful of dried, ugly, greyish lumps.

"Is that what you burn in the fire to make people sleepy?" Kannujaq asked.

"That's a mushroom," Siaq said grimly, "that is very dangerous. It can make one permanently stupid—even kill, if used improperly. But an *angakoq*, like myself or Siku, can prepare small amounts of it properly."

"But if we made a solution of the stuff," Siku grinned, "it would be very deadly, indeed."

"Is there enough to saturate some meat with?" Kannujaq asked.

"I have three bags here," said Siku.

Siaq ran off to retrieve her own stores.

It took a little over a day to ready everything, and the Tunit needed a great deal of convincing. Kannujaq was adamant about securing their promise that they would help out. Everyone's movements were orchestrated and rehearsed. The homes nearest the beach were left abandoned, storage areas full of meat. As many Tunit as possible would share homes nearest the hills, allowing them a head start if the raiders were sighted. They were not to move far, but only to take cover near the base of the hills.

Kannujaq alone would creep back to the camp to see if the Shining One's men took the bait. If so, he would signal.

There was no back-up plan.

The days were long now, so it was late evening when the Shining One returned in creeping dusk.

One by one, the great boat's torches sprang to life as it reached the shore, to harsh cries of, "Skraeling!"

The camp, and especially Kannujaq himself, had been nervous and watchful. All was set, and cries of alarm spread faster than flame among the Tunit, who were soon running. Kannujaq ran alongside them, desperately hoping that the Tunit would be able to summon their courage when the time came.

His greatest fear was that the raiders would not behave as planned. Siku and Siaq had prepared a kind of rancid-smelling tea out of their mushrooms, assuring Kannujaq that it would be undetectable on meat saturated with it. They were wrong. Kannujaq himself had sampled some of it. No peculiar scent, but its flavour was off. His stomach had begun to lurch soon afterward.

Maybe the raiders are less observant, he hoped.

They reached the hills, and could see commotion down by the beach, most likely the raiders kicking in the short Tunit walls, ripping tops off homes, stamping through cook-fires. Kannujaq gave them time, letting the reddish grey of evening come on. After the amount of time it might have taken for someone to boil up soup, he began to creep back down.

Lucky my clothes have become sooty, like the Tunit.

It seemed to take forever to get down there, but at last he was at the edge of the community. Fortunately, there were large rocks about, enough for him to move among cover.

The Shining One was easy to spot. There was that gleaming face by torchlight, the man who never seemed to stray far from his boat. As before, he was arguing with one of his own. He was frustrated by something. At last, he tore off the gleaming shell upon his head and face and cast it upon the stones of the beach.

His giant servant watched him climb back into the boat, retrieving something near its stern. Then the Shining One stretched himself out, drinking something in hand.

The servant shook his head and left his leader there, joining the other raiders at a fire they had constructed. For fuel, they were burning what precious few tools the Tunit had made, from driftwood, over generations.

Yet they are eating, Kannujaq noted. They had found the meat, but the poison would take some time to work. He needed patience, as in hunting a seal.

It was a sudden thing when it happened. They were still laughing, but their movements were becoming syrupy, disjointed. Whenever one arose, he teetered dangerously.

Then one of them vomited. The others laughed at this, crazily, before they did the same. The mad pitch of their laughter increased, until they fell—first to knees, then fully upon the ground. Many began gesturing, calling out at empty air.

Soon the dozen of them were down, some convulsing. One lay still. Others were laughing or weeping uncontrollably.

Kannujaq unravelled the bull-roarer in his hand. He whirled the noise-maker round and round, calling the Tunit.

Where are they, Kannujaq thought. *Now! Now! I can't do it alone!*

Finally, Tunit men appeared next to him, long bear spears in hand. They stood stunned by what they saw, and Kannujaq roared at them to get moving.

He did not watch as they stabbed the giants. His objective was the boat. He ordered several Tunit men to join him and do as he did.

Kannujaq threw himself against the bow of the boat, and the Tunit men did likewise. Together they began to shove it backward, away from the shore, trying to get it out into the water.

Kannujaq's one concern was the Shining One himself. He had assumed that the man would join his fellows in feasting, but he had been wrong. Instead, the man seemed to have gone to sleep in the stern, after guzzling tea all evening.

They didn't get the boat out in time.

There was a dry, rasping sound—that of a weapon being drawn— and the Shining One appeared with a bellow. Kannujaq barely fell away from the boat as a great blade bit into the gunwale nearest his face.

But the Tunit had managed to push the vessel out. There, in the water, the great loon-thing rocked, and Kannujaq knew that the Shining One could not man it by himself.

The Tunit had finished the giants, and many were standing along the beach now, watching the helpless leader of the raiders drift ever further outward. Kannujaq opened his mouth to tell the Tunit to fetch bows, but one glance told him that they were already sickened with murder.

As was he.

So they all watched, stared as a current tugged at the vessel, lazily turning it away from the coast. There stood the Shining One, no longer shining, but staring back at Kannujaq. It was a strange thing that there was no hatred in those ice-blue eyes, but only despair, and resignation.

In that moment, Kannujaq recognized the colour of those eyes and knew. The Shining One had never come here for plunder. Siaq had kept a secret from all.

The sea raiders had always had enough weapons and tools to spare. The objects Angula had stolen meant nothing to them. As with Kannujaq, what most mattered was kin. Kannujaq was looking at a fellow stranger in these lands, a newcomer, one who has known that dread of the unknown against him. Perhaps his people were not faring well here.

This was a man with nothing left, whose greatest fear—as with all men—was that he would fade away, leaving no trace of his passing. And it was such desperation that had driven his attempts to retrieve his only lasting legacy.

His son.

It was telling that there was no real celebrating over the defeat of the raiders. The Tunit simply wanted to put it all behind them, returning to their shy Tunit ways.

Kannujaq never spoke about what he knew of Siaq, that she had once had a husband from beyond the sea. Nor did he ever speak of what he knew of Siku, whose *angakoq* eyes had come from his father.

Kannujaq offered to bring Siaq and Siku away with him. Yet, just as he knew he could never live like a Tunik, so Siaq said that she was no longer comfortable among her own.

Siku, however, took up Kannujaq's offer eagerly. The blue-eyed *angakoq*, it seemed, had never felt comfortable among the Tunit. And he seemed to like the idea of sledding.

So it was that, in the early evening, when the scant remaining snow was cooling, Kannujaq and Siku made ready to depart. And as Siku watched Kannujaq tighten the lashings on his sled, the boy asked him, somewhat haltingly, "What . . . am I to say my mother is, if not a Tunik? What are we?"

"I don't know," Kannujaq replied. But he thought about a word his grandfather had used. "Perhaps we are *Inuit*."

Siku's look was blank. He had grown up with the Tunit dialect, and the word was a foreign one.

"It means something like 'those living here now,'" Kannujaq said with a grin.

But Kannujaq was troubled by his last memory of the Shining One, his boat swept away on odd currents. Was this the destiny of all strangers in this land? Was it the destiny of his kind?

Perhaps the Tunit would eventually speak of his people only in legend.

Kannujaq had no way of knowing that, while the Viking colony in Greenland would fade from existence, his own descendants would travel freely over the next three centuries, settling not only in Greenland but over all the old Tunit lands. The world would grow much colder, as in the time of his ancestors, and his kind would be the only survivors here. And they would speak of Tunit only in their own legends.

But Kannujaq's mind never strayed far from the present. His musings were eclipsed by annoyance that Siku had disposed of the raider artifacts. The *angakoq* had felt they were evil and was convinced that the sea should have them.

Kannujaq wondered how long they could travel before Siku noticed everything lashed to the sled. The boy had forgotten about Angula's knife, which Kannujaq had snuck back and retrieved. It would be ideal for *iglu* building in the winter.

Like his people, Kannujaq remained, above all else, practical.

BASIL JOHNSTON

The Wampum Belt Tells Us . . .

CONTRIBUTOR'S NOTE

IN 1968 I WAS INVITED to an Indian display mounted by the grade 5 students of Churchill Avenue Public School in North York, Toronto, as a grand finale to their five-week in-depth study of Indians. Students, parents, and teachers were justifiably proud of the exhibition.

The entire library was one large, open gallery. It was a veritable feast of Native memorabilia. Against the walls were tables bearing an array of pictures, maps, and artifacts, both genuine and plastic. Posters and several large pictures of Indian chiefs and warriors adorned the walls. At one end of the library was a large canvas teepee; in front, a tripod made of saplings meant to represent an outdoor fireplace. Students, faces painted in warlike colours and wearing paper headdresses, mingled with the guests, whom they conducted about the exhibits while explaining what they knew of their respective First Nations. All of them wore nameplates of the tribes whom they represented: ALGONQUIN, IROQUOIS, SIOUX, HURON, OJIBWAY. In front of the teepee stood a grim-looking grade 5 chief, his arms folded. Like the rest of the Indians, he had his face painted in hostile colours. I went directly to him.

"How!" I said in greeting.

The Blackfoot chief looked at me quizzically.

"Why so glum, Chief?" I asked. Before replying, the chief looked around to make sure that there were no teachers within hearing, and then whispered "I'm bored."

"How so, Chief?"

"Sir! Don't tell anybody, but I'm bored. I'm tired of Indians. You see, sir, I always wanted to be an Indian, and when we started this unit on Indians I thought I'd learn something. When we began this unit we had to choose a special project from social organization, hunting and fishing, food preparation, clothing, dwellings, and transportation. I chose dwellings"—and at this point the little chief exhaled in exasperation—"and that's all me and my committee did for five weeks, sir! We studied and researched teepees, igloos, longhouses, lodges, wigwams. We read books, encyclopedias, went to the library, looked at pictures, and drew sketches. Then we had to make a teepee. Is that all there is to Indians, sir?"

Two comments hit home. "Is that all there is?" and "I always wanted to be an Indian" affected me enormously and profoundly. Now, there is nothing particularly unusual about wanting to be an Indian. In fact, back in the 1960s a youngster's wish to be an Indian was as common as wanting to become a fireman, policeman, nurse, or actress. And children could not give a rational reason for wanting to be an Indian. It was the mystique, perhaps a romantic notion derived from a picture, that attracted wannabe Indians.

That youngster had a dream, preposterous as it may seem to adults, worth pursuing because it represented something real. And dreams and visions are necessary to create and to accomplish. When his school offered a five-week in-depth unit on Indians, that boy looked forward to the program that would teach him all he wanted to know and needed to know that would enable him to turn his dream into reality and become a living, breathing Indian. But the course let him down. He learned about social organizations, subsistence, food, fashion, dwellings, and migration. But he uncovered nothing about the true nature of Indians. He was exasperated. Despite his disappointment, he still clung to hope. His question and tone pleaded for some assurance that "Indians" were so much more, and that it was still worthwhile to dream.

His plea was reminiscent of another boy's plea to Joe Jackson, one of the Chicago White Sox baseball players accused of deliberately losing games in the 1918 World Series, to "say it ain't so, Joe." Faith had to be restored.

To long to be an Indian, as this youngster longed to be, may be dismissed as nothing more than a childhood fancy, a phase. But the longing to be an "Indian" is not confined to youth today.

Just a little over five hundred years ago this boy's ancestors came to this continent when Columbus, blown off course, landed in the Caribbean. Not long after him came Cortés, Pizarro, Cartier, and Cabot seeking a western passage to the Far East with its silver, silks, and spices. Here on this continent, these adventurers saw lands and riches, customs and practices that they had not seen or heard of in their part of the world. Within a few short years these adventurers, their crews, and their sponsors abandoned their pursuit of the Far East and its riches. They wanted what the North American Indians had; they longed to be like the Indians.

The Wampum Belt Tells Us. . .

For hundreds of years before the coming of the White people, the Wampum Belt, a chronicle of a people's history, had few new symbols woven into its fabric. It was as if nothing worth recording had taken place, no wars, nothing but peace. The last event to be recorded was the battle between the Anishinaubae and Cat Nations. Since then nothing.

At first these landings of White people were not taken seriously by most—bad navigation, bad seamanship; but others saw them as a fulfillment of a prophecy. Neither the White people nor the North American Indians saw them as events that would alter the political, social, and economic life of western Europe and that of the Indians of the New World.

But there were troubles from the start, troubles to the south. The White people didn't continue on to the Far East as they had intended—they stayed. After them came shipload upon shipload of other White people. Their numbers and strength grew. Within a few generations these bands grew to nationhood, bigger and stronger than the North American Indian nations.

They grew as did the Weendigoes in Anishinaubae mythology. Whereas the Weendigoes of mythology roamed the land only in winter and could be thwarted, this new breed roamed the land the year round, ravenous and voracious beyond belief, devouring not only the flesh, blood, and bones of its victims but their souls and spirits as well. Unable ever to allay their never-ending hunger, the new Weendigoes ravaged the land and its forests and fed upon animals.

As if there were not enough blood and flesh and bones for them all, the Weendigoes turned on one another. The English Weendigo forced the French Weendigo to give in; the American Weendigo rose up against its English father and forced it back to Europe, and then fought the Spanish Weendigo and sent it reeling into Central America.

The American Weendigo became a nation. Still it wasn't satisfied. It needed more land, just a little more and then it would be satisfied, happy, glutted. It went westward, killing, destroying the Indians who fought back to keep what the Great Mystery had given them. "Just a little more," the Weendigo promised the Indians of the Ohio Valley. "Just a little more, then more."

North of Lake Erie and Lake Ontario, the Anishinaubae peoples were uneasy. There were rumours that the American Weendigo coveted the land that the English Weendigo still retained on this continent.

In the spring of 1812 a messenger from Christian Island arrived in Couchiching, where the Anishinaubae peoples of the Lake Simcoe region had their summer town. The messenger, called a *mazhinawae* by the Anishinaubae peoples, told the chief and his people that the people at Christian Island had received word from the Owen Sound Anishinaubae that Tecumseh wanted all warriors to gather in Couchiching in one hundred days. Tecumseh himself would attend the meeting.

There was no time to lose. The Lake Simcoe Anishinaubae peoples sent their courier to Parry Island. Couriers went from village to village along the north shore to Manitoulin Island, Sault Ste. Marie, Temagami, Nipissing, Golden Lake, and the Kawarthas, inviting warriors to assemble at Couchiching to hear what Tecumseh had to say.

At the end of July, three hundred warriors were assembled at the Couchiching Narrows, among them Newash, Waukey, Madawayash, Bisto, Metigwab, Tomah, Aissance, Copegog, Kitchi-cosinau, Naningishkung, Zauw-indib, Kitchi-cheemaun, Kitchi-noodin, Manitowaubi, Chechauk, Paudash, Zhingwauk, Waukegijig, Pitwanikwat, Abitung, Nagonash, and some such as Kinoshmeg and Webokamigad, whose fathers had taken part in the siege of Detroit under Pontiac fifty years earlier. All wore their hair in the style of a bristling ridge that ran from the forehead to the nape of the neck; on either side of the ridge, the hair was shaved to the scalp. Their faces were painted in red and black, the colours of blood and death. In their hands they carried war clubs; some had guns. They were ready to kill or die.

Last to arrive was Wauwunoosh, Tecumseh's courier from the Lake St. Clair area: Tecumseh himself was unable to come, he'd been called to southern Ohio to drive out the Long Knives who had encroached upon Indian land.

That evening after they'd all eaten their meal, the warriors and the Couchiching Anishinaubae peoples assembled in a large open glade, waiting for their chiefs to get the evening's program underway. Old Aissance, who had taken part in the siege of Detroit half a century earlier and who was now the principal chief of the Lake Simcoe Anishinaubae peoples, opened the meeting with a brief welcoming speech. "It is a memorable occasion . . . and to commemorate this day I will ask Abeedaussimoh, our *mazhinawae* and keeper of our Wampum Belt, to tell the story of our peoples and so to remind us who we are and what the Great Mystery has given us."

In the old days the *mazhinawae* recited the history of the Anishinaubae peoples at the outset of winter and the storytelling season and on special occasions such as the present. With the Wampum Belt draped over his arm, Abeedaussimoh, pointing to two figures of two canoes with masts fore and aft worked into the belt, began.

"More than three hundred years ago a ship and its crew were driven off course by the wind and the fates onto the southern shores of

77

this continent. Nearly half a century later, Jacques Cartier, working in the pay of the King of France to find a northern passage that would shorten the distance from Europe to Asia, chanced upon the northern shores of the gulf of the St. Lawrence River."

The arrival of bearded White men created a stir among the people of the Land of the Great Turtle. Some thought that the coming of the men with pale skin and hair upon their faces was the fulfillment of a prophecy. Others were not awed.

The Indians greeted the strangers and welcomed them ashore and treated them as guests, brought them food and drink. "But—" the *mazhinawae* paused, pointing to an image of a man with a stick— "when the Indians asked to board the vessel to inspect its quarters, the captain of the vessel ordered a crew member to fire the thunderstick, as ancestors called the gun."

There was a tremendous explosion. Half a dozen seagulls fell dead into the water. Indians screamed. Not a few soiled their loincloths, front and back. Panic-stricken, the Indians raced ashore. For days afterwards their ears rang and their eyes blurred.

Word of bearded White men and their thundersticks was carried inland to other Indians. In no time most of the inland Indians knew about the aliens.

After leaving the terror-stricken Indians and the northern shore of the St. Lawrence River, Jacques Cartier and his expedition sailed south to the Gaspé. From here he swung west and upstream until he came to an island in the middle of the river. Cartier and his ship couldn't go any further upriver because the river was too shallow and the rapids too strong. Cartier and some of his men went ashore and planted a cross on the crest of a high hill, claiming all the land for the King of France and naming the place Mont Réal.

Here the *mazhinawae* put his finger on the image of a cross.

"You know," he said, "the Houdenassaunee were ruffled by the erection of this post. To the Houdenassaunee and to many other people of Turtle Island, a post in the ground is a mark of death, the mark of the grave of a dead person. What the white-skin, bearded aliens did was a sacrilege that bodes evil and . . . death. It's a bad sign."

Next the belt shows ships going back. On board are two young Indians.

Before he went back to his own country, Cartier asked Donnacona, chief of Hochelaga, to let his two sons accompany the expedition on its return home, so that they could see France and its great cities and its civilization. Cartier promised to bring the two boys back with him when he returned the next year. At first Donnacona wouldn't hear of it, but his two boys badgered him until he agreed to let them go . . . but only if Cartier would leave two of his men with the Houdenassaunee.

When Donnacona's sons came back with Cartier the following year, they were quite proficient in French. Their tongues were kept wagging describing the glitter of France and the fancy costumes and wigs worn by all the White people. Indians, they said, could never live like that. They told their father why the stick-wavers, as they called the French, erected the cross. They said that the cross was an emblem meaning that France was claiming ownership of all the land. When he heard his sons' explanation, Donnacona declared that the Houdenassaunee would never allow the White people to take their land.

On the same day that his sons came home, Donnacona sent Jean Michel Parisé and Albert Lebrun, the two young Frenchmen who had stayed behind, back to Cartier's crew. During their stay in Hochelaga, both Parisé and Lebrun had learned enough Mohawk to allow them to get by. They had also made some friends. On one of their visits to Hochelaga, Donnacona told them that Cartier and his crew were no longer welcome. Cartier was mystified and upset by the coolness of the chief's message: "Better that you go home and never come back. The sooner the better . . . before the north wind blows."

Cartier sailed downriver to Stadacona, where he established his headquarters. From here he spent the next few weeks exploring the north and south shores of the St. Lawrence River. When he finally decided to go back to France, it was too late. Here in Stadacona the Indians advised

Cartier not to risk going back at this time of the year: "Better you wait till spring. Soon the north winds will blow."

The *mazhinawae* passed his finger over an oval figure enclosing several teepees. He continued.

Cartier had no choice but to stay in the Land of the Great Turtle. He put his men to work constructing a fort. While the bearded White men sawed, hammered, sweated, and cursed, the Indians looked on open-mouthed, wide-eyed. Never had they seen a chief drive men as Cartier drove his; he himself was driven by some spirit deep within his being. He worked his men from dawn to dusk without rest. From their seldom changing diet of cod, it appeared that the stick-wavers would eat nothing but cod all winter.

Once every two weeks or so Cartier allowed his men some meat. Whenever the stick-wavers needed meat, Cartier sent Parisé and Lebrun to Stadacona to ask the Indians there to take them hunting. These two young men in their early twenties, having acquired a taste for liberty, were more than willing to get away from the drudgery of hewing, sawing, and hammering logs and timbers and regimented living.

The *mazhinawae* held up the sash, in the middle of which were two human figures exchanging merchandise that was indiscernible.

For the people of Stadacona it was time to venture upriver to a great sea and then inland to visit a people who grew corn in their fields. In preparation for the trading mission, the chief and the people of Stadacona sent an advance party ahead of the main trading mission to deliver word that the people of Stadacona needed corn and to find out what the Waendaut wanted in exchange. The chief asked Cartier if he would allow Parisé and Lebrun to go with the advance party. The round trip, the chief guessed, would take, depending on the weather, maybe a month.

Here Abeedaussimoh showed his listeners a rough sketch of two canoes surrounded by six canoes.

What the chief, the *mazhinawae* carried on, didn't tell Cartier was the reason that he wanted an armed escort. The chief was afraid that his advance party might meet up with marauding Mohawks out to avenge a raid conducted by some Adirondack warriors. Meeting up with warriors was always touchy business. Then there were the Odauwau, who kept the rivers and portages under surveillance and wouldn't allow anyone to pass without exacting a toll from travellers; they acted as if they owned the waterways and the land.

At first Cartier was unwilling to let two of his men go; he needed them. But when the Stadacona chief glared and growled at him, Cartier changed his mind. To retain the goodwill of the chief and his people, Cartier let Parisé and Lebrun go.

"Now you boys be careful," Cartier warned his men as he shook their hands.

The advance party was made up of ten men in two canoes. As toll payment the party took caribou pelts, merchandise preferred by the Odauwau.

At Hochelaga the party took the south shore for easier portage, carrying their canoes and goods along the shore until they came to deeper waters. They boarded their canoes well beyond the rapids and resumed their westward journey. The party had not gone much beyond the confluence of the St. Lawrence and the Ottawa Rivers when they were hailed by loud voices coming from six canoes that bore down upon them from the north shore. The chief muttered, "You'd think that these vigilantes would sleep once in a while." The advance party stopped paddling and waited.

"Where are you going?" the Odauwau chief asked in Mohawk.

"We're going to the land of the Waendaut to inquire about the corn crop."

Neither Parisé nor Lebrun understood what was going on.

"You got something worthwhile for us? If you have, we'll let you pass. If not, you can get your buns back home."

By now the advance party was surrounded by Odauwau canoes. In each canoe were four warriors, their hair so arranged that it stood straight up, bristling like the quills of a porcupine.

"Come with us," the Odauwau war chief said, nodding his head to indicate the north shore. Then, looking at the two young bewhiskered men, he asked, "And where did you pick up these hairy banshees?"

"Oh! Them!" the advance party chief answered. "They're our guests. White men," and he went on to explain how these men and their companions had come to this land from another land and that they were looking for a way to the Far East. "We brought them along to show them the country."

"Ever hear of anything as brainless?" one of the warriors interposed. "Going west to get to the east? To get to the east, you go east," the warriors said laughing.

"Are they really manitous?" another warrior wanted to know.

"Do they look like manitous?" the advance party chief harrumphed. "Wah!"

"Well! Never know. They can change form, I heard . . . and some of these manitous have hairy faces."

"I don't think that these ones are manitous . . . too backward. Don't know much, and what little they know about the woods, they learned from the people at Hochelaga where they spent the winter before. But they learn pretty fast."

"Ooohn!" the Odauwau chief muttered. "Is that so."

Upriver on the north shore men, women, and children gathered to see what the travellers had brought with them as payment for their continued passage. But when they saw the shaggy-faced White men, the men, women, and children were more taken with these "apparitions" than they were with the caribou pelts.

"These figures on the sash, a man and woman, remind us of what happened next," said the *mazhinawae*.

As the traders from Stadacona and the Odauwau warriors were seated to bargain what toll should be paid, a boy reached out for one of the White men's faces. Parisé, thinking that the boy was about to pull his beard, slapped the boy's hand away. The boy yelped, "He hit me! he hit me!"

The boy's father was at Parisé's throat and would have cut the man's neck had it not been for the quick action of the warriors, who drew the man to one side. There were voices raised. "Serves him right."

The father of the boy raised his own voice. "He hit my boy! He's not going to get away with it."

Parisé and Lebrun were paralyzed with fear. They looked wildly about them for some avenue of escape but there was none. They were surrounded by warriors. Silently they prayed.

"Calm down! Calm down!" the Odauwau chief shouted to restore order and to settle frayed nerves that were rubbed rawer by demands "to bury a hatchet in their skulls" and "leave them alone."

"Get a hatchet! Get a hatchet!"

"A hatchet! A hatchet," an old woman spat out. "That's all that you think of. A hatchet will not settle anything. A hatchet will only hatch ghosts . . . and more ghosts . . . These strangers came here not as enemies, but as passersby. We ought to receive them as guests."

This plea did little to quell the uproar. While the men argued for and against blood, the same old woman raised her voice to draw the chief's attention. His attention gained, the chief raised his arm and in a loud voice called, "Quiet! Pitchinaessih has something to say!" The crowd settled down.

"I want to adopt this boy," Pitchinaessih said, pointing to Parisé. "Since my son died some years ago I've had no one to look after me. I've got no one to care for. I'd like to take this boy into my home. I would like all of you to look on him as my son, as your friend . . . as one of us."

"All agree?" the chief asked.

"Ho! Ho! Ho!" the voices piped up in agreement.

"Welcome, brother," the chief said to Parisé, whose hand he took, and he led him to Pitchinaessih. Parisé went along willingly, not knowing what was going on. A thought that he might be married to the old woman might have flitted through his mind.

Men, women, and children came over to welcome the newest member of the community and to congratulate Pitchinaessih on getting a son. Even the man whose son's hand Parisé had slapped away offered a welcome, a lukewarm welcome. But at least it was a welcome. There was nothing that he could do to reverse the Anishinaubae custom of adoptions.

The chief of the Stadacona advance party protested. "Don't do this! What will I tell our chief? His chief? They'll come after you with their thundersticks."

"Tell them," the Anishinaubae chief answered, "that they ran away . . . captured by Mohawks . . . They drowned . . . They fell in love. Tell them anything, but don't tell them that they are here or else we'll never let you further inland ever again."

"But," the chief of the advance party objected, "you didn't ask the young man if he wanted to stay or to come back with us. His chief trusted us to take them back."

"Did you want to go further inland for your corn, or do you want to go back to your village now?" the Anishinaubae chief asked. "Your choice."

The advance party chief bit his tongue. He had no choice.

The Anishinaubae chief didn't wait for an answer. He turned to his people. "As chief and an Anishinaubae, I'll adopt the other young man as my son and give him to Nauneediss, a young widow who needs a husband and a father for her two children." Then, turning to the chief of the advance party, he said, "You'd better be on your way, otherwise you'll be late."

The chief of the advance party ground his teeth as he and his party boarded their canoes. Just before shoving off they pitched on shore the satchels belonging to Parisé and Lebrun. Only then did the two young Frenchmen awaken to what was taking place. They sprang forward, but the warriors held them back. They struggled to break free. They yelled, "Our guns! Our guns! At least leave us our guns!" But their outcries were as useless as their struggles.

Abeedaussimoh went on to the next images on the sash, men lying on the ground sick, with a medicine man standing among them; then men up on their feet.

"The advance party," said Abeedaussimoh as he picked up the thread of his story, "went on inland, made their request for corn and the amount from the Waendaut, then returned to Stadacona. The chief of the advance party told the chief of his community what had happened to their two White companions. When the chief of Stadacona told Cartier, by means of gestures, that the two men who had accompanied his advance party had run off, Cartier blew his top. He cursed, yelled, clenched his fists, and kicked a sawhorse. He was a picture of frustration, trying to get the chief to understand.

But while the chief couldn't understand what Cartier said, he understood the White man's wrath. After he'd endured Cartier's *"maudites,"* *"mardes,"* and *"enfants d'chiennes,"* the chief shrugged his shoulders and walked away, leaving Cartier to fume and rail at the heavens. How would Cartier explain this when he returned to France?

Back to supervising the construction of their buildings and the fort went Cartier. Meanwhile the chief of Stadacona sent a trading mission inland to obtain a winter supply of corn from the Waendaut.

For those who remained behind, there was nothing more fascinating than to watch the construction of the fort. They gossiped and marvelled at the size of buildings such as they had never before seen. But the building of such dwellings wasn't the only aspect of the bearded White men that drew the attention of the Indians. They could not get over how these men could get along without helpmates. They asked one another, "How do they get along without women? Do they care about women? Do they have wives? Girlfriends? Brothers? Sisters? And if they have families, loved ones, how can they leave them behind?"

When Cartier and his men finished construction of their buildings and erected a palisade around them, they retreated inside, coming out only once in a while to fish for cod or to ask the Indians for meat. The north wind blew, bringing snow and cold. None of the people of Stadacona were invited or allowed inside the fort.

At home the Indians complained. "We let them in our land and let them come into our homes and villages . . . but they won't let us into their homes."

Before too long the bearded White men came into Stadacona to say that their fires were going out and that they were cold. The Indians showed the stick-wavers what kinds of wood made the warmest fires and brought them warm clothing, jackets, mittens, moccasins, leggings, and caps made of buckskin and beaver; they brought warm comfortable bedding, bear rugs, rabbit blankets. The Indians brought these struggling "civilized" bearded White men dried and smoked and fresh meats, but the bearded White men continued to eat their salted cod, boiled.

About mid-winter most of the White men began to bleed from their noses and ears. The men who had not yet fallen sick came to the Indians with their tale of woe, asking for help. Yes, these civilized men asked the Indians for help.

The medicine men were invited into the fort to look at the sick. One glance was all the medicine men needed to know what ailed the stricken men. It was scurvy, a condition brought on by an insufficient intake of greens in the system. It was an ailment easy enough to remedy.

Near at hand were stands of cedar, balsam, pine, and spruce rich in vitamin C coursing through their roots, trunks, limbs, and needles, bearing the life-giving "strength of the earth" that no living creature can do without. The medicine men made a beverage from the greens and gave it to the sick men to drink. Within a week the men stopped bleeding and recovered.

Abeedaussimoh went on to the next set of figures, two bearded men in the company of Indians listening to a storyteller.

For the first two years of their adoption, Parisé and Lebrun were kept under pretty close watch, but after that, in their third year as members of the community, they had as much freedom to come and go as any other member of the village. Both were married and the parents of children, and both were quite proficient in the Anishinaubae language. When asked if they ever wanted to return to their country, both said, "No, never would we ever return to a life of servitude and hunger."

In the meantime both had received Anishinaubae names, really corruptions of their real names: Parisé became Pau-eehnse, an elf who dwelt on the shores of the lakes; Lebrun became Nebaunaubae, a merman. They wore loincloths, moccasins, leggings, jackets, like any other Indian. The two men were as good woodsmen as any Anishinaubae.

By the third winter the two men were in demand as storytellers; people wanted to hear about their country and what had brought them to the Land of the Great Turtle. After three years both men were enough in command of the language to enable them to take part in the storytelling sessions.

The storytelling season always commenced with the account of creation told by one of the leading narrators in the village. This long story was followed by a recitation of the history of the nation.

Two weeks went by before the storyteller came to the prophecy that foretold the coming of bearded White men to this continent. It was this narrative that many older people wanted to hear, to see what their adopted White men would say and do. Then they could hear Pau-eehnse and Nebaunaubae talk about what life was really like in the old world.

And this is the story that he told. I've heard that it was Daebaudjimoot, our nation's first storyteller, who first told this story. The muses who foresaw the future put the story in his mind. He told his listeners: "One day bearded men with pale complexions will come to our land. They'll arrive on board great wooden canoes ten times longer than our longest canoes. At either end of these long canoes will stand tall timbers. From the limbs of these timbers will hang blankets for catching the wind that will whisk this great canoe along as quickly as a cloud. The White man's canoe will not need paddlers.

"In the beginning only a few ships will arrive, on board not many men. For this reason our people will not take them as threats. They'll accept the strangers' word that they are bound for another land lying well beyond the western horizon and that they will resume their journey once they have found a passage and replenished their provisions.

"However, in no time these White people will forget that they were going to the Far East to find its riches for which they had sacrificed so much. They'll find something on our land far more precious than fine textiles, shiny stones, or spices. But wait. Wait for a few years. Then our ancestors will see ship after ship, bringing shiploads of men and women to our shores. They'll come like flocks of geese in their fall and spring migration flights. Flock after flock will arrive and set down in our lands. There will be no turning them back.

"Some of our children and grandchildren will stand up to these strangers, but when they do it will be too late, and their bows and arrows, war clubs, and medicines will be no match for the weapons of the White men, whose warriors will be armed with thundersticks that will sound like thunder as they unleash thunderbolts that kill. Their warriors will need do no more than point a thunderstick at another warrior, and that warrior will fall and die the moment the bolt strikes him.

"With weapons such as these, the White people will drive our people and our descendants from their homes and hunting grounds to lands where deer can scarce find room or food to eat, and where corn can barely take root. The White people will herd our people into pens as our kin, the People of the Weirs, channel trout and whitefish into cages. The White people will then take possession of the greater part of the lands and build immense villages upon them.

"Over the years the White people will prosper while our people will grow ever poorer. Though our people and our kin and other nations of our race may forsake our heritage and take up the ways of the White people, it won't do them much good. It will not be until our grandchildren and their descendants return to their values and traditions and beliefs that they will regain the strength and the heart to master new challenges . . . otherwise they will vanish as smoke vanishes into the sky."

"Preposterous!" the listeners snorted.

"Is that true?" some listeners asked Pau-eehnse and Nebaunaubae.

"No. Our people are just looking for a passage that would serve as a shortcut to the Far East and save months of travel."

"Why would you want to go to the Far East?" a questioner asked. "Why not stay at home with your families?"

"Our commander was commissioned by the first chief of our country to find a shorter way to the Far East than by going south. If our commander found a way, he and those of his crew would receive a reward . . . that would make life easier for us."

"What is a reward, and what would you have done with it?"

Pau-eehnse and Nebaunaubae had difficulty explaining what reward and money were; the listeners had equal difficulty understanding what the terms meant.

"What would 'reward' . . . 'money' have done for you?" the questioner asked again.

"I could have moved to a city and learned a trade and had a better life," Pau-eehnse explained.

"Why'd you want a better life? Wasn't your life at home good? happy? . . . Are you happy now?"

"Yes," Pau-eehnse rejoined quickly. "Since living here with you I've been happy. I have everything that I never had in my home, everything that I could never have."

"Tell us what your life was like in France."

"I was born in the country," Pau-eehnse began, "the son of a serf working the land for my master. We were peasants, poor people." Pau-eehnse went on to describe how the dwelling that was his home was a hovel compared with the homes of the well-off. "Like other serfs, my father worked the land and looked after his master's flocks and did other work as required by the master. Work, work, work. Yet for all his work my father could never provide enough for us. Always we were short of something, especially food and clothing; we were cold, sick . . . miserable. My parents never went anywhere. The master of the manor would not allow his serfs—his slaves, really—to leave the land. They were rooted to the land as the tree is planted in the earth and cannot move. Most of the people in our country were serfs, chattels that belonged to the land that belonged to a master. Our masters were of the upper class, the rest of us belonged to the lower class, worthless. You, my friends," Pau-eehnse said to his listeners, "are lucky. You don't know how lucky you are. You can come and go as you please. You don't have masters to tell you what to do, what not to do. You are your own masters. You are free."

"How then did your masters become masters?" another listener wanted to know.

"I don't know," Pau-eehnse said with a shake of his head.

"I'm not sure," Nebaunaubae broke in, "but I heard a priest say that God gave all power to the King and mastery over all the land and all living creatures dwelling upon it. The King then subdivided his kingdom into several provinces over which he placed members of his families and relatives to govern on his behalf."

"Not many masters, then?"

"No, but they are very powerful, almost as powerful as the King. They live like kings in palaces where they eat fine meals, drink fine wines, sleep in soft beds, wear fine bright clothes, dance to fine music. These men and women are free.

"They look down on the rest of us as backward and unworthy, while we must look up to them as our superiors. We're not allowed to speak to them unless they speak to us first or give us permission to say something. And we must bow, genuflect, kiss the hands of our masters, and lick their boots if they command us to do that."

Turning to the chief and looking at each of his listeners in turn, Nebaunaubae continued, "You are fortunate. You talk to your chief as if you were of the same rank. You walk, work, and eat with your chief. You go to him as he comes to you. You argue with him as if he were no better than anyone else. You don't bow down to him or kiss his hand. He doesn't command you to do this or forbid you from doing that. No one is greater, no one lesser. You're all equal. My countrymen would envy you. You are— we are—fortunate."

"Yes, we are fortunate," the chief agreed. "I cannot imagine any man or woman of our nation bowing or taking orders from me or another man or woman." Then he lapsed into silence, contemplating what he'd just heard.

"Chief!" Nebaunaubae spoke to the chief. "For you and your people, who owns the land?"

"It belongs to Kizhae-Manitou. Whatever the Master of Life has created belongs to the Master. The Master put us on the land that we live on. The Master gave it not to one but to all, including the birds, the animals, and the insects.

"All beings created were born with a right to a place upon the bosom of Earth Mother, to a share in her bounty. Only by having a place somewhere can creatures fulfill their duties to the earth, to plants, to one another, and to humankind. Without birds, animals, insects, and fish, humans would not long survive.

"When a person is born he is entitled to a place on the land and a share in the produce of the earth, and when that person is ready to settle down, he may select any parcel of land that is vacant for his own use for as long as he lives, or until he abandons it. He must choose a parcel that is empty. This land will belong to him and, if he is married, to his wife and his family. He can then say 'ae-indauyaun,' my home; his family will say 'ae-indauyaung,' our home. The man's kin and neighbours will say 'w'ae-indaut,' his home, his dwelling place, in recognition that the dwelling and the land that the building stands on belongs to that man and his family. Women have the same rights as do men. This is our custom, the way we do things. But the land belongs to all the people. For as long as a person occupies a parcel of land, it is his, but the moment that he abandons it and moves to another place, the land reverts to the people.

"Birds and animals have the same need for a place that is their own, and they also have a right to the harvest of the earth."

"That's the way it should be," Pau-eehnse broke in, "but in our country the serfs work for the master. At harvest time the master takes a serf's produce, as much as he thinks he will need. After him comes the priest to take his portion. Always the serf is left with less than will meet his own needs. You don't have a similar practice."

"The chief can get his own. We're not supposed to look after him; he's supposed to look after us," a listener added.

The next figure on the sash was that of a man in black robes. It reminded the storyteller of Nana'b'oozoo's first vision quest and how Nana'b'oozoo had not gone through with it. The story piqued Nebaunaubae's interest in his adoptive people's beliefs. "In my country," he began, "we don't have vision quests, we don't smoke pipes, we don't offer tobacco, we don't drum or chant or have fetishes such as you have. These practices would be regarded as pagan. When our leader Cartier came over here the second time, he brought a priest. The priest was shocked and he felt sorry for the poor Indians. He said, 'Those poor savage pagans, they don't have churches, priests, or a holy book to read. They don't know about God and, not knowing God, will never get to heaven. Instead they'll all go to limbo or to the everlasting fires of hell.'"

"What's a church? What's a priest? What's a holy book? What's prayer? What's baptism? What's contrition?" the listeners asked.

Nebaunaubae explained.

"No, we don't have any of those things," the chief said ruefully. "All we have is Mother Earth. She shows us birth, growth, life, death, and rebirth. She teaches us that life and being come from a seed that breaks its casement and grows and gives life, then dies, and its seed continues the cycle. Mother Earth shows us in her mountains, valleys, forests, meadows, lakes, and rivers that there is a Master of Life. She tells us through her other children, the eagle, deer, butterfly, whitefish, what we ought to do and what we ought not to do as we follow the Path of Life. We watch and we listen. The earth is our book.

"It's also our church. Every part is 'holy,' made so by the act of creation. Wherever we may be, we talk to the Great Mystery."

"How do you know what to say?" Nebaunaubae wanted to know.

"We know. We just know. Our heart and, on occasion, our mind will tell us what to say. Only you know what you want and need; only you know what to say; no one else does. And so you talk to the Great Mystery or to one of your ancestors or to one of the manitous in your own words."

"Do you ever quarrel about your beliefs?" Nebaunaubae asked.

"No, we don't quarrel about prayers and beliefs. Prayers are between a person and the Great Mystery or one of the manitous; they are personal and confidential. Same thing with beliefs. We do have different understandings, but it is the Great Mystery who has given us these different understandings. For who is to say that one person has a better understanding and another less? Will the Great Mystery prefer the person to whom He has given more talent to understand and neglect the one to whom He has given less?" After a moment's reflection, he turned to Nebaunaubae. "Why do you ask? How do your people talk to the Great Mystery?"

Nebaunaubae told the listeners that God sent his only son down to the Holy Land to save mankind by teaching it the right way to live, and that the Holy Land people crucified Him for this teaching. "Why?" the audience wanted to know. "Didn't God do anything to save His son, to punish His killers?"

"Later Jesus Christ's teachings were written down in a book," Nebaunaubae continued. "Right from the start men quarrelled about God's teachings. To put an end to these disputes a priesthood of wise and holy men learned in the hidden meanings of the Holy Book was set up. Only these men were competent to interpret the teachings of Christ and to guide the people along the path of righteousness. These wise and holy men built churches to which people were required to go once a week to hear the word of God. Learning and ever more learning didn't put a stop to the disputes over the word of God. The wise and holy men disagreed. Even laymen drew different meanings from the Holy Book. The men who differed from the teachings of the Roman Catholic church founded their own religions and built their own churches. For starting their own religions, these men and women provoked the wrath of the Catholic church fathers who, along with the government, persecuted and killed the Protestant Huguenots.

"France wasn't the only country that wouldn't put up with different beliefs. In England, the model of tolerance and enlightenment—the English church—persecuted the Catholics.

"We heard our priest say that missionaries would reap a rich harvest among the Indians."

The chief harrumphed, "And they'll sow seeds of squabbling, adding more fuel to the fire. As if we haven't already enough to quarrel about."

Next evening Pau-eehnse asked, "I'm curious. What are these dreams, these visions that you talk about? Why are they so important?"

The storyteller explained, going over ordinary dreams that most people have, some people more frequently than others. These had meaning. He said that the Houdenassaunee saw dreams as "the unfulfilled desires of the spirit."

"Dreams," he went on, "are meetings of the spirits of the living and the spirits of our ancestors in the World of Dream. The spirits of dreamers may even meet manitous and other spirits of the living in that stage of existence." The storyteller explained that some men could conjure up spirits and summon them to the presence of the world of men and women. When the storyteller had finished going over the "Shaking of the Earth" rite, he went over the ordinary dream that men and women indulge in, "the dream of a better life." To illustrate this point he related the story of two young friends who, seeing the crimson hills in the horizon, were led to believe that the land in the distance was much more beautiful than their surroundings. They left their village to make their home in the crimson hills. Each evening, after walking the entire day, the two friends were no nearer to the crimson hills than they had been the previous day. The land of the crimson hills was always on the horizon, as distant as before. Years later the boys, now men, returned to their village. They had gone around the world. Their home and their land had been the land of crimson earlier that day.

The storyteller told another story, a story of four young men who dreamed of a better life for their people, who were cold, hungry, destitute, as if they had been forsaken by their Maker.

"The friends set out seeking a land where there was food aplenty and fair weather, and where there was no illness and the people were happy.

They went on following the path of the sun. They came to a great river over which they were ferried by a riverman. Well beyond the river they came to the lodge of a bedridden woman. They looked after her until she recovered. When the friends were ready to resume their journey, the old woman told them to go back home to their people. She knew what they were seeking. And she would give them what their kindness deserved, medicine for their people. To each of the young men the old woman gave a small packet, which they were not to open and take until they returned to their village. They followed her advice, and taking their medicine was the first act the young men performed when they got home. But nothing happened, nothing changed during their lifetime. Their people were as poor as before, and the young men felt that they had been betrayed by the old woman. Only after they died did their graves yield the gifts that changed the lives of their people. The graves yielded evergreens, birchbark, flint, and tobacco that changed the lot of people who had once been cold, hungry, and sickly."

"At home," Pau-eehnse remarked, "we could never indulge in such dreams. My father and my mother were serfs. A serf I would be, and to die in servitude was my destiny. That is not a dream; it was the reality. I dream that I remain here, never to go back. But I do wish that I could see my parents."

Nebaunaubae nodded. "I don't want to go back. I wish that our people had what we have here."

During that storytelling season the chief and his people were absorbed by the master-slave relationship that Pau-eehnse and Nebaunaubae had described. They found it hard to believe that in a country as civilized and Christian as France, one man and his family owned all the land, and that his friends owned men and women and made them work, and that men, holy men, quarrelled about their beliefs and even killed those who differed with them. None could dream of a better life, except after death.

On the Wampum Belt was a fleet of ships. With these figures as his cue, the storyteller resumed his narrative.

"It was not long, no more than ten years since Parisé and Lebrun had been adopted by the Odauwau, that, unknown to them, what Daebaudjimoot had foretold was coming to pass. Shipload after shipload of bearded White men and white-complexioned women came to the Land of the Great Turtle. Most came because of a dream. They dreamed of a land where they could practise their beliefs without persecution; they dreamed of land, of a better life."

Next on the Wampum Belt were two stakes with the totems upside-down, the sign of death.

"The Indians in the interior heard rumours of the influx of aliens in the east and reports that the aliens were squatting on the lands of the People of the Dawn, as the Anishinaubae called anyone who lived east of them. Nebaunaubae heard these rumours and, fearful of capture by his country-men, moved further inland to Nipissing with his wife, five sons, two daughters, and twenty-five grandchildren. There he died in his seventy-fifth year. Pau-eehnse also moved inland, to Lake Simcoe, with his family of six boys, brown- and grey-eyed, light-complexioned youngsters. By the time he passed away, there were eighteen grandchildren. In addition to grandchildren, they left behind them stories of their heritage that their descendants kept."

Abeedaussimoh highlighted soldiers firing their guns at warriors. There were bodies on the ground.

Now the aliens were moving inland. They were moving in on the People of the Dawn's lands, massacring the people who defended their lands and their freedoms. These aliens had no sense of right or wrong. They had no respect for the People of the Dawn or their rights or their lives.

And so it went. Chiefs complained, "When the White people came here, they were few and weak. All they wanted, they said, was a little space. Our ancestors gave them space, fed them, and gave them clothing. Soon they became many and strong. They wanted more land, more space. Before long our people were crowded off their ancestral homes and penned in enclosures."

Abeedaussimoh paused and looked up. "I am done," he said. "I have told you what our Wampum Belt has recorded of our people in the Lake

Simcoe area up to this time and what fates await our people in the future."

There were shouts of "How! How! How!" (comparable to "Hear! Hear!") throughout the assembly as Abeedaussimoh rolled up the Wampum Belt before sitting down.

Aissance, the chief, held up his hand for quiet and attention. The crowd settled down. "We will now hear from Wauwunoosh, Tecumseh's courier."

Wauwunoosh, lithe, lean, tall, took his place beside Aissance, who drew back to sit with the other chiefs.

"Neekaumisseedoog, N'dawaemaudoog!" the *mazhinawae* began. "I am Wauwunoosh, Pottawotomi, Tecumseh's courier and brother in arms. I come to you from Tecumseh with greetings and his apologies for not being able to come to deliver his own message. But just as he was about to come away, couriers from his own people living in southern Ohio came to him with word that the Long Knives were encroaching upon their lands. As he was leaving, Tecumseh asked me to come to you, to ask you to join our cause in Ohio and to keep the Long Knives on the east side of the Ohio River . . . Otherwise the Shawnee, Miami, and Illiniwuk, and the Ottawa, Pottawotomi, Chippewa, and Maumee who make up the Anishinaubae peoples will suffer the same fate as our brothers in the east. Tecumseh asks, Where are the Pequot now? Where are the Narragansetts? The Passamaquoddy? The Massachusetts? The Mohicans? Once great nations, they are now but remnants of a once proud people, without land, without home, disdained, unwelcome in the villages and towns of the White people. How their fortunes have changed.

"When the White people first came to these lands, they were few and weak; though they knew a great deal, they knew next to nothing of the land, how to hunt, what to eat, what to wear. They told the Indians that they were looking for goods that would obtain for them a better life at home. Where they came from, they were slaves with masters. Masters made them work and took part of their harvest, leaving them with less than met their needs, so that they were ever hungry and often sick.

"There were deer and wild boars and pheasants in the forests, but they belonged to the King. For a man to kill one of them to feed his starving family was a grave offence. If a man were caught killing one of the King's animals, he could be put away in prison or in a grave. The animals in the forests were better off than were humans. These itinerants told the Indians that the King owned their bodies and their labours and that preachers owned their prayers, beliefs and souls.

"The Indians felt sorry for these hapless itinerants. They gave them some land, showed them how to hunt and grow corn and potatoes, and how to store meat and berries without salting. The itinerants took up land and many of the ways and attitudes of the Indians. Their numbers grew, and as their numbers increased they took up more land by fighting and killing the Indians to whom the Great Mystery had given the land. Now it is the Long Knives who own land, come and go as they please, and take their places by the side of other men and women as our people are accustomed to do. The White people have now what the Indians had. It is now the Indians who have no land, nowhere to go; they look up to army officers and governors and listen to preachers to guide them along the right Path of Life. This is the lot that the Indians of the east coast have come into.

"Unless we, the Shawnee, Kickapoo, Miami, Sauk, Illiniwak, Anishinaubae, Menominee, Winnibego, and all the nations to the south stand up to the Long Knives, we will all suffer the same fate as did our brother Indians along the east coast. Tecumseh wants you to know that the Shawnee will not give up a foot of their land that the Long Knives have demanded. They will not suffer the fate that the Pequots, the Narragansetts, and the other Indians went through. They are going to fight it.

"We, the Pottawotomi-Anishinaubae of Lower Michigan, are going to stand with Tecumseh and the Shawnee. We are asking you to join with us in the Niagara region, there to meet the Long Knives with bullets, arrows, clubs, and courage. We, all of us, must unite as one people if we are to repel the invader and to keep our lands and our way of life."

"How! How! How!" the warriors cried out, then rose to their feet and uttered war whoops. Mingled with the hoots were shouts of defiance. "We will not back down! Blood! Death! Wounds! Drive them out. Send them back to where they came from! The war dance, the war post!"

That night the warriors performed the Dance of War. Next day they were off with Wauwunoosh, leaving behind apprehensive parents, wives, and children.

In Niagara they joined other warriors to fight by the side of a ragtag collection of conscripts to defend Upper Canada against the Long Knives. Without the Indians the defenders would have lost and Upper Canada would have been seized by the Long Knives. But, in the main, it was the Indian warriors who stemmed the Long Knives, and if General Isaac Brock had listened to Tecumseh and the other war chiefs, the defenders would have inflicted an even more decisive blow. Unable to break the Indian resistance, the Long Knives fell back.

Not long after the Battle of Queenston Heights, a courier from the St. Clair River region brought word to Tecumseh that the Long Knives had crossed the St. Clair River and were believed to be making their way toward the small town of London. Tecumseh and his war chiefs made straight for London. Learning that the invaders were still camped well downstream on the banks of the Thames River, Tecumseh and his chiefs prepared a trap. Some days later the invaders walked into the trap. The battle was fierce, both sides suffered heavy losses, but the greatest loss to the Indians was the death of Tecumseh. The invaders turned tail and went back to their country. The Indians won and they lost. Though they drove the Long Knives back to their own country and saved the fledgling nation from falling into the control of the United States, victory wasn't enough to fulfill their own dreams of keeping their lands and their way of life.

Within a few years the colonial government directing Canada's affairs turned on the Indians, took their lands, and herded them on to reserves, and they were no longer free to come and go as they were once accustomed to do, for they no longer had anywhere to go. They now had

Indian agents as masters. Missionaries came among them to tell them what was right and what was not. They were now no better off than the Pequots or the Narragansetts. In fighting for the White man's freedom, the Indians lost theirs.

The old Anishinaubae prophecy was fulfilled.

After the Battles of Queenston Heights and the Thames, these events might have been commemorated on the Wampum Belt, but the belt was either lost or hidden and is now forgotten. Few Anishinaubae people remember their history, and they rely upon European historians to remind them of what happened.

But the fate of the Indians was commemorated in story. A storyteller dreamed of a mighty struggle between a snake and a man. And this is the tale that he told.

Our people's lot is exemplified in a story that grew out of their desperation. A man out hunting one day heard a cry of distress in the distance. There he went. When he came at last to the place where the anguished calls came from, the hunter found a monstrous serpent entangled in the underbrush.

The moment the snake saw the man, he pleaded, "My friend, set me free. Have pity on me."

"No! You might turn on me!" the man explained as he refused.

"My friend! What kind of creature do you think I am?" The snake sounded hurt. "Why think so ill of me? Do you not think that I ought to be grateful for having my life spared and that I would do everything to do you a good turn for having saved my life?"

"Yes!" the man agreed. "I suppose you ought to be, but I'm afraid."

"Never! Never! Never!" the snake protested. "Never would I turn on you if you were to set me free. Think! Suppose you were caught fast as I am. And suppose someone came along and set you free. Would you turn on your friend?"

"No," the man said.

"Then no more would I turn on you than you would turn on a person who befriended you," the snake assured the hunter. "My friend! You can set me free and give me life . . . or you can leave me here to die. If you leave me, you may as well kill me now!"

With considerable misgiving the man cut the vines that held the snake fast. The moment the snake crawled free, he sprang on the man and coiled himself around his friend and, after nearly crushing him, pushed him into the entanglement where the snake himself had been held bound. And the snake left him there.

TANTOO CARDINAL

There Is a Place

CONTRIBUTOR'S NOTE

I CHOSE THIS TIME IN Métis history, 1915 to 1928, because it was a time of hopelessness. Métis and non-status were essentially illiterate. Nomadic lifestyle and non-tax-based land use left them without educational privileges. In the majority of cases, the money wasn't there to provide the clothing and materials to hold the children beyond ridicule and discrimination in the white schools.

Métis industry on the rivers was dying. The railroad was bringing in white settlers in numbers never before seen. Commercial fisheries began, along with the jigger—which allowed fishing all winter. Stocks were depleted. Jobs that would have gone to Métis were now going to white settlers or immigrants. Licensing for traplines and taxes on furs further pinched the Métis trapper.

The history of Red River and Batoche was forgotten. The new immigrants knew nothing of it, nor did they care—a proud history forgotten.

Now we had illiteracy, landlessness, and disease to consider in a new world where we had no place. We were obsolete.

Meetings were beginning. A few determined souls, without education, were pondering what could be done for the children. In 1928 a meeting was held in Fishing Lake, Alberta, where a non-status Cree teacher applied his education to help organize the movement that would produce the Métis settlements of Alberta by 1935.

There Is a Place

It was one of those long quiets—me sitting at the old pine table and her washing up the dishes by the stove—when the kettle let us know the water was boiling good. Adeline grabbed it up with both hands (it must have been half the size of her, that kettle) and poured the water into the old teapot next to me. She threw a handful of tea on top of the leaves already filling the pot.

"Here you go, Francis, half-breed tea. Half black, half muskeg, the only kind the company sells out here in the bush," she said. She put the lid on to let it steep. "Drink up and wash down dinner. You needed it—looks like the muskrats were pretty skinny where you've been."

My belly was full. I was tired, like I was ready to crawl under the table and fall asleep like an old dog. I just cupped my hands around my empty mug and tried to shake the feeling. "It's good to get a square meal and some tea without having to listen to a sermon for it."

"Not in this house, but if you talk about those priests around Adolphus you'll hear preaching for certain." Adeline went back to washing the dishes.

"I should help him mend those nets. There's still good light left to get some work done." I said it, but I wasn't sure I could get up off my chair.

"No," Adeline said. "Not 'til you tell me where you've been for the last year and a half."

I didn't want to think about it. Piecework and drinking. I'd seen a lot, but it all tossed together in my mind and none of it I wanted to tell her. And as soon as I started thinking, I started remembering why I was here, and it did a good job of waking me right up again.

I looked up at her, watching me with those leathery eyes. Might as well get to it. "Have my boys been hard on you?" I asked her.

"They're good. Little devils. Keep us busy, stop us from getting too old," she said. "We always tell them about you. You'll see them soon enough—had we known you were coming, we wouldn't have let them go to town with the Prudens."

Daniel and Francis Jr., I could see their faces. Or how they looked when I saw them last. I wondered if they'd know me. How mad they would be for how I left them. They're too young to know my thinking, and my story. But Adeline would understand, and I had been practising in my head all the way up to the cabin how I'd tell her and what she had to know.

"It's good the way you're keeping them. You know I was eleven when I went to live with my grandpa. When my mother died"— I couldn't match those eyes so I watched the teapot instead—"they told me she had died of consumption. No one had even told me she was sick. She just didn't come to visit me every week like she used to. I remember, I felt like I didn't belong anywhere. It was bad when my dad, died but this time . . ."

"You were out at the mission school. Lucien had to go up to tell you."

"Sister Agnes held onto me. She wouldn't let me go with Uncle Lucien. She said she was worried for my soul. Uncle Lucien told her, 'We will tend to his soul. He needs the Spirit of God all right, he needs his family.'"

I could catch her out of the corner of my eye, still watching me. "So he took me out of the mission school and took me home to Grandpa."

"Your grandpa was a better one for spirits than the Spirit of God. Lucien always was quite the talker." She had gone back to washing, and I could look up and talk again.

"Well, that school was no good for me anyhow. They never let me forget I was a half-breed and lucky to be there. My mom had to give them money for me to go to school, and she did."

"I remember. I used to see her at the Bay every once in a while, selling her jackets and moccasins and mukluks. She did such beautiful work. She was a hard-working woman."

"My uncles got the moose hides and deer hides for her after Dad died. They would bring fish and fresh meat by the mission school whenever they got some, but still the priests and nuns never let me forget that I didn't belong. Some of the kids at school were jealous that my mom came to visit me. They would beat me up and call me names. When they stole priest food from the pantry, they would never give me any."

Adeline snorted. "Those priests stole that food in the first place."

"Most priests are good people. They've always been good to me."

She turned around, the soaking rag in her hand dripping on the floor.

"You ask Adolphus. He still remembers St. Paul de Métis."

"St. Paul? Wasn't that a long time ago? Must be twenty-five years."

"Well, you think about what happened to us. When the government and the Church went round telling people that they were setting aside land for us—that we'd have a community, our community, with a trade school and a church and everything else. We moved everything, sold everything we couldn't move, to start over. The land wasn't broken yet, and clearing the land nearly killed him, it was so much work, and still having to get crops in. And what happened? The Church never gave us title to our land, and once we built the place up they threw us out. Replaced us with a pack of Frenchmen with nothing to show for it. We're not going to forgive that, or forget."

I didn't know what to say. Adeline was always tight-lipped when it came to the mission schools. I knew she and Adolphus had spent some time in one in their younger days. When it sunk in, when I saw her standing there lost in anger, I felt a real fear build up. I couldn't say a word about the boys. I couldn't meet her eyes.

Finally she spoke. "That tea is ready for pouring." In relief, I poured myself a cup, mixed in some sugar, and took a sip. It had been a long time since I'd tasted good bush tea. For a moment it felt like it was ten years ago and I was sitting at this table with Catherine. Adeline couldn't let me stay in that place too long, though, and she was at it again.

"Wah! You're still in your own world. Pour a cup for Adolphus and bring it out to him. Then you can come back and tell me about your hard life."

I could feel myself burning as I made up the tea for Adolphus. I burned against her, even knowing that she was right. I could barely look after myself. That's why she and Adolphus were raising my boys, so they wouldn't be stuck being raised like I was. Lucien hadn't known how much Grandpa had changed since Grandma died. He wasn't very well and he didn't seem to care about life as much. Maybe Lucien figured I would be good for Grandpa. I had tried to help him, back then, to do what needed to be done, but it was never right or enough.

Sometimes Grandpa would take me along to his poker games. He would play for two or three days at a time sometimes. I would have to come home and look after the horses though. He was happy when he was on a lucky streak. Sometimes he would leave me at home to cut wood or haul water, or whatever had to be done. Then I knew he would be getting into the homebrew and come home in a rage. I hated those times, Grandpa yelling, telling me I was "no good for nothing," even though the wood was up and the water was there. He would yell and scream for a while, then he would go to bed and sleep, or he would cry, grab me, and cry all over me. I know why he did it, I couldn't blame him. We'd both lost my mother and my grandmother, and he'd lost others besides, lost himself. And him crying was better than the belt.

In those days, I had been happy only when Uncle Lucien took me upriver on the steamer. He was the captain and he would keep me up in the cabin with him. He taught me about the water, the currents, how the light on the waves told a story. I loved that world. He told me I had good water sense. He started to teach me how to navigate, and I was good at it. By the time I was fourteen I was working full-time on the boats, in the man's world. Uncle would take me to dances. In time I wasn't just a kid any more, and I was a good dancer. The ladies liked me. They made me feel like I was someone they wanted. I had fun with them. I spent my money on them and my poker games. That's the way money goes, I was never good at keeping it around.

There was one girl, Flora. She would look for me when we docked in Lac La Biche. I knew her from the mission too. She always wanted to take me home to her house. She had a big family. They would play music and sing and dance. Her mom would make sure I had lots to eat. Then one night her dad pulled me aside and wanted to know what my intentions were. It took me a moment to figure out what he was asking.

"I'm not looking for a wife," I had told him.

"Then get out of here and don't come back," he had told me.

So I did. I went back to get my jacket. I told Flora I was leaving.

"Sing one more song before you go," she had said.

"I won't be coming back here any more," I told her. "Your dad doesn't want me around."

"Why?" she asked.

The whole world closes off when you have to be cruel like that. I just said what I needed to say: "Because I don't want to get married."

She was so hurt. Her face just kind of fell apart.

"You're better off for it," I told her. "I wouldn't make a good husband for anyone."

Better to be back on the water. Anything I could do, someone else could do just as well or better. Except for navigation. I was one of the best. The men treated me with respect when it came to that. And my uncle was proud for what he had taught me. I went back to the docks. We were making our last run before freeze-up.

That's what I was thinking of as I walked the dirt path down to the river where Adolphus had his work shed, a mug in each hand. The sun was already back behind the poplars, and I could hear the loons calling to one another on the lake. There was a peace in Adolphus's easygoing ways that I needed right now. He hadn't said much over dinner, leaving the news catch-up to Adeline.

He gave a little whistle of greeting when he heard my approach.

"There's the boy again. Something put a smile on your face, there. Is that mine?" Adolphus was mending his nets, sitting down on an old stump next to the shed with his moccasin rubbers off and the cloth jacket Adeline had made him lying on the grass beside him. He took the steaming mug into his hands and blew across it.

"Thinking about the old days on the water," I said.

A smile lit his face. "Those were old days."

"Remember when you had me here?"

"Yeah. About every time your grandpa threw you out." He laughed.

"You always treated me good."

"Well, it's always good to have another pair of hands. You chopped enough wood for your food. And this shack . . . " He patted the shed. "Adeline didn't even have to yell at you to get the job done. And the boys weren't old enough back then, Catherine was just a girl—it was always good having you around."

"I remember one day when two of the mares had got through the fence and were gone, and Grandpa—he was so hot he came after me with a whip. And after that I followed their trail—"

"And here they were!" Adolphus laughed. "I remember seeing them walk up the trail and I said to Adeline, 'Put down some more settings, we got two more orphans for us to look after.'"

"I guess they were tired of Grandpa too."

"When your grandpa was around, even the mosquitoes tried to move in with us to get away from him."

"I remember when I came to catch them, Adeline came out with some cookies that she had baked. She said to me, 'I know your grandpa's mean to you,' she said. 'It's not right.' I remember that—that was the only time I'd ever cried in front of a woman, besides my mom."

"She has a good heart."

"I wouldn't come here enough to visit. I always—I didn't want to bother you. But just to know that someone else was there . . ."

"We prayed for you. Still do. Figured you need it, especially since you've been riding the rails."

"Prayed? I've never seen you in church."

"Just because we don't go in the church doesn't mean we don't pray," he said.

Adolphus knew so much about a world I knew nothing about. Old stories, things people didn't talk about any more. When I was a kid, he'd mostly tell me about the animals and how they behaved. He would show me things that would tell you what the weather would be like. He was always watching, always aware. All that he would show me came in handy when I went out into the world because I came to recognize "the weather" in some people. I guess my grandpa helped to put me on guard too. I could tell when someone was going to turn stormy or if they were bad terrain. Most people are warm but I learned not to let my guard down, watch the signs.

That's why it surprised me when Adolphus got hurt when we were back at the dock in Lac La Biche. He and Pierre had been unloading some crates when one fell on Adolphus's leg and broke it. The nuns fixed him up; we borrowed a team from Bertrand, and I drove him home to Adeline and Catherine. I drove up to their house with her dad in the back of the wagon. I remember seeing that there was this beautiful young woman at the place, looking up at us from cutting up moose meat for drying in the smokehouse.

Adeline was standing out on the front step. I could see she recognized Bertrand's horses but she was surprised to see me driving the team. Adolphus was laid out in the back of the wagon drinking whisky to deaden the pain. "Adeline's out here," I told him. He groaned, emptied the last of the bottle, and tried to shove it under his blankets.

"Hello, this house," he said, and then he passed out.

Adeline came up to take a look at him. He didn't do it often, but she'd seen this before, especially when he got off at the end of the season with the rest of the boys. She was going to let him sleep it off in the wagon. Then the girl joined her. I didn't recognize her for Catherine at first, she had grown so much. Last time I'd seen her she was a seven-year-old girl with tomboy knees. She was beautiful now, and something else. I felt she could tell something was wrong with her father just from looking at me.

"What's wrong with Papa?" she asked.

"Well, he emptied that whisky bottle for one," Adeline said.

"He's got a broken leg," I told her.

Adeline pulled off the blanket to see the brace the nuns had put on Adolphus's leg.

"All right, let's bring him in."

Adeline collected a couple of tent poles from the house. Catherine grabbed a blanket from the wagon box. They threw together a stretcher and we all three manoeuvred Adolphus onto it and into the house. Seeing him cared for like that, I thought how lucky he was to have a family like that. No wonder he wouldn't let the nuns keep him overnight. He wanted to get home to these women who loved him. Catherine and her mother worked together like veterans, sharing few words and getting everything done. Adolphus didn't come to in the whole trip to his bed.

"There, let him rest now for a couple of weeks maybe. That's a long time for Adolphus to hold still," Adeline said after they were finished.

"They told him at the mission to stay off it for a month at least."

Adeline just laughed.

I had thought about staying around and helping out so Adolphus could rest easier. But then again, things were well looked after as it stood, and neither Adolphus nor me had been here for weeks. I wanted a reason to stay but couldn't think of one, so I went out to take the team back to Bertrand. It would be dark soon but the horses knew the way. I figured I could camp at Bertrand's and head out to Prudens' ranch in the morning.

Adeline caught me heading out. "You stay here tonight," she said. "Bertrand's got lots of horses. He doesn't need to see them tonight. You can take them back in the morning. You have something to eat and rest up."

Adeline went to the stove as Catherine went into the sleeping room and came back with some blankets. She began fixing me a bed on the floor on the far side of the room.

"Was he drinking when he got hurt?" Adeline asked me.

"No, working," I said. I told them what had happened while they fixed the table with moose stew and bannock. Adeline caught me up on all the news. I can't remember everything we talked about. That was around the time that my cousin George took over grandpa's homestead and started farming. He did that for a year before he was back to building boats. And the train was running passengers in by then, it was the start of harder times. There were so many white people around; it was tough for a Métis to get a job. "White people stick together," I had told them.

"Maybe it's because they have more schooling," Catherine said.

"Then they would be hiring the Treaties if that was it," said Adeline. "A lot of Treaties have schooling. It's true; they stick to themselves if they can. Before, they used to make sure they were our friends. They needed us. They didn't know their way around the bush like us. Remember those pitiful people that came and settled just west of us here by the river? They could farm all right, but they weren't that good at hunting. They were so happy when we would drop some meat off for them every once in a while. I guess they were getting tired of fish."

"Maybe it's good there are so many white people here," said Catherine. "They built a school now."

"I don't know about that," said Adeline. "Most of them still think we're too stupid to learn. They still act like they're better than us."

"Not when they need us," Catherine said. "They don't think we're too stupid when they're sick or having a baby, eh? Remember when Mr. Lafontaine came pounding on our door in the middle of the night?"

"That poor woman, I had to reach in for that baby. Now that little boy is always hanging around with George's boys. He thinks he's Métis. He talks Cree pretty good too, eh?"

By now the table was cleared. Catherine poured tea for us and picked up the moccasins she was working on. I could see that she did beautiful, tight beadwork. She could get a good dollar for that. Catherine was so attentive to whatever she was doing, so skilled. And she had the kindness of her mother and her father. I couldn't stop watching her.

"Do you have the medicine you need to make sure Papa heals in a strong way, Momma?"

"Yes. Remember the plants I had you dig when we were out picking blueberries the last time? Those are the ones we will use tomorrow."

"You said they were for blood."

"For bones too."

I figured I could head out in the morning, but I still didn't want to. When I woke up the next morning, Catherine was already building the fire in the cookstove. Adolphus and Adeline were already awake; I could hear them talking in the next room. It was a little embarrassing—I should have been the first one up and building the fire. I put my boots on and joined Catherine. She just smiled at me and handed me the water pail without saying a word.

Later that morning I paid Adolphus a visit. He looked like he had been doing some thinking.

"How you doing, partner?" I asked him.

"It looks like I'm tied up to the post here for a while. It's a bad time of year to be held up."

"I'm not in any rush to get out to Prudens'," I told him. "I was thinking of coming back to see how my cousin George is making out. Adeline was telling me he might be having a hard time. Is there anything you need me to bring back for you from town?"

They needed a few supplies since we hadn't stopped to pick any up. Adolphus was in too much pain to think about it at the time. Catherine offered to follow me. We hitched up the teams. Having her behind me, driving the team, it felt like we were already together. Even then I felt like we belonged to each other. She was sweet to watch, so shy in town. I felt like I should protect her. I felt then that I had to have that woman in my life. When we got back, that's what I told Adolphus.

"You will have to show me how you are going to look after her," he said. "You have no house. You have no horse. You have no boat. You have nothing."

I told him, "I can work. I have never had anybody I cared about. I want to be with her. I want to take care of her. I want to see that no harm comes to her."

"I believe you," he told me, taking hold of my arm and looking up at me. "But you'll have to show me."

So I started to work. It was easy when you could see why you were doing it, and with each day I got to know Catherine, the surer I was. Adeline told me, "She has a gift. The Spirits love her well. She helps me with my medicines. She has dreams. Sometimes that's not easy to live with. You might want to run away." Catherine said, "I know you belong to me. You will think it through." I would go through each day thinking about how I could show them that I was the man I needed to be.

Catherine and I looked after the trapline until Adolphus was back on his feet, then it was he and I that worked it. It was the start of more rough times. White trappers were moving into the country in bigger numbers than there had ever been. They would poach our traps, fix their own with poisons. Adolphus was angry and disgusted. He couldn't just give up trapping, because it was the way he had always supported his family through the winter, but by the end of the season he was planning on moving further north to get away from them.

By then I had developed a plan. I had helped my cousin George build a few skiffs, enough to earn my own, and went to Adolphus with my idea. We went into business. We would trade up and down the river from our skiff. Adolphus knew furs and I knew the water. We would trade goods for furs and dried fish. We bought and sold with trappers, farmers, and ranchers all along the river. We did a good business. I earned my way into the family. Catherine and I were married that December.

We were so happy. I had never been so content. I was a new man. Jean Francis was born in October of the following year. We continued to do good business on the river. Soon Catherine and Adeline were travelling and trading with us as well.

When Jean Francis was two we had a hard time when Catherine miscarried. Adeline was the strength for us. She had been through this before. You never forget it, but we moved on. Two years later we had Daniel. This time all went well, we thought. We had taken such good care of Catherine to be sure the baby had the best chance. But when he was about ten months old Catherine began to feel weak. She and Adeline stayed home with the children that summer. By the time Adolphus and I came back from our trading trip, Catherine was bedridden, coughing, pale and weak. She had consumption. Nothing Adeline could do was helping. That's when I saw Flora again. She was now a nun and had come to help with Catherine full-time.

I was stunned and in shock. I was numb. I didn't know what to think. How was this possible? Adeline had medicine. Flora had another medicine, and Catherine was so strong. She didn't want to leave us. She had her family to live for. We told ourselves she would make it.

That last night I had fallen asleep on a chair with my head on her bed. I awoke at the feel of her fingers stroking my head. I looked at her. Her eyes were filled with the deepest sadness I had ever seen. Tears were flowing down her face.

"Francis, I heard my owl," she told me.

"When? I didn't hear anything."

"Last night. Everybody was sleeping. No one heard but me. It was for me."

I felt a fear, and then a panic. She's going. She's leaving us. I fell beside her and held her and held her. We cried together.

"I can't go on without you," I said.

"You have to, for the boys. They will need you more than ever."

"I can't think about that right now. How can I be any good to them without you? I'm no good without you."

"Don't say that. You're good."

"I was no good until I met you. Ask your papa."

"He was just making sure you were good for me," she said as she touched my face and ran her fingers through my hair.

"I will be gone but I will never leave you. I will be here always to help you raise our babies. Remember that and believe it. I know. I see them all waiting for me on the other side," she said.

Once her owl had come she wasn't fighting any more.

I was crazy in my grief. I was living in a world that was here and not here. When we laid her in the ground I was broken. I was in so much pain. I couldn't bear it. I was broken and empty once again. I was no good. I was lost in my own insane world.

I was no good to my children like this. I couldn't eat. I couldn't sleep. I was in rage, agony, and sorrow, and in devastated hopelessness. I couldn't seem to come back. I didn't want to come back. I wanted to die along with her.

Adeline tried to comfort me even in her grief. "She's not in pain any more, Francis. Remember how she suffered. Take some comfort in knowing she is well now."

I couldn't hear that. I blamed myself. I'm sure she picked up the sickness on one of our trading trips. I raged at the greedy, selfish, ugly white man who was taking our land and our jobs, and who would rather see us dead. Adolphus tried to stop me from going to that place in my heart. "If you hate, it will kill you. Think of your children. They miss their mother too and they need their dad."

I was poison. I had to take myself away from those I loved. I heard the train whistle blow. "There's my owl," I said to myself. I threw myself into an open boxcar. "Take me. Take me, I don't care where."

"So tell me. Where did you go when you went to wandering around?"

Adolphus looked up from over the top of his mug, leaned back onto the side of the shed. "Must be some stories come from when a man travels like that."

"Well, I was travelling with Louis for a while there. He was sitting in the shadows in the boxcar I jumped into, with his big jug of moonshine!"

"That's right. We heard he was gone about the same time you were. Crazy right from when he was a boy."

"He told me his woman threw him out after that white man who was boss of the survey crew fired him."

"Yeah, I remember. The boss wanted to bring in his brother-in-law. Not a lot of folks from around here still working for that team," Adolphus said. "They all came from somewhere else."

"Louis told me that it was because he lost his gun at Sylvester's poker game."

Adolphus laughed. "That's probably true."

"We made plans to work for some ranchers around Edmonton and take it from there. For a while we were thinking of maybe finding a train going to Winnipeg and go back to the old country—Rupert's Land, Louis called it. He said he was named for Riel but he hasn't been able to find his army."

"His uncle was in Riel's army in 1869, you know. They came up here the same time as Laurent Garneau."

"I remember him telling that to me. I asked him, 'Don't you know the war is over?' and he says, 'Well, in the name of dog tail soup! I guess I should be recovering my casualties.' I told him he's crazy. He said, 'I'm a man of vision. There are two of you in front of me right now.'"

"I think you were spending too much time with him."

"We had some wild times. We fell off the train just outside Dunvegan and slept the night in the bushes. Back then it was around harvest, so there was plenty of work. Don't have much to show for it, though, but it was pretty easy living. We even had the opportunity for a few scrimmages from time to time."

"So what happened to him then? Did he come back with you?"

"No. Well, we split up when I got a ranching job and Louis went off with a threshing crew. We would meet up at the bar but it wasn't long before he disappeared for a while. And that was hard. I don't need to tell you, I had a lot of pain, and it started coming back then."

"I knew that. It was always hard for you."

I couldn't tell him how things went from there. I was drinking, more and more. I always made it to work because I didn't want to lose my booze ticket. Waking up was its own hell. I had to have my "medicine" to start the day, just enough to get me out of the bunkhouse. Not enough to get in the way. When the day was done I could do it right. Finally it got to the point where I needed more and more to get out the door. Then it was over. I had to go and find another job. It wasn't easy. The boats weren't working like they used to. I didn't have enough education to brag about, and my hard living was clear enough that most folks wouldn't give me a second glance, much less hire me.

Then I found Louis again. This time it was from the shadows under the bridge. He had his army. They would pool their findings and their thievings and make another day. He still had his grin but his body wasn't interested in big plans, even though his mind still made them. When I saw him, torn up and wasted away, that was the first time I realized how I looked.

"I was lost, lost for a long while there."

I looked up at Adolphus. It was hard finding the words I needed to say.

"It's good you're back. I've been thinking about you. Bertrand's been around, trying to get meetings going about getting Métis land again. There may be something for you if you stay here for a while."

He was so kind. I had to tell him what had brought me back.

"I had this dream, one of those dreams that felt so real it felt like it really happened." I could see Adolphus knew what I was talking about. "I was walking with Catherine along the edge of a lake. It was that old comfortable feeling, yet in the back of my mind I knew she was gone. She was beautiful and healthy and happy. She smiled at me and told me, 'Our boys must know the world. There's so much for them to be aware of.' She touched my face and she was gone."

Adolphus leaned forward. "That's a vision, for sure."

"I didn't open my eyes right away when I woke up. I wanted to savour the feeling of her presence. I could even remember her smell. I thought about my boys but this time I let their memory enter me, to be with her. All of us, we were all together for a brief moment and for the first time in a long time I let the tears flow. I cried until I felt like I'd just finished a hard day's work."

Adolphus took a sip of his tea. "They have to know the world. What does that mean?"

I looked up at him. "That's what I was thinking. How could they see the world? Right now I have nothing to give them. I got up that morning at first light, washed myself in the river, straightened up my clothes as best I could, and just walked. I walked toward the city buildings. I needed to clear my head. I didn't know where I was going but I had a sense. And when I turned the corner I saw two nuns walking in my direction. One of them said, 'Francis!' It was Flora."

"Flora?"

"Joseph Callioux's daughter, the sister that was here helping us when Catherine was sick. She saw what rough shape I was in and took me in. The convent gave me some fresh clothes and a good breakfast. She's a teacher there now. I showed her my picture of the boys. She told me, 'You bring them to me. I will take care of them as though they were my own.'"

"A convent school? What are you asking?" I sensed something darkening in Adolphus.

Just then from up the hill I heard the sound of two boys. I felt a joy rising in my heart as I got up. It was Jean Francis and Daniel. I bent down to meet them and soon they were on top of me, grabbing, laughing, and I was in the middle of it all, crying.

JOVETTE MARCHESSAULT

TRANSLATED BY YVONNE M. KLEIN

The Moon of the Dancing Suns

CONTRIBUTOR'S NOTE

THE PERIOD OF THE Second World War was one of extraordinary misfortune. The skies appeared impenetrable and normal life seemed to be turned upside-down. It was as though the business of living had become transfixed while Death galloped rapidly around the world.

"The Moon of the Dancing Suns" is a kind of memorial that I am dedicating to the First Nations and their children. The wealth of courage, bravery, and loyalty that they displayed during our wars has been obscured, but it is our duty to do justice to the First Nations.

I presume that someday, in the light of an eternal day, when humans no longer see through the eyes of thieves, this wealth will finally be revealed.

The Moon of the Dancing Suns

MI TAKU OYASIN.[*]
We are all linked to one another.

A voice swells in the light of the moon that shines in the darkness. It speaks to Tobie with all the sweetness of an old soul no longer possessed of an earthly voice. It speaks with so overwhelming a tenderness that he feels his heart, his entire being, open and expand. His first thought is that this might be the voice of his father, absent for so long a time, who is using this means to give him a sign from the invisible world where he sometimes likes to turn his steps, saying that it was there that he felt truly at home. His father is off fighting for freedom, just as Tobie's grandfather and all of his uncles did during the First World War. Even if they are not always recognized as full citizens, thousands of Natives have once again voluntarily joined up. Reserves everywhere are emptied of almost all their warriors, who have become soldiers alongside the millions of soldiers who

---

*Words spoken at the conclusion of every Lakota tobacco ceremony.

are fighting from east to west on front lines so far-flung that they could be given the names of rivers.

When Canada entered the war against Germany on September 10, 1939, Tobie's father became part of the Devil's Scouts, the Twenty-second Canadian Regiment. One evening, after reading one of his father's infrequent letters, Tobie asks his mother: "What do they use scouts for?"

"They are used to look hell in the eye, to be the only one to hear the tragic cry of a poor soldier dying in the gloom as he roars out his despair. A scout is a poor exhausted body, a freezing soul living in the mud, one who burrows out tunnels and undergoes the worst of hardships."

"My father is a scout for pain and grief," Tobie concludes after a silence.

"One day he will show you a beautiful, shining road known to no one else," his mother adds, turning over and lying down, her breath coming short.

Even in this time of war and rumour, of depression and illness, Tobie's mother views everything with eyes that transform the colour of things, especially whatever Tobie most fears. She never uses a low human word for a thing from above. She tries to give to everything both its human value and its divine weight. She is Native, a descendant of the Métis of western Canada. Her ancestors were both Indian and French, while those of her husband were Lakotas who had lived in every latitude of the Canadian and American west, in a condition of permanent war with the Cree and the Ojibwas, who were amply supplied with firearms by the French. For almost a century, the Lakotas went from one bloody war to another even more bloody one, culminating in 1890 in the massacre of two hundred Natives, including women and children, at Wounded Knee.

But the Métis and the Lakotas of the old days were familiar with an unforgettable epoch during which they still could stand full of wonder before the grassy ocean of the Great Plains. The winds that blew from the four quarters, the clouds, the beams of sunlight, all drew pictures in the tall grass, which bent and sprang back hypnotically and without end.

"On second thought," Tobie says to himself, "that isn't my father's voice I hear on moonlit nights. His voice is so vast that it could almost make the leaves fall from the trees in autumn. Nor is it my mother's voice. When she speaks, she often uses a haunted tone, a voice filled with the conviction that death is nigh or . . . that a miraculous cure is about to occur. My mother carries with her a bottomless fund of hope."

The mere thought of this inexhaustible fund, which is of course related to the paradise of the braves or the heaven of all the saints in the White people's calendar, fills him with a surge of sweetness and peace for a brief moment. But as a barrier it is too frail to hold back that wall of silence which would crush him and make him give in to despair.

When his father went off of his own free will, Tobie felt abandoned and betrayed. Even if he does know, in the depths of his soul, that his father has never ceased loving him and his mother, he does not know how to forgive him for racing off as if nothing else mattered to this warrior but the war. He left his family with pitifully little on which to live, and what he left was dwindling away. He writes them the occasional letter in which it seems that the war is a source of satisfaction that is lost on Tobie. In order to help himself forgive, Tobie has decided to watch over his father's vacant place at table, his spot at the window, his boots, his tools, and his turquoise necklace. In the depths of his memory, and without knowing exactly why, Tobie stands guard over his father and learns how to forgive him. In his father's absence, it is Tobie who takes care of his mother, trying to ease her pain. In return, she gives him that smile of hers which is so necessary to those who care for dying souls.

As if he expects an even greater sorrow, he raises his face toward the moon shining high in the sky and murmurs in a voice that hardly can be heard, an infinitely humble voice, "Spotless moon, snowy moon, do not desert me. Without you, my heart would be crushed and my head would throb like a drum." Tobie is a child. He is barely twelve years old.

As answer to his prayer, a joy-filled child's voice makes a dazzling breach in his black and evil sadness. It is little Anaië coming toward him. She is running through the woods and she is out of breath. The very first time that Tobie laid eyes on this little girl, he swore to himself that he would be her protector. He saw in her eyes a shimmering flash of blue, and he thought that no one, no one should ever have the right to dim that ray. It is a terrible responsibility to take on the task of protecting another, especially if that person is a child ... But mysterious arrangements are made in the deeps of time and heaven. From that moment on, who can say who is protecting whom?

Little Anaië is a Cree. Her parents, like Tobie's, no longer live on the reserve. They are not status Indians and so to a certain degree they do not exist. But if they were to live on the reserve, they would not have a much greater existence. After they left the reserve, they still continued to live within the sacred circle, the circle of life and death. "Within the sacred circle, the earth is not ordinary soil; it is dust compounded of the blood, the flesh, and the bones of our ancestors," say members of the Crow tribe. The earth of the sacred circle is an enormous ossuary in which are neatly piled the bones of millions of those who have died. When you chant the death threnody, accompanied by the sound of the drums, you can hear the full song of the dead, their tireless voices of silence, rising from the centre of the earth.

Little Anaië has recovered her breath enough to carol, "It's going to snow! It's going to snow in flakes as big as your nose, your eyes, and your ears! The snowflakes will whirl and dance in the white wind!"

Taking her hands out from under her cape, she catches flakes of snow and Tobie thinks, with a shiver, that she is also grasping his heart. Little Anaië is a devotee of snow, which she thinks is the most extraordinary, most beautiful thing in all the world. She claims that the first time snow fell on her, it enveloped her forever. It settled over her, like a halo.

Because of this and for other reasons, the little girl is not a well-liked child. This dense, profound shade hovers over her—she is useless! Everything seems to present difficulties to her. She fumbles, hesitates, and makes mistakes about even the simplest of things. She has trouble passing her exams at school and at home, she cannot pick up a plate without breaking it, nor can she make bannock or decorate the moccasins of her two brothers or her father's tobacco pouch with beads. Her mother worries that she will never make a good wife.

If her natural inabilities loom large in the eyes of all, her preoccupation with the supernatural escapes them. She is absorbed by the invisible, a presence so near to her that almost without wishing to, she can place her steps inside the tracks it leaves. Her natural forgetfulness, her moments of supernatural absorption provide her with a phenomenal life that seems ridiculous to wary, petty adults. When she is out of doors, she always seems to be wasting time, to be forever retracing her steps, but she is patience itself, as if she senses that the unfathomable paths over which she is drawn are of extraordinary length.

Before he left for the front, her father said in a troubled voice, "My daughter's moccasins must cease circling the camp. If she wishes to, she can go to the ends of the earth, all the way to the mountains, to the far waters."

These were his final words before travelling to Quebec City to board a great ship that would take him overseas. From this moment on, he would experience other things, undergo different emotions. He is a soldier and, like every true soldier, he will sacrifice himself completely and remain faithful to his country right to the end. He will give unstintingly until there is nothing left to give. And since he has never received anything from that country of his, he does not have to add it all up, as if he were afraid of giving too much. He would be ashamed to do the arithmetic; his spirit is too lofty for that.

Several seasons later, little Anaië dreamed she saw him in a great square where hundreds of corpses were laid out on the planks and the cobblestones. Her father was among these bodies, his eyes bloody, his chest split open. Feeling suddenly invulnerable, she ventured, trembling, right to that terrible threshold where he lay. A chaplain had just arrived to offer a last blessing.

"Oh, I feel much better," said her father, who was already dead. "If you will bless my battalion, Father, we can then return to the battle."

But the chaplain, who could not hear the voices of those who had died, went on his way without stopping.

That night, without knowing it, going forward across the vastness of the worlds, Anaië had crossed the gigantic boundary line that divides the living from the dead. And after having been present at her father's struggle to win back his life, she thought she could make out the creeping forms that slowly stole up upon the cadavers—repulsive forms with neither flesh nor meat, like demons trying to enshroud each dead man in a shadowy scarf.

It was a feeling of glacial cold accompanied by a violent shaking that woke her in the middle of the night to throw herself at the foot of her bed. On her knees, her teeth chattering, she prayed until dawn, imploring the Ancients to grant repose to the souls of her father and all the soldiers. Anaië was certain that no moment of human forgetfulness, no snowfall yet to come, would ever be capable of eradicating this dream.

"The Milky Way is falling down," chants Tobie, dancing with the snowflakes. Then, stopping still, troubled, he asked, "Why are you crying?"

Throwing herself with both abandon and trust toward Tobie, crying into his shoulder, the little girl tells him the dream that haunts her still.

"When I cry," she says, blowing her nose in Tobie's handkerchief, "it's as if I am lending a little of my own spirit to my father.

"Oh! See how the Snow Moon shines. I think she looks brighter and brighter," she adds. "It's a moon in bud. She seems to be full but it is in fact a swelling."

"She will be in blossom for the night of the Solstice," says Tobie, sticking out his tongue to swallow a snowflake.

"Do you believe she will speak? Do you think she will sing?" asks Anaië, sounding concerned.

"When she is in flower, she will grant everything! But that's a secret, Anaië." Tobie sinks his gaze into the immense and starry night, as if he wants to exhaust all speculation, and Anaië whispers in his ear, "She surrounds the earth with her bounty. She will help you."

"It has stopped snowing. It was only a passing cloud that came by to give my friend Anaië some pleasure."

"Listen, Tobie! Listen!" she says, suddenly alert. "What is that?"

It seems to be a sound coming from the outside, at once very close and very far away. A sound the children hear within themselves, like a thought, but so clear and musical that it gives the impression of beating on the air. In the silence of the night, this voice accompanied by music passes with an extraordinary swiftness, and the mark that it leaves on Tobie and Anaië gives no sign of effort. The children, the young people, listen without saying a word.

"Kateri! Kateri!"

This time, it is the voice of a young boy calling for help for what he believes he has lost.

"Jérémie . . . ," Anaië says to herself.

Breathing hard, a young Mohawk appears inside the circle of the clearing, his face creased with fatigue and distorted from worry. It is Jérémie. He is thirteen years old and lives with his father, a widower who left the reserve after his wife died.

"Kateri disappeared two days ago. No one knows where she has hidden herself. Even I have lost all trace of her. I did know that she wanted to go away."

Jérémie is speaking from within a kind of utter stillness, a stillness of the air and of time. Deeply moved, they allow themselves to be filled with the inflections of Jérémie's voice. These inflections they recognize well, as they are those that are the most comforting. They are those that are the best guide to your interior transformation. This is love.

"I was supposed to meet her at Aspen Point. She was looking for aspen bark for her grandmother's cataracts . . . I got there too late. When I got back home, there was her father. He was talking to my father. Kateri was nowhere . . . nowhere . . . Her father seemed to think it was my fault. He came back again that evening to question me. He was wearing his peacekeeper's uniform. As he was leaving, he said, 'When the whole world is tossing and turning in the nightmare of war, deaths come quickly.'"

Lacking words, he turns to gestures. With his face streaming with tears, Jérémie beats his chest in inconsolable sorrow and with surges of harrowing affection, as if he has lost Kateri forever.

"I was a coward," Jérémie goes on after swallowing a great gulp of air. "I told her father that I didn't know a thing and that anyway, this girl was not my type. If something horrible has happened to her, there will have to be an investigation, and her father will find out in the end that I did know something. I myself will be an accomplice, the one who stood by and did nothing. That's worse than anything else, because it is so cowardly a way to behave."

Jérémie weeps burning tears and Anaië wants to throw herself down on her knees without any false shame to comfort him and promise him that they will find Kateri.

All of a sudden, a clear and joyful voice cries, "What kind of Indians are you? You never even heard me coming!"

Parting the branches of a fir tree that were hiding him from view, David, Tobie's best friend, appears. He is fourteen years old and from a family that has been White for a number of generations. But David often takes pride in his distant ancestors, the Ojibwas, whose sad and marvellous history he knows by heart.

"Kateri has disappeared," cries Jérémie inconsolably.

"I know she has disappeared. Her father came to our house. My friends, I know no more about it than you who are standing here in a circle beneath the falling snow, but I would like to say what I think."

"She was walking in the direction of the city," Jérémie exclaims, raising his head. "Montreal is a city of mazes, alleys, train stations, bus stations, and bridges. And of horrifying, evil things! Young people, children, disappear there every day."

"As for myself, I think she has followed a different path," says Tobie.

"What path is that?" Jérémie asks in a despairing voice.

"The Blessing Path," says Tobie. "When a cure is needed, that is the path to choose."

"She is sick and I never knew?" asks Jérémie.

"Jérémie, the Blessing Path can be used to invoke peace and harmony throughout the world. Or it can be used at a birth, at the entrance into the world of human beings. We are all sick of the war," says Tobie.

"If Kateri has chosen the Blessing Path, I believe I know where she is hiding."

"Me, too, Anaië, I think I know—just fifteen minutes' walk away from here, in the middle of a wood, there is a chapel where they close the doors every equinox," says David, taking his place in the circle.

"David is right!" cries Anaië, clapping her hands. "Kateri has taken refuge in the Chapel of Healing. She is safe."

"The Chapel of Healing," Tobie repeats to himself. "Oh, how I love that name! It is the name of a resting place which confers its own incommunicable grace."

"Kateri among the Black Robes! Don't even think of it. She detests them," complains Jérémie.

"She is not with the Black Robes, she is with the Sparrows," Anaië answers, flaring up. "That is, with the Franciscans, who are as poor as any sparrow."

"I myself like all sorts of sparrows," says David. "Even those who wear a very rough brown wool tunic, cinched with a cord. It's the same colour as the earth."

"Like sparrows, they beg for their supper. I say that when sparrows fly to heaven, they go to carry our earth there," says Anaië, transfigured.

"And like sparrows, they never lay a hand on money. To them, it is as if they were touching excrement," David finishes in an admiring voice.

"Hey, I don't have anything against sparrows," Jérémie mutters, a little confused.

"Let's follow after Kateri," Tobie says, giving the signal.

In the clear lunar light, with hearts swollen with hope, they walk on. Instinctively, they understand the need for silence.

Before reaching their goal, they have to cross a broad wild meadow where the grass grows so high and so thick that it would be impenetrable at summer's end. But now the snow clothes, covers, and cloaks it all. The snow has laid low the vegetation that is growing in thick clumps, the sort that has large horned stems, alongside the cleverer ones that belong to heal-all and other vigorous and hardy plants that bear a thousand names and can cure when they are properly applied.

"In summer, all the flowers are swollen with sap and honey for the bees, the butterflies, and the hummingbirds," little Anaië thinks. "The Moon of the Long Snows is the Mother of All Grasses."

"I feel cold in all my parts and I am beginning to wonder if I shall ever be warm again. We must go forward despite the frost nipping at our heels. I have got to move faster or I am going to fall into the snow and go to sleep like the earth. Kateri needs me . . . indeed, is counting on me," Jérémie whispers very low.

"Friends, when we come back again to the Blessing Path, we must be sure to bring seeds to scatter as a treat for the birds," David says.

Sniffing the air, Jérémie makes a sudden stop.

"Someone has made a smoky fire, a fire of smoke!"

The chapel has just appeared at the bend in the meadow, surrounded by great pines, heavy with snow, that bend over its roof. Silver birches make a shining border against a dark background of fir trees.

"You can see footsteps in the snow," observes Tobie. "Two people have passed this way."

"There is a light within," murmurs David.

Now forgetting the frosty chill, the children, the young people, drink deeply from a sudden wellspring of invisible warmth and dash toward the great door, a door that must weigh several hundred pounds . . . Amazingly, it weighs nothing at all: it is only a couple of planks held together by a few crosspieces, easy to open. Jérémie tugs with all his might but the door resists. David comes to lend a hand, but to no avail. Holding on with all the strength in its lintels, the door utters a kind of moan.

"Listen!" says little Anaië, "the door is speaking!"

Rooted in its resistance, the door emits a long, long shriek. Jérémie and David retreat, a bit afraid.

"It is saying that we must not be too hasty . . . We must pause for a moment," little Anaië adds.

A second later, after a push that comes from within, the door finally opens.

"Well, you've taken your own sweet time," says Kateri, who is standing in the doorway.

She spreads wide her arms to welcome them. The children, the young people, hesitate between outside and in, between winter and sanctuary, surprised and uneasy, all save David, who goes to church with his parents.

Quite close to where the altar rises up and dominates the remainder of the space, someone has left a thick straw mattress on the ground, on the pine floorboards. On the altar steps themselves, placed at different heights, can be seen tall sure-footed candlesticks from which warmly coloured beeswax candles spring upward. Slender in form, they rise up in space to be transformed into a gentle light. Far above, their flames flicker.

In the half-light surrounding the altar, several statues can be seen, endowed by the candlelight with a pulsating presence. A few feet from the statue of Saint Francis of Assisi, his arms filled with birds singing with him his canticle "Brother Sun," a little pot-bellied stove pours forth a lovely warmth. The children, the young people, are sitting down. They have made a circle between the great candlesticks and the pot-bellied stove. Before beginning on her tale, which she tells with great effect, Kateri feeds the fire. Into its fiery maw she tosses sticks that she takes from a bundle made up of branches, slender pieces of wood, and twigs. The fire crackles, scented with the odours of the forest, and the flames leap up. As well, a light flows from the fire, and even if the air is still cold in the sanctuary, it seems easy enough to have a warm heart.

They wait for Kateri to begin her tale. No one asks a question, not even Jérémie, who feigns a certain detachment. Kateri is almost twelve years old, and when she is calm, as she is tonight, when nothing appears to shadow her heart, she becomes brilliant and translucent. When she wants to, she can make of herself a mirror for those who look at her. She knows how to reflect back to you what it is that lies hidden even deeper than your own being, the profound reality of the world of your soul. If she trusts you, she may even allow you to dive to the bottom of her heart, but you may go no farther than she wishes you to. Her friends find the simple recollection of her name extraordinarily invigorating. There are times when Kateri's energy runs so strong that you feel you are floating in her wake. She has hair as dark as a crow's wing, a dusky complexion, and eyes the colour of obsidian. When you see her, you cannot but think that this little girl has, like the majestic black pines that ceaselessly thrust themselves toward the sky, the capacity to grow indefinitely. They rise and taper as they rise until they form a fine point in the sky.

As Kateri continues her narrative, Tobie observes his friends. They are all hanging on her every word, especially David, whose face, at certain points in the tale, is crossed by shafts of light.

Tobie thinks he can remember that David once told him that in his family there was a long tradition of storytelling. "The finest gift that you can make to friends or guests is the enchantment of a good story. You must take care always to have one ready."

"My friends," muses Tobie, "are more alive than all the people I run across in the course of the day. I wonder sometimes if all those people have not come from the graveyard, dressed up in clothes that make them only look as though they were human."

Now that Kateri has finished her story, comments and questions explode.

"Oh, yes, Jérémie, my father, the peacekeeper, raised his hand against me one too many times, that hand of his as large as a great snow shovel, but my mother held back his arm!"

"The things you've told us have lodged themselves close to my heart," stammers Jérémie, mist in his eyes.

"This meeting in the middle of the woods when it was already growing dark is . . . miraculous!" David exclaims. "Especially since Brother Léon never goes out at night because of his failing sight."

"Never mind his failing sight! He was the one who spied me in the first place," Kateri says with a laugh.

"No one in the world is more practical than the invisible," muses little Anaïe aloud.

"What did he say to you?"

"David, he asked me why I was crying. I said that I never cried, even though I was a little girl. He smiled sweetly and told me, 'My child, sometimes the heart's clear vision is better than uncertain eyesight such as mine. And sometimes too such vision can even be enhanced by a kind of magnificent discernment that allows the recognition of all kinds of tears—tears of despair, tears of compassion, tears of love . . . and tears of repentance.'

"Then I asked him, 'Brother Léon, how do tears appear to you?' He replied, 'My dear child, they always look to me like sometimes shadowy, sometimes luminous rivers on their way to losing themselves, in what unnamed gulfs I do not know.'"

"Do you see him every day?" Jérémie wants to know.

"Since he offered me this shelter, I see him once or twice a day. He brings me a bit to eat—some bread, a boiled egg, cold water."

"And what do you give him in exchange?" Jérémie cannot stop himself from asking, his voice thick with jealousy.

"I give him our medicine for his poor eyes," Kateri replies, without letting herself be troubled by the question.

Turning toward little Anaië, Kateri gives her a medicine bag filled with aspen bark shavings.

"There is enough medicine in there to cure my grandmother's cataracts. I'm entrusting you with this bag. . . . You will give it to her. Don't be afraid; she won't say anything to my father."

Then she turns toward Tobie and hands him two little parcels containing a fragrant substance wrapped in birchbark.

"Brother Léon and I have gathered balsam gum and black pine resin . . . This is for your mother's lungs."

As he takes the presents of Brother Léon and Kateri, Tobie is confused and deeply moved. He has the idea that he has witnessed something extremely good, as good as a fount of tenderness, like a flame . . . Tobie is discovering universal interconnectedness, so often hidden by social falsehood.

"If one day I have lost everything else, I hope that I will never be without friends like you," Tobie says.

Now it is his turn to have misty eyes.

"It is already time to go," David exclaims regretfully. "Day is about to break."

"Tonight is the night of the Solstice," little Anaië recalls.

"We should meet again in the clearing," Tobie suggests.

"At the moment that the Moon of the Long Snows rises," Anaië insists.

"I shall be there," promises Kateri.

The marvellous door breathes a melancholy sigh as the children, the young people, pass under its lintel to return to a world seething with war.

"I am a night crow. I am alone of my kind," Kateri thinks as she closes the door with the sense that she is solitude's chosen one.

Outside, the snow swirls in flurries and the wind harvests it and shapes it into dunes. The children, the young people, walk along at a quick and joyous pace; then, all of a sudden, Jérémie seems to falter at the first difficulty and his gait, despite the encouragement of the others, becomes slower and slower. When he gets to the point where the ground begins to rise, Jérémie falls down and says he can go no farther.

Anaië believes she can see Jérémie's own thoughts moving about him. He wants to return to Kateri, but his thoughts are clotting together so powerfully that they seem to present an insurmountable obstacle. Anaië trembles as though Jérémie were about to fall to pieces before her eyes.

"This is a unique moment, a most mysterious instant," she calls silently to him. "If you are not deaf, go back to the chapel."

Jérémie at last gets up and, shaking his head, turns his steps with a light heart in the direction of the chapel. After following him with their eyes, the children, the young people, press on once again.

At last they reach the clearing, where the children, the young people, separate with the sense of having passed a night of exceptional sweetness bathed in moonlight.

Tobie makes haste to find his mother. Every morning, he makes her a nice hot cup of tea and a piece of toast and, on good days, even a dish of stewed fruit. After washing herself, his mother goes back to bed, already exhausted by the effort. Tobie hopes she has not coughed in the night, that she was able to slip into the sweet slowness of sleep.

David's parents, Anaïe's mother, and Jérémie's father are not yet back from work. They are mercenary hands working by night in a factory making bombs and munitions, operating around the clock. The work is stupefying, exhausting, and dangerous. Everything there is so mean that it would be a mistake to speak of wages; they earned a pittance.

White people have invented a word of hellish harshness to describe a certain form of labour in commerce and industry: "sweatshop." But what sweat is this? Sweating blood in accordance with the system? In order to make their way in such establishments, mercenaries have to be ready to rip their own flesh into tatters when necessary as they graft thorns on their finger ends. Such a thing would cause the hinges of the earth to groan. But the soul understands, the soul that knows more than we do.

From dusk to dawn, through the streets of the village, in its various spaces, in the forest openings, Kateri's mother and father have searched for their older daughter. This is their ordeal and it seems that, as far as they are concerned, everything except what belongs to Kateri's world has disappeared. An odd silence reigns between this father and this mother, a silence louder than all the sounds of the whole village. However much they cry out, the silence, the interminable silence, keeps them enclosed within the walls of their grief.

"My daughter has disappeared into the glacial night and my heart violently contracts when I think of her, and I think of her all the time. I am a peacekeeper and I know what goes on in the villages and on the reserves. Death waits everywhere in his own particular way. I know that in most cases, Death goes only where he is allowed to go. Strangest of all is that, when Death is kept waiting at the door until the dying person is ready to go, Kateri is obstinate enough to slam the door in Death's face. Kateri's disappearance has brought my wife and me closer together . . . When I speak to her, I speak more gently . . . She listens to me very attentively, then she starts to cry once again. Someday, that little scourge will find out how many tears she has cost her mother. Her mother, a woman so proud that she has never asked anything of anyone, is now following me about like a beggar, while asking all those she passes for the charity of a mere hope.

"I'm looking for my daughter. Listen! Look! Here she is in a photo. It was taken on her eleventh birthday. If you've come across her, you'd surely recognize her. Wouldn't you? But it's got so cold, you might have forgotten already . . . I know that my head is confused, my memories are all mixed up because of the cold. I beg you, look again at her face so you can engrave it on your memory. I'm leaving now, it's so cold . . . Heat is a treasure we must keep safe . . . When you see my daughter, the one called Kateri, tell her that my house contains an endless source of warmth.

"My wife is begging someone to grant her the alms of a single hope for our future, she has told me. I wonder whether anyone can hear her as she is crying so hard. I am holding her by the hand because she cannot see very clearly, thanks to her tears.

"Before my daughter disappeared, I rarely cried. So I had a vast storehouse of tears inside me and I didn't even know it. I should have cried more, I should have cried ahead of time, before the sorrow that is to come.

"My wife looks as though she has aged ten years overnight. When she bends over those children who are sleeping wrapped up in newspaper, with their tears frozen to their cheeks and icicles in their hair, she looks as though her whole life has passed in a single moment. When I look around, with a poor horrified glance at the world, I feel that hell itself is spilling across the earth.

"Wherever the children are, there is a stench of putrefaction, and the walls of even slightly obscure places are covered with horrible stains and running with freezing drops that make me think of my own tears . . ."

"Husband, what have we done to our children? What have we done to our children?"

When Kateri opens her eyes, it is daylight and Jérémie is standing at the foot of her straw mattress, with a pale smile on his lips. Kateri immediately understands what has happened in his heart and asks in a most gentle voice: "Jérémie, where is Chamia?"

Chamia was Jérémie's little dog, a dog that ran far and near and came back tirelessly . . . a dog that would travel the road a hundred times to come back to you. Jérémie understands that his little dog never tired because to Chamia, the road was never the same. He also believes that, with the aid of the full moon's light, the little dog could see at a single glance the great procession of all the roads of the immense earth. Even that did not discourage the little dog—on the contrary, it only gave renewed strength to its heart and legs.

"Some day," thinks Jérémie, "I too will be stronger than the road, stronger than exhaustion."

"Where is Chamia?" Kateri asks again. "We never see you together any more."

"My father killed him," Jérémie answers in a muffled voice. "He said he was sick, that he was too old . . . He put a shot through his head. My father was lying! He's a liar! Chamia was only seven years old, not old for a little dog who was never sick."

A shiver comes over Kateri, a shiver that looks like a shudder of dread.

"Kateri, I'm afraid. When my father looks at me . . . I am thirteen years old and I can't help wondering if he isn't figuring my age like the age of a dog! I don't understand any more. Everything he does or says, everything that bursts out of his mouth, seems cruel and dangerous."

"We have to feed the fire," says Kateri. "Later, we'll go collect branches and small logs. It should be a fine day."

In the house where Tobie lives, a woman has just spoken the same words.

"It should be a fine day, a day newly washed by the moon and the sun, a radiant day. I hear Tobie in the kitchen . . . I smell bread toasting . . . My son is good and he is brave. It is thanks to him that I can find the strength to grit my teeth and keep on going. I know that the sun will one day rise on a better day."

On the reserve, a man crazed with rage and grief has come to knock on the door of the house belonging to Kateri's father. He is using the butt of his gun. It seems as though he wants to burst it into a million pieces. Just when it seems that it is on the verge of giving up the ghost, the door opens and there stands a man, also holding a gun.

"You bastard, give me back my son!" Jérémie's father bellows at the man standing in front of him.

"I don't know where your son is. I didn't even know he too was gone," Kateri's father answers, pointing his gun at the father of his daughter's best friend.

"You've put Jérémie in jail in revenge for your daughter's disappearance!"

"I don't put children in jail!"

"You're just lying! I want to beat you up!"

"My sons, I have two objections," says a voice from afar that is speaking as it comes closer. "In the first place, you are going to hurt yourselves; in the second, I don't see what good will come of your putting a bullet in your bodies."

It is the voice of an Elder. The news has spread like wildfire through the reserve, and door after door opens as the Elders walk with solemn and deliberate steps toward the two men who are about to kill each other.

"What are we going to do with you when you are dead?" one grandmother asks, her throat trembling. "You are neither hare nor rabbit."

"If you want to try out your guns, pick a target about the same size as you are . . . If you hit it, let the other guy know," a grandfather says.

"When our children disappear, our duty is to bring them back home, offering them peace and justice, love and beauty. And no quarrelling on their account," says another grandmother.

"I am searching for my daughter day and night . . ."

"I have looked for my son all morning . . ."

"You are looking for your children with thoughts that make your hearts grow smaller!" says another grandfather.

"We are all linked to one another and each of us must be responsible for everyone else. Like our sons and daughters on the battlefield, we, the Elders, no longer sleep nor dream. The world is drunk on blood and our souls are drowned in sadness," moan the grandmothers.

"I have heard nothing from my granddaughter for months . . . She and her friends enlisted in the army to take care of the wounded and console the dying . . . Sometimes I see her running through the palpable darkness of the battlefield," says the eldest of all the grandmothers.

"In the olden days, our people had a secret power to comfort their children's souls and keep off impending danger," says a grandfather, holding his breast as if an invisible arrow had pierced him to the heart.

"We must leave it up to those who watch over us, according to the way of our tradition," the Elders chant, bonding themselves to one another. "If we do not . . ."

"If we do not?" The two fathers, armed with guns, ask in a single troubled voice.

When there is silence, it is Kateri's grandmother who answers: "If we do not, then we would rather that this very old world come to an end and that everything return to nothingness."

The band of Elders, united in a great circle, nod their heads as they listen to the old woman's answer, for she has been coming closer to the world of the Spirits for a very long time.

She continues her words: "My brothers and sisters, I have had a vision. You will certainly be amazed to hear me speak of vision in these times when the world is strangely and so rapidly darkened by so many dying in fear and bitterness. But listen to me speak of this vision—see the Great Spirit in our children."

"If you see with a pure and humble heart, this is a great vision," maintains another of the grandfathers, an old soldier of the First World War who left an arm and a leg on the battlefield in a blood-filled rut.

"Our children, our young people," Kateri's grandmother goes on, "with their actions, their language, and their absences are protesting against the darkness, against the foulness, against death."

She pronounces these last words while examining Jérémie's father down to the depths of his being . . . It must make his head swim so that he comes to lay his gun at the feet of one of the grandmothers . . . Having done that, he then asks her and all those gathered there to hear him and counsel him.

"By what evil spirit, by what demon, am I possessed?" asks Jérémie's father.

"Everyone, at least once in his life, comes in contact with a demon, an evil spirit in human form," says Kateri's father.

"But under what circumstances did you meet him, my son?" ask the grandmothers.

"When my wife was alive, she and I often used to go picking wild berries . . . Last summer, on the anniversary of her death, I went back to where we used to go. Just before noon, when the sun in the sky said that it was time to make lunch for my son, I turned back. Suddenly, I sensed a presence. Up ahead, by the edge of the path, a man was sitting motionless upon a large boulder. To get back home, I had to pass in front of him . . . To go around him would have meant a loss of face . . . A terrible foreboding swept over me as I went forward . . . But he did not appear threatening and bore no distinguishing marks. The closer I came, the more a blank horror seized me . . . When he turned his head to watch me approaching with his eyes like dark chasms, I saw that his gaze came from death itself . . . I passed him by, avoiding looking at him. I heard his voice hissing, 'I will have you, go on. I will have you.' As I heard this voice, horrible visions cast themselves on me and made me throw my hands in the air in my despair. I was a prisoner, I belonged to this evil spirit, to these visions of horror . . . I fell to the ground, unconscious, all my strength spent. When I opened my eyes, the sun was setting and the man, the evil spirit, had disappeared . . . "

"And what of the stone on which he sat?" a grandmother wants to know.

"*Pfft* . . . Gone up in smoke, just like him. Since that day, I have been in pain as though I'd been hit by the cries and howls of the dead. I spend my time cursing life, this bitch of a life, and that damn dog that my son prefers to his father . . ."

"When you curse, you are not doing your job as a father," the grandfathers chant as they close the circle around the two men again.

"To curse is to give up on everything," chant the grandmothers in their turn. "We are intended to dispense blessings, to kiss our children's hair and foreheads and cheeks. To embrace each and every one of our days on this earth."

"A father's lips, a mother's lips, are softer than the finest cloth," Kateri's grandmother chants.

"My wife says that we never say enough to our children or enough about them," Kateri's father murmurs as he places his gun on the snow, at his mother's feet.

"My life has been full of curses," moans Jérémie's father. "My son has turned from his father . . . He does not want my suffering," he moans even louder. "He is afraid!"

"Children, my son, are not afraid of suffering, not of the kind of suffering that is shared by all and is not lost. They are with us in this sort of suffering. But the suffering that you express, it is sterile suffering because you throw it back onto others. Your suffering," says Kateri's grandmother, looking at him with those eyes that induce dizziness, "that suffering that you bear inside you is a sterile and hellish suffering, a suffering that demands that you be ready for anything, even murder, to put an end to it."

"My son can't know anything about that . . . It's a secret . . . my secret," Jérémie's father answers, with a cracked laugh like a crow.

"Children, young people, play with their fathers' secrets the way the fathers play with the ammunition for their guns," the grandmothers chant, in their voices the light breeze of a secret dove.

Kateri's father is shaking Jérémie's father.

"My brother, give your son the gift of a living father who has triumphed over despair and his demons. Only by remaining alive can one come to the end of his life! Come with us, my wife and me, and look for our children . . ."

"Our people have walked for many years along the Trail of Tears," says a grandfather, raising his arms toward the sky. "Our lives have become lives like dead branches that, despite everything, creak under the tread of our sons and daughters who with wild eyes march across the battlefields that reach farther than rivers. At night, when I am sleeping and my thoughts take a rest from the material world and I approach the Spirit, I hear their moans. Their souls are in danger! We must gather all our strength and prepare a great ritual. The sun will travel more swiftly today as it is the Solstice . . ."

Kateri's father and Jérémie's father stand and object: "First we must find our children!"

"This very night, our children, our young people, will celebrate the Solstice in a secret place," says Kateri's grandmother. "Little Anaië confided that to me."

At day's end, all is ready in the clearing. The children, the young people, have piled up more than enough branches and small logs for a great bonfire that night. Seated on old stumps, clasping one another tightly, they wait for David, who is late . . . But here he is, and he is not alone: someone is walking behind him, his hand resting on David's shoulder . . .

"It is Brother Léon!" Kateri exclaims joyously.

"Look at that sky!" David cries. "It is the Archangel Gabriel spreading his evening wings. His wings are broad enough to mount to the sky—with one, he fashions the deep crimson of dusk, with the other, the rosy wreath of dawn. Brother Léon taught me that."

Rapt, enchanted, the children, the young people, behold the faintly crimson light of this one moment, and the blossoming Moon beholds it too. At last Tobie lights the fire, which crackles, speaks up, while the smoke, perfumed with the incense of pines and fir trees, rises toward the stars. With the help of the blaze, the atmosphere of trust between Brother Léon and the children, the young people, has increased. Each one there decides to reveal to the rest something he treasures. Tobie displays thick buffalo-hide gloves. "For the Lakotas, the bison is the animal that gives the greatest part of itself so that the people may live. When they need food, the bison offers its flesh, and when they need shelter, the bison provides its hide to make garments and tepees." When he left his father's house, Jérémie took with him his treasure—two rattles, one made of insect cocoons containing grains of sand, the other a turtle shell with small pebbles. As for David, he pulls six little buckskin pouches filled with birdseed from his backpack, giving one to each in turn.

"In anticipation of the next time we walk on the Blessing Path," he says, his voice filled with emotion.

Kateri shows her empty hands . . . She has brought nothing with her. Little Anaië, with a peculiar smile, decides to skip her turn: "Brother Léon, you go first," she says.

From under his cape, he brings forth an icon of the Theotokos, or the Mother of God, painted on a wooden board small enough that he can hold it in his large hand.

"I brought this for you," he says, giving the icon to Kateri. "She was painted in Russia, where I was born."

By the light of the flames, Kateri can be seen to blush.

"She is very beautiful. Thank you," she says simply.

"And you, little Anaië," Brother Léon says seriously, his voice lightly accented. "Have you a surprise in store for us?"

Anaië's treasure is wrapped in a beaded buckskin. She unwraps something that looks like a bow from which a piece of string dangles. There is also a long arrow.

"This is my father's musical bow," she says. "He taught me how to play it."

Grasping the dangling string between her teeth, she draws it tight and then strikes it with the arrow, causing it to vibrate. With her mouth acting as a resonating chamber, she produces sounds as old as the world itself. Standing erect, she plays and plays. The creature Moon in the sky lights the creature Earth, and the children, the young people, listen only to this music that has the power to make the whole world dance! Jérémie shakes his rattles and clear waves, solemn waves, pulse through the palpable expanse of night. They dance, circling the fire. As he leaps into the air, Tobie thinks he sees his mother, as beautiful as a young bride, smiling radiantly at him. Jérémie sees his father welcoming him with open arms . . . Kateri sees her father and her mother both sending her a thousand kisses.

Hidden in the forest at the edge of the clearing, the Elders witness the children, the young people, dancing. Tobie's mother is there—she is wrapped up in furs to keep her from the cold and comfortably tucked up in a sleigh that Kateri's father and Jérémie's father have taken turns to draw to this spot. As they promised Kateri's grandmother, the people of the reserve remain perfectly still, without making the slightest movement to disturb the air—on this night, only the Moon of the Long Snows and the children, the young people, are allowed to move. Watching their dance, Tobie's mother thinks deep inside herself, "It is as if the suns are dancing."

At the instant of the Solstice, Kateri is absolutely still. Quivering like a winged creature clad in a golden beam of light, she begins to sing the dirge "Death of a Warrior." The musical bow and the rattles accompany her as she intones the sad lamentation. All those present think they hear very clearly the beat of the drums along with the plainsong of the dead souls coming from the heart of the earth. When Kateri finishes her song, another voice arises . . . Appearing as a white shape, it descends from the Moon.

The grandmothers think, "It is the magnificent Daughter of Heaven."

The grandfathers think, "It is White Bison Woman, who taught us the seven sacred ceremonies."

Kateri's grandmother thinks, "It is the Great White Star, come from the Land of the Dead, to be a guide to our daughters and our sons."

Brother Léon thinks, "It is Gabriel, the Angel of the Moon, the guardian of human and animal mothers and new-borns, who is beginning his task of tenderness and love. How the blessings enlarge and spread!"

When this singer of a hundred names raises her ethereal voice, a matchless silence reigns. Hearing this *solestial* voice, surrounded by her divine song, every voice is silent and the demons seem to retreat into their caves.

"At last, those who have died on the field of battle are walking on the Blessing Path," say the Elders, who do not expect to see more winters.

Withdrawing in silence, they return to the reserve.

At dawn, under a pink sky and a pale moon, the children, the young people, part, each setting off along the path while feeding the birds. It will be a beautiful day.

Neither Tobie's nor Anaië's father ever returned. Like so many other Natives, they were buried in the lovely Canadian military cemeteries somewhere in Europe.

"Kahgee pohn noten took," the Crees say. This means "The battle is over."

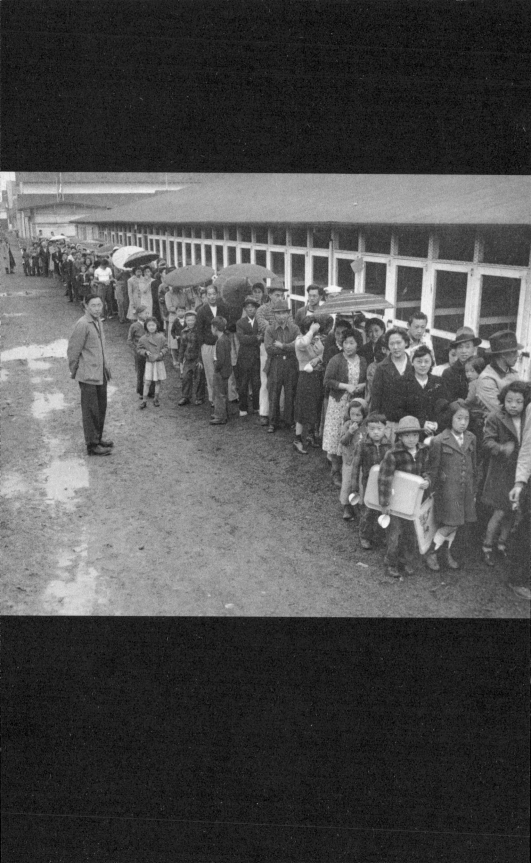

THOMAS KING

Coyote and the Enemy Aliens

CONTRIBUTOR'S NOTE

IT'S NEVER A GOOD IDEA to ask writers why they wrote something. We're such great liars. When anyone asks me that question, I have three answers I generally haul out.

One, I did it for the money.

Two, I wrote it because the topic moved me.

And three (my favourite), I wrote it to change the world.

It's not that these are bullshit answers, though, in part, they are. It's just that I have absolutely no interest in trying to figure out my reasons. I'm not even sure why I write, though I can't imagine giving it up. I suspect it was never my choice in the first place, which makes the question of why I write and what I write sound deliciously mysterious. Perhaps even mystical.

And, of course, that's bullshit, too.

But there is a moment in the creative process (in my creative process, at least) when something falls into my lap.

As it were.

Sometimes it's a phrase that I can use for a title. Sometimes it's a story I've heard. Sometimes it's an injustice (God knows there are enough of those). Sometimes it's a joke. Sometimes it's a recipe. Sometimes it's a personal demon that's gotten loose (I hate it when that happens). Sometimes it's little more than a sad thought or a vague gesture.

Who cares? I don't. I'm just happy that whatever comes along comes my way.

I know the story of the Japanese internment in Canada. I know it as most Canadians know it.

In pieces.

From a distance.

But whenever I hear the story, I think about Indians, for the treatment the Canadian government afforded Japanese people during the Second World War is strikingly similar to the treatment that the Canadian government has always afforded Native people, and whenever I hear either of these stories, a strange thing happens.

I think of the other.

I'm not suggesting that Native people have suffered the way the Japanese suffered or that the Japanese suffered the way Native people have. I'm simply suggesting that hatred and greed produce much the same sort of results, no matter who we practise on.

So never ask a writer why he wrote something.

You've been warned.

Coyote and the Enemy Aliens

You know, everyone likes a good story. Yes, that's true. My friend Napioa comes by my place. My good place. My good place by the river. Sometimes that Napioa comes by my good place and says, Tell us a good story. So I do. Sometimes I tell those good stories from the Indian time. And sometimes I tell those good stories from the European time. Grown-up stories. Baby stories.

Sometimes I take a nap.

Sometimes I tell Coyote stories. Boy, you got to be careful with those Coyote stories. When I tell those Coyote stories, you got to stay awake. You got to keep those toes under that chair. I can tell you that.

You better do that now. Those toes. No, later is no good.

OK, so I'm going to tell a Coyote story. Maybe you heard that story before. Maybe not.

Coyote was going west. That's how I like to start that story. Coyote story. Coyote was going west, and when he gets to my place, he stops. My good place. By the river.

That was in the European time. In 1940. Maybe it was 1944. No, it was 1942.

Coyote comes to my house in 1941. Hello, says that Coyote. Maybe you have some tea for me. Maybe you have some food for me. Maybe you have a newspaper for me to read.

Sure, I says. I have all those things.

So Coyote drinks my tea. And that one eats my food. And that one reads my newspaper.

Hooray, says that Coyote. I have found a job in the newspaper.

Maybe you're wondering who would hire Coyote.

I thought so.

OK. I'll ask.

Who would hire Coyote. I says.

The Whitemen, says Coyote. The Whitemen are looking for a Coyote.

Oh boy. Coyote and the Whitemen. That's pretty scary.

It's over on that coast, says Coyote. In that west. That's where my job is.

Good, I says. Then I won't have to move.

But I am so hungry, says Coyote. I don't know if I can get to that coast, unless I get something good to eat.

OK, I says, I will feed you so you can get to that coast.

And I don't have a good shirt, says Coyote. I really need a good shirt, so the Whitemen will see that I'm a good worker.

OK, I says, I will give you my good shirt.

Oh, oh, oh, says Coyote, how will I get there? It's a very long ways, and my feet are quite sensitive.

You still got those toes tucked under that chair? You better keep your hands in your pocket too. Just in case Coyote notices you sitting there. And don't make any noise. If that Coyote sees that somebody is listening to him, that one will never leave.

OK, I tell Coyote, I will call Billy Frank. My friend Billy Frank goes to the coast. He drives that pickup to that coast to go on that vacation. Maybe he will take you when he goes on that vacation.

Hooray, says Coyote. Hooray!

So Billy Frank takes Coyote to that coast. And that's the end of the story.

No, I was only fooling. That's not the end of the story. There's more. Stick around. Have some tea. Don't move those toes. Coyote is still around here somewhere.

Ho, ho. So a lot of things happen. All of a sudden, everyone is fighting. Mostly those White people. They like to fight, you know. They fight with one another. And then they fight with those other people. And pretty soon everyone is fighting. Even some of us Indians are fighting.

You're probably think that Coyote is fighting, too.

Is that what you were thinking?

It's OK, you can tell me.

So Coyote comes back. I warned you about this. Coyote comes back, and he is driving a pretty good truck.

Yoo-hoo, says Coyote, come and see my pretty good truck.

Yes, I says, that's a pretty good truck, all right. That job you got must be a pretty good job.

Oh, yes, says Coyote, that job is the best job I have ever had.

That pretty good truck that Coyote is driving says "Kogawa Seafood" on the door. Ho, that Coyote. Always looking for something to eat.

Where did you get that pretty good truck, I says.

Coyote stole me, says that pretty good truck.

No, I didn't, says Coyote.

Yes, you did, says that pretty good truck.

Don't talk to that silly truck, Coyote tells me.

What's wrong with talking to trucks, I says. Everybody talks to trucks.

Not any more, says Coyote, and that one lowers his eyes, so he looks like he is sitting on a secret. Talking to Enemy Alien trucks is against the law.

Enemy Alien Trucks? Holy, I says. That sounds serious.

National security, says Coyote. If someone saw you talking to an Enemy Alien truck, I might have to arrest you.

I'm not an Enemy Alien, says that truck.

Yes, you are, says Coyote.

No, I'm not, says that truck.

So Coyote and that pretty good truck says "Kogawa Seafood" on the door argue about Enemy Aliens. They argue about that for a long time. All day. Two days. Three. One week. They keep everyone awake. Nobody on the reserve can sleep. Even the dogs are awake.

Knock it off, those dogs says. You're keeping everyone awake.

I haven't heard of any Enemy Aliens, I tell Coyote.

Oh, says Coyote, they're all over the place. But you don't have to worry. You don't have to run away. You don't have to hide under your bed.

That's good news, I says.

Oh, yes, says Coyote. Now that I'm on the job, the world is a safer place.

No, it's not, says that pretty good truck.

Yes, it is, says Coyote. And those two start arguing again.

I don't know about you but all this arguing is making me dizzy. Maybe we should have some tea. Maybe we should have some dinner. Maybe we should watch that television show where everyone goes to that island, practise their bad manners. Maybe we should go to sleep. You can sleep on the couch.

So when I wake up, that pretty good truck is gone. But Coyote is still here.

Where is your pretty good Enemy Alien truck, I ask Coyote.

Oh, says Coyote, I had to sell that one. That's the law now. All Enemy Alien Property must be confiscated. All Enemy Alien Property must be sold. That's my job. And that Coyote shows me a piece of paper says "Order-in-Council 469."

Boy, I says, that paper has a nice voice.

Order-in-Council 469, says that paper. All hail, Order-in-Council 469.

Boy, I says, that paper sounds pretty important.

It is, says Coyote. That paper says that I am the Custodian of Enemy Alien Property.

Coyote is the Custodian of Enemy Alien Property, says that paper. All hail Coyote, Custodian of Enemy Alien Property.

That job sounds pretty important, I says.

It is the most important job in the world. says Coyote.

Is it more important than being truthful, I says.

Oh, yes, says Coyote.

Is it more important than being reliable, I says.

Absolutely, says Coyote.

Is it more important than being fair, I says.

Probably, says Coyote.

Is it more important than being generous, I says.

It certainly is, says Coyote.

Holy, I says, that is one pretty important job, all right. How do you do that pretty important job?

Well, says Coyote, first I find all the Enemy Aliens. Then I confiscate their property. Then I sell their property. Say, you want to buy some Enemy Alien Property?

Enemy Alien Property. Yes, that's what that Coyote said. Sure, I don't mind asking. You keep sitting in that chair. Keep those toes under that chair. And stay awake. You start snoring, and that Coyote is going to hear you for sure.

So, I ask Coyote, what kind of Enemy Alien Property do you have for sale?

Oh, says Coyote, I have everything. You want a sewing machine? How about a set of dresser drawers? I have a bunch of radios. Cameras? A refrigerator? Blankets? Teakettles? A wheelbarrow? A house. Maybe you need an easy chair. I got lots of bicycles. Maybe you need a new car. Maybe you need a fishing boat.

A fishing boat? You have a fishing boat for sale?

Ho, ho, says that Coyote, I have more than one. How many would you like?

How many do you have, I says.

Eighteen hundred and four, says Coyote.

That's a lot of fishing boats, I says.

It's a hard job, says Coyote. But someone has to be paid to do it. Maybe you need a pretty good kimono.

No, I says, I don't need a pretty good kimono.

Come on, says Coyote. Let's go see the Enemy Alien Property.

So I go with Coyote. But we don't go in that pretty good truck says "Kogawa Seafood" on the door because Coyote has sold it. But that Coyote has another pretty good truck says "Okada General Store" on the door.

You sure have a lot of pretty good trucks, I says.

Oh, yes, says Coyote, I am an excellent Custodian of Enemy Alien Property.

So Coyote starts driving. He drives to those mountains. And that one drives into those valleys. And then he drives to that Pacific National Exhibition in that Vancouver city.

I am lost, I tell Coyote. Where are we now?

Hastings Park, says Coyote.

That Hastings Park is a big place. Big buildings. Big signs. That big sign says "Livestock Building."

Livestock? All right. So, I ask Coyote, you got any Enemy Alien Horses? That's what I ask. You got any Enemy Alien Horses? I could use a good Enemy Alien Horse.

That Coyote checks that list of Enemy Alien Property. That one checks it again. No, he says, there are no Enemy Alien Horses.

Enemy Alien Cows? I ask Coyote.

No, says Coyote, no Enemy Alien Cows.

Chickens?

No.

Sheep?

No.

Holy, that's all the livestock I can remember. So, I ask that Coyote, what do you keep in that Livestock Building?

Enemy Aliens, says Coyote. That's where we keep the Enemy Aliens.

Boy, that Coyote likes to tell stories. Sometimes he tells stories that smell bad. Sometimes he tells stories that have been stretched. Sometimes he tells stories that bite your toes. Coyote stories.

That's one good Coyote story, I tell Coyote. Enemy Aliens in a Livestock Building.

No, no, says Coyote. This story is not a good Coyote story. This story is a good Canadian story.

Canadian story. Coyote story. Sometimes it's hard to tell the difference. All those words begin with c.

Callous, carnage, catastrophe, chicanery.

Boy, I got to take a breath. There, that's better.

Cold-blooded, complicit, concoct, condemn.

No, we're not done yet.

Condescend, confabulate, confiscate, conflate, connive.

No, not yet.

Conspire, convolute, crazy, crooked, cruel, crush.

Holy, I almost forgot cupidity.

No, no, says Coyote. Those words are the wrong words. The word you're looking for is "legal."

Boy, you're right, I tell Coyote. That legal is a good word. You can do a lot with that one. That's one of those magic words. White magic. Legal. Lots of other White magic words.

Patriotic, Good, Private, Freedom, Dignity, Efficient, Profitable, Truth, Security, National, Integrity, Public, Prosperity, Justice, Property.

Sometime you can put two magic words together. National Security, Public Good, Private Property.

Stop, stop, says Coyote. All these words are giving me a headache. We only need one word for Enemy Aliens. And that one word is legal.

So Coyote takes me into the Livestock Building and that one shows me the Enemy Aliens.

Boy, I says, you caught a big bunch of them.

You bet, says Coyote.

But what is that smell, I ask Coyote.

Pigs and cows and horses, says Coyote. We had to move the pigs and cows and horses out so we could move the Enemy Aliens in.

That is certainly a strong smell, I says.

It certainly is, says Coyote. We better leave before we get sick.

Maybe the Enemy Aliens would like to leave, too, I tell Coyote. So they don't get sick from the pigs and cows and horses used to live here.

Enemy Aliens don't mind that smell, says Coyote. They're not like you and me.

They look like you and me, I says.

Oh, no, says Coyote, you are mistaken. They look like Enemy Aliens.

So that Coyote shows me all those sights. That one shows me that big building with all that glass. And that one shows me that other big building with all that glass. And then that one shows me that other big building with all that glass.

Boy, I tell Coyote, that's a lot of big buildings with glass.

You want to see another big building with glass? says Coyote.

No, I says, that's enough big buildings with glass for me.

Okay, says Coyote, let's go see that Enemy Alien Property. Maybe we can find you some silverware.

So that Coyote shows me that Enemy Alien Property.

Holy, I tell Coyote. It looks like you confiscated everything.

Yes, says Coyote. The Whitemen have given me a commendation that I can hang on my wall.

Boy, there's another one of those words begins with *c*.

See anything you like? says Coyote. I can give you a really good deal on family heirlooms.

But just as that Coyote is showing me those good deals on those family heirlooms, he gets that phone call. This is before they got those phones you can walk around the house with, and this is before those phones you can carry in your pocket. Call any place you like for thirty cents a minute, plus those roaming charges. This is the time when those phones are nailed on those walls, when those real women place that call for you, when you have to stand right next to them.

No, not the real women.

So that Coyote stands next to that phone and that one nods his head and that one smiles and that one makes happy noises.

Good news, says that Coyote. The Whitemen have given me another job.

Boy, I says, you are one busy Coyote.

Yes, says Coyote, and I have a new slogan. You want to hear it?

You want to hear Coyote's new slogan? No, I don't want to hear it either. But if we say no, we may hurt Coyote's feelings and then that one is going to cry and make a lot of noise and keep everyone awake. Yes, that one will keep the dogs awake, too.

So I tell Coyote, OK, you tell us your new slogan.

OK, says Coyote. Here it is. "Let our slogan be for British Columbia: 'No Japs from the Rockies to the seas.'"

Ho! That's your new slogan?

Ian Alistair Mackenzie, says Coyote. It's Ian Alistair Mackenzie's slogan.

He must be important, I tell Coyote. All Whitemen with three names are important.

He's the Whiteman in charge of making up slogans, says Coyote. But that one is not a good poet. If he was a good poet, he would have said, "Let our slogan for British Columbia be: No Japs from the Rockies to the sea."

Look at that, I says. Now that slogan rhymes.

Be, sea, says that slogan. Be, sea.

Oh, yes, says Coyote, all good slogans rhyme. You want to hear some of Ian Alistair Mackenzie's other slogans?

Is that your new job, I say. Making those Ian Alistair Mackenzie slogans rhyme?

Oh, no, says Coyote, my new job is to Disperse Enemy Aliens.

No, I don't know what "disperse" means. Lots of those words begin with "dis." Disdain, Disappear, Distress, Disaster, Disillusioned, Disappointed, Disingenuous, Distrust.

Disperse.

No, I don't think we should ask Coyote. OK, but don't blame me if things get messed up.

Come on, says Coyote, we got to get those Enemy Aliens dispersed.

So Coyote gets all the Women Enemy Aliens and the Children Enemy Aliens out of that Livestock Building smells like horses and cows and sheep, and that one gets those Men Enemy Aliens with those targets painted on their backs from that other place, and that Coyote puts all the Enemy Aliens into the back of his pretty good truck says "Okada General Store" on the door.

It's pretty crowded, I can tell you that.

OK, says that Coyote, let's start dispersing.

So that Coyote drives that truck into that valley, and then that one drives that truck into those mountains, and then that one drives that truck onto those prairies, and that one doesn't stop driving until he gets to my place.

My good place. My good place by the river.

Holy, I says, there is my good place.

Yes, says Coyote, this is a good place, all right. Maybe this is a good place to disperse the Enemy Aliens.

Sure, I says, we got lots of room.

So Coyote gets all of the Enemy Aliens out of the truck, and I call my friend Napioa and my friend Billy Frank. Ho, I tell my friends, we got guests.

OK, my friend Napioa and my friend Billy Frank tell me. We'll call the rest of the People. Maybe we'll eat some food. Maybe we'll drink some tea. Maybe we'll sing a welcoming song.

169

A party? says Coyote. I love parties!

But you know what? Some of those Enemy Aliens look pretty sad. Some of those Enemy Aliens look pretty scared. And some of those Enemy Aliens with the targets on their backs look pretty angry.

Boy, I tell Coyote, those Enemy Aliens don't look too happy.

And after everything I've done for them, says Coyote. And just as that Coyote says this, a big car comes along.

Ho, I says, that is one important-looking car.

Yes, I am, says that important-looking car.

Did you come for the Enemy Alien party? I ask that important-looking car.

No, says that important-looking car, I am looking for Coyote.

Did I get a promotion? says that Coyote. And that one polishes his teeth with his tongue.

Get in, says that important-looking car. We got some secret stuff to talk about.

So Coyote gets in that important-looking car, and I go find the food, and now some of the Enemy Aliens are feeling a little better.

You know, that Billy Frank tells me, this story about the Enemy Aliens have their property taken away by Coyote and the Whitemen and get moved from their homes to someplace else reminds me of another story.

Yes, I tell Billy Frank, me, too.

You remember how that story goes, says Billy Frank.

No, I says, but maybe if we think about it, that story will come back.

So we eat some food, and we drink some tea, and Billy Frank and Napioa warm up that drum, and we have a couple of songs.

So pretty soon, that Coyote gets out of that important-looking car. And those RCMPs get out of that important-looking car. And those politician guys get out of that important-looking car, singing O Canada. But they don't sing so good.

Holy, says Billy Frank. We're going to have to get more food.

Okay, says Coyote, all the Enemy Aliens back in the truck!

Let's not be hasty, I tell Coyote. The party is just starting.

No time to party with Enemy Aliens, says Coyote. I got a new job.

Another job? Boy, that Coyote is one busy Coyote.

What is your new job? I ask Coyote.

I got to take the Enemy Aliens to their new homes, says Coyote.

They can stay here, I says. We got lots of room.

Oh, no, says Coyote, that would be too dangerous. We got to take the Enemy Aliens who look sad and the Enemy Aliens who look scared to that Sugar Beet Farms. We going to give them jobs.

OK, I says, working on the Sugar Beet Farms is pretty good money.

We're not going to pay them, says Coyote. Those Enemy Aliens have to work for free, so they can show us that they are loyal citizens.

Boy, I tell Billy Frank, those citizenship tests are tough.

What's a citizen? says Billy Frank.

What about those Enemy Aliens with the targets painted on their back, who look pretty angry?

Oh, says Coyote, those are the Dangerous Enemy Aliens. Those Dangerous Enemy Aliens are going to Angler, Ontario.

Holy, I says, those Enemy Aliens must be real dangerous have to go to Ontario. Have any of the Enemy Aliens caused any troubles?

Not yet, says Coyote, but you can't be too careful.

So that Coyote goes to the centre of the party and stands by the drum, and that one holds up his hands.

Okay, says Coyote, all the Enemy Aliens back in the truck.

But you know what? Nobody gets in the truck.

Maybe they didn't hear me, says Coyote. And this time he says it really loud. All the Enemy Aliens back in the truck!

But nobody gets in the truck.

OK, says Coyote, we going to have to do this the hard way. And Coyote and the RCMPs grab Billy Frank.

Enemy Alien, says that Coyote and those RCMPs.

Silly Coyote, I says, that's not an Enemy Alien. That's Billy Frank.

Are you sure, says Coyote. He certainly looks like an Enemy Alien.

I'm Billy Frank, says Billy Frank.

So that Coyote and the RCMPs grab another Enemy Alien.

No, I says, that's not an Enemy Alien, either. That's my friend Napioa.

Nonsense, says Coyote, I know an Enemy Alien when I see one, and Coyote and the RCMPs grab everyone they see. Those politicians stand behind that important-looking car singing O Canada and waving flags.

Enemy Alien.

No, I says, that's Leroy Jumping Bull's cousin Cecil.

Enemy Alien.

No, I says, that's Martha Redcrow. She's married to Cecil Jumping Bull's nephew, Wilfred.

I wouldn't stand too close to this story if I were you. Coyote and the RCMPs might grab you. Yes, I'd sit in the corner where those ones can't see you.

Enemy Alien.

No, I says, that's Maurice Moses. He's Leroy Jumping Bull's grandson. Leroy's daughter Celeste had twins.

Enemy Alien.

No, I says, that's Arnold Standing Horse. He takes those tourists into those mountains go hunting.

That silly Coyote even grabs me.

Hey, I says, let me go.

Oops, says Coyote, oops.

You got to stop grabbing everybody, I says.

But Coyote and the RCMPs don't do that. And pretty soon that Coyote has that pretty good truck filled with Enemy Aliens, and that one has that pretty good truck filled with Indians.

I have more Enemy Aliens than when I started, says Coyote. I must be better than I thought.

You got to keep the Indians and the Enemy Aliens straight, I tell Coyote. Otherwise you're going to mess up this story.

And just then the RCMPs grab that Coyote.

Enemy Alien.

No, no, says Coyote. I'm Coyote.

Enemy Alien, shout those RCMPs. O Canada, sing those politicians. And everybody drives off in that important-looking car and Coyote's pretty good truck says "Okada General Store" on the door.

And I don't see that Coyote again.

So that Coyote comes by my place. My good place by the river.

Yes, this is still the same story. Yes, that Coyote has been gone a while, but now that one is coming back. Sure, I know where Coyote and the Indians and the Enemy Aliens go. No, they don't go to Florida to play that golf, wrestle that alligator. No, they don't go on that cruise to those islands, everybody sits in the sun and drinks out of big nuts. No, they don't give those Enemy Aliens back their Enemy Alien property either.

Hello, says that Coyote. Maybe you have some tea. Maybe you have some food. Maybe you have a newspaper for me to read.

Sure, I says. Sit down. Where's that pretty good truck says "Okada General Store" on the door?

The Whitemen took my pretty good truck, says Coyote. And they took all my Enemy Alien Property. And they took all my Enemy Aliens.

Holy, I says, those Whitemen like to take everything.

Yes, says Coyote, that's true. And that one drinks my tea. And that one eats my food. And that one reads my newspaper.

Hooray, says that Coyote. I have found another job.

Boy, I says, it is dangerous to read newspapers.

This job is better than the other one, says Coyote.

You going to round up more Enemy Aliens? I says.

No, says Coyote. I'm going to that New Mexico. I'm going to that Los Alamos place in New Mexico, help those Whitemen want to make the world safe for freedom.

OK, I says, that sounds pretty good. That New Mexico is mostly that desert and those mountains. Nothing much in that Los Alamos place that Coyote can mess up.

Yes, now Coyote is gone. Yes, now those toes are safe. Yes, that's the end of the story. Well, you should have asked Coyote while he was here. Maybe if you hurry, you can catch him before he gets to that New Mexico.

No, I'm going to stay here. That Coyote will come back. That one always comes back. Somebody's got to be here to make sure he doesn't do something foolish.

I can tell you that.

TOMSON HIGHWAY

Hearts and Flowers

CONTRIBUTOR'S NOTE

I CHOSE TO WRITE on the subject of Canada's Native people winning the right to vote in federal elections for two reasons. The first is that we, the group of writers whose work you see in these pages, were asked to write a story or an essay for this project based on, or woven around, an important, that is to say, a pivotal, event in the history of Canada's Native people. This, of course, would mean—I started thinking right away—going back in history perhaps even as far as the storied arrival of Christopher Columbus in North America in 1492. My problem, however, is that I—to date anyway—have never been particularly good at writing what one might call "period pieces." I've only really been truly comfortable writing about the "here and now"—that is to say, what is happening today. Or at least, what has happened during *my* lifetime, meaning what I myself remember happening, even if only vaguely.

Well, nothing *that* important has happened to the Native people of Canada this year or last, or even this last decade, at least nothing truly earth-shattering or universally transformational, at least nothing that

I know of. As I was thinking all of this, moreover, the notion that I really should be writing about, and around, an event that took place while I was alive, just kept coming back to me. That is to say, this "event" had to be an event that I myself, if only vaguely, would remember, and what's more, it had to be an event that was indeed "universally transformational." It had to be an event that changed *all* our lives, clean across the country, in a manner that was significant, powerful, and permanent, and "all" meaning, of course, the Native people of Canada. And that event, I came to decide, was the day—the 31st of March, 1960—when we, as a "nation," as a people, as human beings, got the right to vote.

I was eight years old in 1960, the year Prime Minister John Diefenbaker finally was successful in pushing through the legislation whereby we, as a people, got the right to vote in federal elections—the law whereby we, as a people, were able to decide our own fates, as it were, or, at the very least, help decide the fate and the direction our own country was and would be taking in the world at large. It dawned on me, moreover, that a people are not truly considered full-status human beings until their intelligence is recognized as being that of human beings, in which case they can then participate in the way their own country is run, the way their lives are decided for them. I think what also helped in this whole thinking process for me, personally, what pushed me along, was that I had just seen, in France, a play entitled *Controversy at Valladolid*, written only recently and considered a classic of modern French drama. In it a group of Roman Catholic clerics and intellectuals, fifty years after "the fact of Columbus," are arguing, in the context of a major international forum, whether the "Indians of the Americas" are or are not human (for you see, in those days, the Pope considered that we had no souls, that we were equivalent, in effect, to wild, savage animals, like jungle cats or mink).

At any rate, all this thinking eventually crystallized into this little story that I've had stashed away inside my head for a very long time, a story that, like too many of my stories, tends to be a little on the autobiographical side, shall we say. But it's a story, nonetheless, that I've always wanted to record because it is, in point of fact, about a little Cree Indian boy who changes the world with–and this at the risk of sounding just a touch self-important—the power of art. That is to say, it is about the "universally transformational" power of a simple, and perhaps forbidden, piece of music called "Hearts and Flowers," and the boy who dares play it . . . on that fateful night when his people, finally, are recognized as human.

And *that* was the second, and final, reason why I chose to write about this subject *and* in this manner.

Hearts and Flowers

Daniel Daylight sits inside Mr. Tipper's travelling car. It is cold—not cold, though, like outside; of this fact Daniel Daylight is quite certain. He looks out through the window on his right and, as always, sees white forest rushing by; maybe rabbits will bound past on that snowbank in the trees, he sits thinking. He has seen them, after all, on past Thursdays just like this one. It is dark, too. Not pitch-black, though, for that half moon hangs unhidden, making snow—on the road, on the roadside, rocks, ground, trees (mostly spruce though some birch and some poplar)—glow, as with dust made of silver, Daniel Daylight sits there thinking. Daniel Daylight, at age eight, is on his way to his piano lesson in Prince William, Manitoba.

Twenty miles lie between the Watson Lake Indian Residential School, where resides Daniel Daylight, and Prince William, where he takes his weekly lesson. The Watson Lake Indian Residential School, after all, has no one to teach him how to play the piano, while Prince William has elderly and kind Mrs. Hay. So his teacher in Grade Three at the Watson Lake Indian Residential School, Mr. Tipper, drives him every Thursday, 6:00 p.m. on the nose, to his piano teacher's house, Mrs. Hay's, in Prince William.

Orange brick and cement from the top to the bottom, held in by a steel mesh fence, then by forest (mostly spruce though some birch and some poplar), the Watson Lake Indian Residential School stands like a fort on the south shore of a lake called Watson Lake, 550 miles north of Winnipeg, Mr. Tipper's place of birth. Prince William, quite by contrast, is a town that stands on the south bank of a river called the Moostoos River, just across from which sprawls a village called Waskeechoos (though "settlement" is a noun more accurate, Mr. Tipper has explained on previous Thursdays, for no "village" can be seen, only houses peeking out of the forest here and there). Waskeechoos, on the north bank of the muddy Moostoos River, is an Indian reserve, Mr. Tipper has informed Daniel Daylight, not unlike the one from which hails Daniel Daylight: Minstik Lake, Manitoba, 350 miles north of Waskeechoos, Prince William, and the Watson Lake Indian Residential School. It takes half an hour for Daniel Daylight to make the journey every week, in Mr. Tipper's travelling car, from the Watson Lake Indian Residential School south through the heart of Waskeechoos and across the Moostoos River to Prince William, so he has time on his hands for reflection (so, at least, Mr. Tipper calls such thinking).

Daniel Daylight likes these trips. For one thing, he gets to practise what he knows of the language they call English with elderly and kind Mrs. Hay, with the waiters at the Nip House or at Wong's (where he sometimes goes for snacks with Mr. Tipper once he's finished with his lesson), and with friends of Mr. Tipper whom he meets at the Nip House or at Wong's. He enjoys speaking English just as he enjoys speaking Cree with the students at the residential school (though, of course, mother tongues need no practice, not like English with its *v*'s that make one's teeth come right out and bite one's lower lip). Daniel Daylight, for another thing, likes to ride in "travelling cars" (as he calls them for the *v* in "travel"). Standing at the northern tip of a lake called Minstik Lake, the Minstik Lake Indian Reserve, after all, has no cars and no trucks, just dogsleds in the winter, canoes in the summer. A third reason why

Daniel Daylight likes these trips is that he enjoys being dazzled by the lights of a city like Prince William (for to him, the railway depot is a city of one million, not a town of five thousand) with its streets, its cafés, hotels, stores, and huge churches with tall steeples, whereas Minstik Lake, with its six hundred people, has no streets, no cafés, no hotels, just dirt paths, one small store, and one church. Daniel Daylight, for a fourth thing, likes these trips because Mr. Tipper's travelling car has a radio that plays songs that he can learn in his head. When it stops playing music, furthermore, it plays *spoken* English words, which, of course, he can practise understanding. Tonight, for example, people living in the east of the country (Mr. Tipper has explained) are discussing voting patterns of the nation (Mr. Tipper has explained), even though Daniel Daylight knows the word "vote" for one reason: it begins with the sound that forces one to sink one's teeth deep into one's lower lip and then growl. Sound, that is to say, thrills Daniel Daylight. Which is why, best of all, Daniel Daylight likes these trips: because he gets to play the piano. He gets to play, for elderly and kind Mrs. Hay, "Sonatina" by Clementi, which he now knows well enough to play page 1 from the top to the bottom without stopping. He gets to play, for the third time this winter, "Pirates of the Pacific," with the bass that sounds like a drumbeat. He gets to play, this week, for the first time, *with* Jenny Dean, the duet— for four hands—called "Hearts and Flowers."

"Jenny Dean is a white girl," he has overheard someone say at the Nip House, just a few days before Christmas, in fact, when he was there having fries and Coca-Cola with Mr. Tipper. "Daniel Daylight is an *Indian*. A Cree Indian. Indian boys do *not* play the piano with white girls," he has overheard one white girl whisper *loudly* to another over Coca-Cola in a bottle, "not here in our Prince William, not anywhere on earth or in heaven." Daniel Daylight let it pass. He, after all, was eight years old, not thirty-one like Mr. Tipper; what could he have done to the girl who had made such a statement? Bop her on the head with her bottle? Shove a french fry up her nose? Scratch her face? Besides, neither Jenny Dean's parents, Mrs. Hay, nor Mr. Tipper seemed to mind the notion of Jenny

Dean making music with a boy whose father was a *Cree* caribou hunter and a celebrated dogsled racer.

"There it is," says Mr. Tipper. And so it is, for the travelling car has just rounded the bend in the road from which the lights of Prince William and the Indian reserve on this side of the river from the town can be seen for the first time. This first view of both town and reserve, to Daniel Daylight, always looks like a spaceship landed on Planet Earth, not unlike the spaceship in the comic book that his older brother, John-Peter Daylight, gave him as a Christmas present twenty-one days ago and that Daniel Daylight keeps hidden under his pillow in the dormitory at the residential school. Daniel Daylight likes, in fact, to imagine all those lights in the distance as exactly that: a spaceship come to take him to a place where exist not Indian people, not white people, just good people and good music. In fact, he can hear in his mind already "Sonatina" by Clementi, key of G, allegro moderato. He can hear "Pirates of the Pacific" with that drumbeat in the bass that goes *boom*. He can hear "Hearts and Flowers." He has practiced all three pieces to the point of exhaustion, after all, in the one room at the residential school that has a piano, what the nuns and the priests call the "library" but, in fact, is a storage room for pencils and erasers, papers, rulers, chalk, and some old spelling books. Feeling on the tips of his fingers all the keys of Mrs. Hay's brown piano, Daniel Daylight sees the sign on the roadside that announces, "Waskeechoos Welcomes You." Mr. Tipper's travelling car speeds past the sign, thus bringing Daniel Daylight onto land that belongs "to the Indians," Mr. Tipper, for some reason, likes proclaiming, as on a radio. "Speed Limit 30 MPH," Daniel Daylight reads on the sign that then follows. The road now mud, dried, cracked, and frozen, potholed and iced, the travelling car first slows down to a crawl, then bumps, rattles, slides.

"Indian people are not human," says Mr. Tipper, dodging first this small patch of ice then that small patch of ice, "at least not according to the government. They cannot vote." Daniel Daylight sits unsurprised—Mr. Tipper's use of English, white as a sheet and from Winnipeg as he may be, is not always perfect, Daniel Daylight has simply come to accept. The young Cree piano player, in any case, does not feel confident enough, in either his grasp of English *or* his age, to say much in rebuttal. His father, after all, speaks maybe ten words of English, his mother just two or three; of his eight living siblings, older all than him, only John-Peter Daylight, who is three grades ahead of Daniel Daylight at the Watson Lake Indian Residential School (and perhaps Florence, who once studied there, too, but quit at just Grade Four), speaks English. No one on the Minstik Lake Indian Reserve where Daniel Daylight was born, for that matter, speaks the language, not even Chief Samba Cheese Weetigo *or* his wife, Salad. Like people right here in Waskeechoos (as Mr. Tipper has informed Daniel Daylight in the past), they speak Cree and Cree only. So how, indeed, *can* they be human, Daniel Daylight asks himself, *if* they don't even know what the word means or looks like on a page?

At the bridge that spans like a giant spider's web the muddy, winding Moostoos River, a bottleneck is fast taking shape. Built mainly for trains, the bridge makes room for car and truck traffic only by means of a one-way lane off to one side. The traffic light glowing red like a charcoal on this side of the crossing, four cars sit at its base humming and putt-putt-putting; the travellers from Watson, as happened last Thursday, will just have to sit there for four or five minutes, much too long for Daniel Daylight, who can't wait to play the piano with Jenny Dean. Preparing, in a sense, for conversing with elderly and kind Mrs. Hay when he gets to her house (for Mrs. Hay's Cree, of course, is like Mr. Tipper's—it does not exist), Daniel Daylight makes a decision: he will practise his English. On Mr. Tipper.

"Human, what it mean, Mr. Tip—" But Mr. Tipper does not let him finish.

"If a man, or a woman, aged twenty-one or older cannot vote," says Mr. Tipper—who, from the side, resembles Elmer Fudd, Bugs Bunny's worst enemy in the comics, thinks Daniel Daylight—"then how on earth can he be human, hmmm, Daniel Daylight?"

"'Vote'?" Daniel Daylight feels himself bite his thick lower lip with both sets of teeth, so unlike Cree which has no such sound or letter, he sits there regretting.

"'Vote' is when a person helps choose the leaders that will make the laws for his country," replies Mr. Tipper. He snorts once and then continues. "Every four years, in Winnipeg where I come from, for instance, the person who has the right to vote will go to a church or a school or some such building that has a hall, step inside a little . . . room—the *voting* booth, this room is called—take a small piece of paper on which are written the names of the four, five, or six people from that region or that neighbourhood who want to go to Ottawa to speak for the people of that region or that neighbourhood." Daniel Daylight is having trouble keeping up with the torrent of words pouring out of Mr. Tipper's mouth. Still, he manages to catch what he thinks Mr. Tipper, in the past, has referred to as "the drift." "The person then votes—that is to say, chooses—by checking off the name of the person on that list who he thinks will best speak for him and his needs, and the person on that list whose name ends up being checked off by the greatest number of people in that region or that neighbourhood is voted, in this way, into power, and that person goes to Ottawa to help our prime minister run our country, is what the word 'vote' means, Daniel Daylight," says Mr. Tipper. "You 'vote' for your leader. *You* decide how *you* want *your* life to be in *your* country. That's what makes you a human. Otherwise, you're not."

The traffic light changes first to yellow, then to green. Daniel Daylight has always taken pleasure in looking at what, to him, is an act of magic. *Thump, thump*, goes the travelling car as it crosses the bridge built for trains. The *thump, thump* stops. And now they're in Prince William (or in land that is human, as Mr. Tipper calls it, where people can "vote," just like in Winnipeg)—paved streets, lights so bright Daniel Daylight has to squint, lights so bright it looks like midafternoon. On Mr. Tipper's car radio, the music is back; some sad, lonely man is howling away about being "cheated" by someone, maybe his wife. To Daniel Daylight, it sounds, for some reason, like the Indians are being cheated.

In Mrs. Hay's living room, Daniel Daylight sits straight-backed at her upright Baldwin piano. Sitting in a chair right beside him, her hairdo white, short, and fluffy, her face as wrinkled as prunes, the elderly and kind human woman smiles at her one Cree student through glasses so thick they could be ashtrays, Daniel Daylight sits there thinking. Scales first, chords next, then arpeggios, key of E. Major. Right hand only, two octaves up: E, G-sharp, B, E, G-sharp, B, E. And two octaves down: E, G-sharp, B, E, G-sharp, B, E. Back up, back down, Mrs. Hay humming softly along, in her cracked, quavery voice, with the tune such as it is. Daniel Daylight cannot help but wonder as he plays his arpeggio in E major if playing the piano will or will not make him human. Left hand next, same arpeggio, only two octaves lower, first up: E, G-sharp, B, E, G-sharp, B, E. And two octaves down: E, G-sharp, B, E, G-sharp, B, E. He is dying to stop right there at the E with the brown stain and confront Mrs. Hay with the question, for Mr. Tipper, as always, has left him with her, alone, at her house for the hour.

"Very good, Danny," says Mrs. Hay, giving him no chance to ask any questions. Only she, of all the people he knows in the world, calls or has called him Danny. Not his five older brothers, not his six older sisters, not his one hundred friends, not even his parents call him "Danny Daylight." Daniel Daylight is not sure he likes it. But he says nothing. In any case, it's too late now; she has called him "Danny" ever since he first walked into her house that fine, sunny day in September almost three years ago. They move on. First "Sonatina" by Clementi, key of G, allegro moderato, a Grade Six piece; of this fact, Daniel Daylight is very proud if only because he has been taking piano lessons for only two and a half years and should, by rights, still be in Grade Three, not Grade Six already.

"It's the 14th of January," says Mrs. Hay as she peers over her glasses at the calendar that hangs on the wall with the picture, right above the calendar's big, black "1960," of her husband, Mr. Hay, driving a train and smiling and waving. "The festival starts on the 29th of March." Daniel Daylight thus has ten weeks to practise and memorize "Sonatina," for that is his solo entry at the festival and he plans nothing less than to win first prize. As he plays "Sonatina," a piece energetic and happy because it, after all, is written in the key of G, major, allegro moderato (meaning, in Italian, "fast, but not too fast," as in "moderate"), Daniel Daylight, in his mind, sees his father, Cheechup Daylight, and his mother, Adelaide, standing in a line at the little wooden church in the village of Minstik Lake, a worn yellow pencil each in hand. They are lining up to vote. At this point in their lives, they are not human, for a sign on their backs says as much: "Non-human." The melody line for Clementi's "Sonatina" soars like a swallow flying up to the clouds, tugging at the heart of Daniel Daylight as with a rope. If he plays it well enough, his parents will surely turn, allegro moderato, into humans, Daniel Daylight prays as he plays. He comes to the end: dominant chord (his right thumb adding the minor seventh) followed, *seemak* (right away), by the tonic. *Thump. Thump.* In the pianist's mind, Cheechup Daylight and his wife, Adelaide, are turned away from the little voting booth by the missionary priest, Father Roy. They are not human. They cannot vote.

"Very good, Danny," says Mrs. Hay. "Jenny should be here in just five minutes," she adds, smiling. "But . . . " And this is where Mrs. Hay, kind as a *koogoom* (grandmother) as she may be, criticizes him and his playing, sometimes in a manner that takes him quite by surprise. He is tensing up at his right temple as he plays, says Mrs. Hay. If he is tensing up, at his right temple, meaning to say that a vein pops up in that region, as she calls it, every time he reaches for a high note, then his right arm is tensing up and if his right arm is tensing up then his right hand is tensing up. Which is why the melody, from measure 17 to measure 21, in particular, sounds not very happy, forced, not quite "there," explains Mrs. Hay. He must try it again. He does, Mrs. Hay, this time, holding her bone-thin, liver-spotted, white right hand, gentle as a puff of absorbent cotton, on Daniel Daylight's thin right wrist, guiding him, as it were, from phrase to phrase to phrase. Better this time, he can feel it: his right arm is not tensing up, not as much anyway. Again, however, as "Sonatina" comes to an end, his parents are turned away from the little cardboard booth at the church that stands on the hill overlooking the northern extremity of Minstik Lake. *Still,* they are not human. *Ding,* goes Mrs. Hay's electric doorbell. And into the vestibule of her back entrance blow a flurry of snow *and* Jenny Dean. Taking off her bulky winter outer-wear—mitts, coat, hat, scarf, boots—her cheeks glow pink from the cold of a mid-January evening in far north Manitoba and her hazel cat-like eyes sparkle as does her blond, curly hair—yes, decides Daniel Daylight, Jenny Dean looks, indeed, like a human.

Now Jenny Dean is sitting on the brown wooden bench right there beside Daniel Daylight. She smells so nice, thinks Daniel Daylight, like snow just fallen on a green spruce bough. The sheet music for the duet Mrs. Hay has chosen as their entry at the festival sits open on the piano's music stand before them. He can feel his red-flannel-sleeved right arm pressing up against the girl's yellow-pullovered left arm. His is the lower part, the part with the bass line and chord structure, hers the higher part, the part with the melody but with the occasional *part* of a chord, meaning that the Cree Indian, non-human pianist, the "Heart," Daniel Daylight, and the white girl human pianist, the "Flower," Jenny Dean, will be sharing chords, in public, from a piece of music called "Hearts and Flowers" written in the key of C, major, andante cantabile—meaning, in Italian, "at a walking pace *and* singing"—by a human woman named Joan C. McCumber.

Water-like, limpid, and calm, the chords start playing, they float, placed with care on the keyboard by Daniel Daylight. The bass sneaks in, the melody begins. Playing octaves, Jenny Dean's hands begin at the two Cs above middle C, arc up to the G in a curve graceful and smooth, then waft back down to the F, move on down to the E, and thence to the D, skip down to the B and swerve back up to the C whence they had started. The melody pauses, Daniel Daylight's series of major chords billow out to fill the silence, the melody resumes with another arcing phrase, filled with sunlight. For Daniel Daylight, two things happen. First, from where he sits, he sees four hands, two brown (non-human), two white (human), playing the piano. He is sure, somehow, that once he and Jenny Dean have mastered the piece and won first prize in the duet section of the music festival, he—and his parents—will be human. They will have the vote. Father Roy will *not* be able to turn Cheechup Daylight and his wife, Adelaide, away from the little voting booth at the little wooden church that overlooks the northern extremity of beautiful, extraordinary Minstik Lake with its ten thousand islands.

One month later, Daniel Daylight sits at a table in a booth at the Nip House on Prince William's main thoroughfare, looking with amazement at the valentine just given him, at Mrs. Hay's, by the human piano player Jenny Dean. Standing upright on the table one foot before him, the card is covered with hearts and flowers. High above it looms the very white face of Mr. Tipper with his Elmer-Fudd-like, round, pudgy nose, and behind Mr. Tipper, a wall made of one giant mirror. On the radio that sits on the counter five tables, and therefore five booths, behind Daniel Daylight, Kitty Wells is singing, "Three Ways to Love You, It's True," his sister, Florence Daylight's, favourite song, the one she sings with her boyfriend, Alec Cook, as they sit there on the shores of Minstik Lake strumming and strumming their two old guitars. Now it is mid-February, the Kiwanis Music Festival looms even closer—just six weeks, Mrs. Hay has informed Daniel Daylight *and* Jenny Dean, so Daniel Daylight is excited to the point where he can't stop slurping, through a straw and as loudly as he can, at his glass half-filled with black Coca-Cola. They are sitting in the "Indians Only" section of the restaurant, Mr. Tipper, for some reason, chooses this moment to explain to Daniel Daylight, his blue eyes peering at the restaurant spread out behind and over Daniel Daylight's shoulder. Daniel Daylight stops his slurping and peers past the rim of the tall thin glass at the wall behind Mr. Tipper, the wall which, of course, is one giant mirror. Darting his eyeballs about like tiny searchlights, he looks for a sign that will, indeed, say "Indians Only."

"There is no sign that says 'Indians only,'" says Mr. Tipper, knowing, as almost always, what is going on inside the mind of Daniel Daylight.

"Indians only . . ." Kitty Wells has stopped singing, Daniel Daylight suddenly observes, and a man's speaking voice has taken over on the radio. Daniel Daylight locks his eyes with Mr. Tipper's—what on earth will the man say next about . . . ?

"Hamburger deluxe, gravy on the side!" yells the big, fat waitress who always scowls at Daniel Daylight, drowning out the voice of the man on the radio, at least temporarily.

" . . . cannot vote," the man on the radio ends his speech.

"You see?" says Mr. Tipper, sipping at his coffee with his thick pur-plish lips. "They're not human, not according to the radio, not according to the government. It is the law."

"Who made the law?" Daniel Daylight feels emboldened to ask Mr. Tipper.

"No one," says Mr. Tipper. "They are unwritten. It's the same thing at the movie house right here in Prince William, the taverns, the bingo hall, even the churches, Baptist, Anglican, *and* Catholic—Indians on one side, whites on the other."

Suddenly ignoring his half-finished plate of french fries with gravy, his Coke, and his valentine, Daniel Daylight twists his back around to look at the rest of the restaurant—looking in the mirror will *not* do: 1) the Nip House has room for at least sixty customers; 2) the fire-engine-red-vinyl-covered booths are not high enough to hide any-one from anyone; 3) true to Mr. Tipper's unwanted observation, white people sit on one side of the restaurant, Indian people on the other. He turns back to the mirror and to Mr. Tipper, who, of course, is the one exception, being as he is a white man sitting with the brown-skinned, black-haired, non-human, Cree Indian pianist Daniel Daylight on the "Indians Only" side of the restaurant. Mr. Tipper must be brave, Daniel Daylight thinks rather sadly, lets go his Coke, and slips his valentine into a pocket of his black woollen parka. Suddenly, he is no longer hungry.

Six weeks later, Daniel Daylight sits inside Mr. Tipper's travelling car with the radio playing, again, country music, a song that Daniel Daylight does not know. He is about to ask when Mr. Tipper asks him, "What they will think when they see you and Jenny Dean playing together at the festival?" Daniel Daylight has no answer, not at the moment anyway, for "They will love our music" sounds somehow hypocritical, facetious, not quite truthful. Again they are going down the winding gravel road, with snow-covered forest rushing by as always, a rabbit bounding past on the snowbank just to the right. Daniel Daylight is on his way, this time, to the Kiwanis Music Festival in Prince William. He is going there to compete in the solo/Grade Six section with his "Sonatina" by Clementi, key of G, allegro moderato, which he now has down note-perfect *and* memorized. More important, however—at least so says Mr. Tipper, and with this notion Daniel Daylight is inclined to agree—he is going there to compete in the duet section of the annual event with the white girl/human, Jenny Dean, in a piece with the title "Hearts and Flowers," written by the human composer Joan C. McCumber.

They come to the Indian reserve called Waskeechoos, the sign that says so just going by and the next one saying "Speed Limit 30 MPH." The travelling car slows down. It bumps, rocks, and rattles. One pot-hole here, two there. Ice. The travelling car slides once, for six inches, then stops. A non-human man walks past, from the town and back to his home in Waskeechoos.

"People can't vote?" asks Daniel Daylight, his English, and his confidence, having bloomed rather nicely in the last two months for, of course, it is now the 31st of March, 1960, the last day of the three-day-long Kiwanis Music Festival, and northern Manitoba is still gripped hard by winter.

"Soon they might," says Mr. Tipper. "I heard on the radio the other day . . ." But the traffic light at the railway bridge has just turned green and Daniel Daylight, in any case, has drifted off already to his own reserve 350 miles north, where his father and his mother are standing in line at the church on the hill that overlooks beautiful, extraordinary Minstik Lake, a worn yellow pencil each in hand. They are getting ready to select a man they can send to Ottawa to speak for Minstik Lake and all its people, perhaps even Chief Samba Cheese Weetigo. Into the line behind and in front of them are crushed all six hundred people of Minstik Lake, even babies. And they are roaring; they want to vote. "Apparently the law is changing," says Mr. Tipper, "soon. Or so I heard on the radio." Good, thinks Daniel Daylight, all these people back there in Waskeechoos, like those people where I come from, will soon be human, he sits there thinking. He doesn't even notice that they are now on "human territory," as Mr. Tipper calls it, for already he can see himself on stage at the Kiwanis Auditorium in downtown Prince William, sitting at the piano beside Jenny Dean, playing music with all his might so his parents, and therefore he, can change from non-human to human. He is glad that Sister St. Alphonse, the principal seamstress at the Watson Lake Indian Residential School, has found him a suit for the evening: black, white shirt, red necktie, black shoes, all, for the moment, under his black woollen parka. His hands, meanwhile, are wrapped in woollen mittens so thick they do *not* stand a chance of getting cold, stiff, or claw-like, he has decided, not when he has to use them, tonight, to make *a point.*

At the Kiwanis Auditorium in downtown Prince William, Daniel Daylight sits in the audience with his back tall and straight, like all good pianists, Mrs. Hay has always insisted. From where he sits, in the middle and on the room's right side, he can see—now that he is two months wiser, courtesy of Mr. Tipper—that the room is, indeed, divided: white people on one side, Indian people on the other, the latter a little on the sparse side. Just like at the Nip House and at Wong's, Daniel Daylight sits there and thinks, *and* at the movies, the bingo hall, the taverns, and the churches—according, anyway, to Mr. Tipper, who has been to all these places. As he sits there waiting for his turn on stage, he can, on the left side of the hall, see Jenny Dean and her parents, with Mrs. Hay, waving at him and waving at him, beckoning him to come to their side. Shyly, he shakes his head. Jenny Dean, with her parents, belongs on the human side, he, with his parents (who are not only non-human but absent) on the other. Only Mr. Tipper sits beside him, and he is not even supposed to be there. On stage, some dreadful music is playing: two human boys at the piano, aged ten years or so (guesses Daniel Daylight), wearing green V-neck sweaters, white shirts, and bowties, their hair yellow as hay, skin white as cake mix. According to the program, they are playing a duet called "Squadrons of the Air" but Daniel Daylight can't really tell; whatever the word "squadrons" means, it sounds like they are dropping bombs from the air on some poor hapless village. Next come two human girls, plump as bran muffins, red-haired, freckled, dressed in Virgin-Mary-blue smocks with long-sleeved white blouses, again aged ten years or so. They haven't even sat down on the bench when they charge like tanks into a duet called "Swaying Daffodils." For Daniel Daylight, the daffodils try desperately to sway first this way and then that but can't quite do it; to him, first they bang around, then leap about, then bang around some more, until they just droop from exhaustion, stems halfbent over, heads hanging down, sad daffodils, unlucky plants. They are next, he, Daniel Daylight, and, she, Jenny Dean.

Daniel Daylight marches down the aisle that separates the Indian section of the huge auditorium from the white section. Jenny Dean joins him from the other side. Two hundred and fifty human people look at them as with the eyes of alligators, Daniel Daylight thinks, for he can feel them on his back, cold and wet and gooey. He shudders, then climbs the steps that lead to the stage and the upright piano, following the eight-year-old white girl Jenny Dean in her fluffy pink cotton dress with the white lace collar and shoulders that puff out like popcorn. They reach the piano. They sit down. From where he sits, Daniel Daylight can see Mr. Tipper looking up at him with eyes, he is sure of it, that say, "Go on, you can do it." Only twenty-five or so Indian people, mostly women, sit scattered around him, also looking up at him but with dark eyes that say nothing. On the room's other side, he can see the eyes that, to him, are screaming, "No, you can't; you can't do it. You can't do it at all." Feeling Jenny Dean's naked left arm pressing up against his own black-suited, white-shirted arm, he takes his right hand off his lap, raises it above the keyboard of the Heintzman upright. He can hear a gasp from the audience. Then he is sure he can hear the white side whispering to one another, "What's he doing there, little Indian boy, brown-skinned boy? His people cannot vote; therefore they are not human. Non-human boys do *not* play the piano, not in public, and not with human girls." Daniel Daylight, however, will have none of it. Instead, gentle as snow on spruce boughs at night, he lets fall his right hand right on the C-major chord.

Water-like, limpid, calm as silence, the chords for "Hearts and Flowers" begin their journey. Placed with care, every note of them, on the keyboard by Daniel Daylight, they float, float like mist. The bass sneaks in, the melody begins. Playing octaves, Jenny Dean's hands begin at the two Cs above middle C, arc up to the G in a curve smooth and graceful, then waft back down to the F, move on down to the E, and thence to the D, skip down to the B and thus swerve back, up to the C whence they had started. The melody pauses, Daniel Daylight's series of major chords billow out to fill the silence, Jenny Dean's elegant melody resumes its journey. In love with the god sound, Daniel Daylight sends his/her* waves, as prayer from the

---

*Like all North American Aboriginal languages (that I know of anyway, and there are a lot, fifty-two in Canada alone!), the Cree language has no gender. According to its structure, therefore, we are all, in a sense, he/shes, as is all of nature (trees, vegetation, even rocks), as is God, one would think. That is why I, for one, have so much trouble just thinking in the English language—because it is a language that is, first and foremost, "motored," as it were, by a theology/mythology that is "monotheistic" in structure, a structure where there is only one God and that god is male and male only. Other world systems are either "polytheistic" or "pantheistic" in structure, having, for instance (now or in the past, as in ancient Greece), room for gods who are female or even male/female, systems where all of nature, including sound, just for instance, simply "bristles," as it were, with divinity.

depths of his heart, the depths of his being, right across the vast auditorium, right through the flesh and bone and blood of some three hundred people, through the walls of the room, beyond them, north across the Moostoos River, through Waskeechoos, north to the Watson Lake Indian Residential School and thus through the lives of the two hundred Indian children who live there, then northward and northward and northward until the sound waves wash up on the shores, and the islands, of vast Minstik Lake. And there, deep inside the blood of Daniel Daylight, where lives Minstik Lake and all her people, Daniel Daylight sees his parents, Cheechup Daylight and his wife, Adelaide, walking up the hill to the little voting booth at the little wooden church that overlooks the northern extremity of beautiful, extra-ordinary Minstik Lake with its ten thousand islands. And Daniel Daylight, with the magic that he weaves like a tiny little master, *wills* his parents to walk right past Father Roy in his great black cassock and into the booth with their worn yellow pencils. And there they vote. Frozen into place by the prayer of Daniel Daylight *and* his "flower," Jenny Dean, Father Roy can do nothing, least of all stop Cheechup Daylight and his wife, Adelaide, from becoming human.

Receiving, on stage, his trophy beside Jenny Dean from a human man in black suit, shirt, and tie—Mayor Bill Hicks of Prince William, has explained Mr. Tipper—Daniel Daylight beams at the crowd that fills, for the most part, the Kiwanis Auditorium in downtown Prince William, Manitoba. Both sides are standing, the Indian side with its two dozen peo-ple, the white side with its 250. And they are clapping. And clapping and clapping. Some of them, in fact, are crying, white and Indian, human and . . . well, they don't look non-human any more, not from where stands exulting—and weeping—the Cree Indian, *human* pianist Daniel Daylight.

Daniel Daylight sits inside Mr. Tipper's travelling car. It is cold—not cold, though, like outside, of this fact Daniel Daylight is quite certain. He looks out through the window on his right and, as always, sees white forest rushing by; maybe rabbits will bound past on that snowbank in the trees, he sits thinking. Snow falling gently, it looks, to Daniel Daylight, like he is being hurtled through the heart of a giant snowflake. In his black-trousered lap, meanwhile, rests his trophy, a ten-inch-tall golden angel with wings outspread and arms wide open, beaming up at her winner through the glow of the travelling car's dashboard lights. On the radio, the music has stopped and people living in the east of the country, explains Mr. Tipper, are discussing a matter that takes Daniel Daylight completely by surprise: the Indian people of Canada, it seems, were given, that day, the 31st of March, 1960, the right to vote in federal elections, in their own country.

"You see?" Daniel Daylight says to Mr. Tipper, his English, and his confidence, having grown quite nicely in just two months. "We are human. I knew it. And you know why I knew it, Mr. Tipper?"

"Why, Daniel Daylight?"

"Because I played it."

LEE MARACLE

Goodbye, Snauq

CONTRIBUTOR'S NOTE

BEFORE 1800, "Downriver Halkomelem"–speaking peoples, my ancestors, inhabited the city of Vancouver. By 1812, the Halkomelem had endured three epidemics caught as a result of the east-west and north-south Indigenous trade routes. At that time, the Halkomelem were part of a group of five friendly tribes (according to court records in the case of *Mathias vs. the Queen*). Following the epidemics the Tsleil Watuth or Downriver Halkomelem were reduced to forty-one souls and invited the Squamish to occupy the Burrard Inlet. They did so. One group led by Khahtsahlanogh, from Lil' wat, occupied what is now False Creek. False Creek or Snauq (meaning sandbar), known to all the neighbouring friendly tribes as the "supermarket of the nation," became a reserve some fifty years after white settlement began. It was sold between 1913 and 1916, and Khahtsahlano, the son of Khahtsahlanogh, and his remaining members were forced to move. This sale was declared illegal in a court case at the turn of the millennium. Although the Tsleil Watuth and the Musqueam originally shared the territory, the courts ruled that the Squamish, because they were the only ones to permanently occupy the village, "owned" it. I am related to Khahtsahlano and the Tsleil Watuth people, and I had always wanted to write the story of Khahtsahlano. He was still alive when I was a child and was much respected by the Squamish, Musqueam, and Tsleil Watuth people as one of the founders of the Allied Tribes of B.C., a group that sought redress for the illegal land grabs by British Columbia in the decades following Confederation. There is still an unresolved ongoing court case involving the Canadian Pacific Railway station at Terminal Avenue and Main Street in False Creek and the Squamish Band.

Researching this story has been both painful and enlightening. For one thing, the formerly friendly tribes that once shared the territory are not quite so friendly with one another today. The Tsleil Watuth and the Musqueam sued the Squamish Band Council, all three claiming ownership of Snauq, and the Tsleil Watuth and the Musqueam lost. The case has convinced me that Canada must face its history through the eyes of those who have been excluded and disadvantaged as a result of it. Severely weakened by epidemic after epidemic and legally excluded from land purchases in the new nation of Canada, the First Nations people have had to make desperate and unfair decisions to assure their survival. The forfeiture of the right to Snauq is, hopefully, the last desperate measure we will need to take before we can be assured of our survival in Canada.

Goodbye, Snauq

Raven has never left this place, but sometimes it feels like she has been negligent, maybe even a little dense. Raven shaped us; we are built for transformation. Our stories prepare us for it. Find freedom in the context you inherit—every context is different: discover consequences and change from within, that is the challenge. Still, there is horror in having had change foisted upon you from outside. Raven did not prepare us for the past 150 years. She must have fallen asleep some time around the first smallpox epidemic, when the Tsleil Watuth Nation nearly perished, and I am not sure she ever woke up.

The halls of this institution are empty. The bright white fluorescent bulbs that dot the ceiling are hidden behind great long light fixtures dimming its length. Not unlike the dimness of a longhouse, but it doesn't feel the same. The dimness of the hallway isn't brightened by a fire in the centre nor warmed by the smell of cedar all around you. There are no electric lights in the longhouse, and so the dimness is natural. The presence of lights coupled with dimness makes the place seem eerie. I trudge down the dim hallway; my small hands clutch a bright white envelope. Generally, letters from "the Queen in right of Canada" are threateningly ensconced in brown envelopes, but this is from a new government—my own govern-ment, the Squamish First Nation government. Its colour is an irony. I received it yesterday, broke into a sweat and a bottle of white wine within five minutes of its receipt. It didn't help. I already knew the contents—even before Canada Post managed to deliver it; Canadian mail is notoriously slow. The television and radio stations were so full of the news that there was no doubt in my mind that this was my government's official letter informing me that "a deal had been brokered." The Squamish Nation had won the Snauq lawsuit and surrendered any further claim for a fee. The numbers are staggering: $92 million. That is more than triple our total GNP, wages and businesses combined.

As I lay in my wine-soaked state, I thought about the future of the Squamish Nation: development dollars, cultural dollars, maybe even lan-guage dollars, healing dollars. I had no right to feel this depressed, to want to be this intoxicated, to want to remove myself from this decision, this moment, or this world. I had no right to want to curse the century in which I was born, the political times in which I live, and certainly I had no right to hate the decision makers, my elected officials, for having brokered the deal. In fact, until we vote on it, until we ratify it, it is a deal only in the-ory. While the wine sloshed its way through the veins in my body to the blood in my brain, pictures of Snauq rolled about. Snauq is now called False Creek. When the Squamish moved there to be closer to the colonial centre, the water was deeper and stretched from the sea to what is now Clark Drive in the east; it covered the current streets from Second Avenue in the south to just below Dunsmuir in the north. There was a sandbar in the middle of it, hence the name Snauq.

I lay on my couch, Russell Wallace's CD *Tso'kam* blaring in the back-ground—Christ, our songs are sad, even the happy ones. Tears rolled down my face. I joined the ranks of ancestors I was trying not to think about. Wine-soaked and howling out old Hank Williams crying songs, laughing in between, tears sloshing across the laughter lines. The '50s. My Ta'ah intervened. Eyes narrowed, she ended the party, cleared out the house, sending all those who had had a little too much to drink home. She confiscated keys from those who were drunk, making sure only the sober drove the block to the reserve. "None of my children are going to get pinched and end up in hoosegow."

My brain, addled with the memory, pulled up another drunken soirée, maybe the first one. A group of men gathered around a whisky keg, their children raped by settlers: they drank until they perished. It was our first run at suicide, and I wondered what inspired their descendants to want to participate in the new society in any way, shape, or form. "Find freedom in the context you inherit." From the shadows Khahtsahlano emerged, eyes dead blind and yet still twinkling, calling out, "Sweetheart, they were so hungry, so thirsty that they drank up almost the whole of Snauq with their dredging machines. They built mills at Yaletown and piled up garbage at the edges of our old supermarket—Snauq. False Creek was so dirty that eventually even the white mans became concerned." I have seen archival pictures of it. They dumped barrels of toxic chemical waste from sawmills, food waste from restaurants, taverns, and tea houses; thousands of metric tons of human sewage joined the other waste daily.

I was drunk. Drunk enough to apologize for my nation, so much good can come of this . . . So why the need for wine to stem the rage?

"The magic of the white man is that he can change everything, everywhere. He even changed the food we eat." Khahtsahlano faced False Creek from the edge of Burrard Inlet, holding his white cane delicately in his hand as he spoke to me. The inlet was almost a mile across at that time, but the dredging and draining of the water shrank it. Even after he died in 1967, the dredging and altering of our homeland was not over. The shoreline is gone; in its place are industries squatting where the sea once was. Lonsdale quay juts out into the tide and elsewhere cemented and land-filled structures occupy the inlet. The sea asparagus that grew in the sand along the shore is gone. There is no more of the camas we once ate. All the berries, medicines, and wild foods are gone. "The womans took care of the food," he said. And now we go to schools like this one and then go to work in other schools, businesses, in band offices or anyplace that we can, so we can purchase food in modern supermarkets. Khahtsahlano was about to say something else. "Go away," I hollered at his picture, and suddenly I was sober.

Snauq is in Musqueam territory, it occurred to me, just across the inlet from Tsleil Watuth, but the Squamish were the only ones to occupy it year-round—some say as early as 1821, others 1824, still others peg the date as somewhere around the 1850s. Before that it was a common garden shared by all the friendly tribes in the area. The fish swam there, taking a breather from their ocean playgrounds, ducks gathered, women culti- vated camas fields and berries abounded. On the sandbar, Musqueam, Tsleil Watuth, and Squamish women tilled the oyster and clam beds to encourage reproduction. Wild cabbage, mushrooms, and other plants were tilled and hoed as well. Summer after summer the nations gathered to harvest, probably to plan marriages, play a few rounds of that old gam- bling game *lahal*.

Not long after the first smallpox epidemic all but decimated the Tsleil Watuth people, the Squamish people came down from their river homes where the snow fell deep all winter to establish a permanent home at False Creek. Chief George—Chipkaym—built the big longhouse. Khahtsalanogh was a young man then. His son, Khahtsahlano, was born there. Khahtsahlano grew up and married Swanamia there. Their children were born there.

"Only three duffles' worth," the skipper of the barge was shouting at the villagers. Swanamia did her best to choke back the tears, fingering each garment, weighing its value, remembering the use of each, and choosing which one to bring and which to leave. Each spoon, handles lovingly carved by Khahtsahlano, each bowl, basket, and bent box had to be evalu- ated for size and affection. Each one required a decision. Her mind watched her husband's hand sharpening his adze, carving the tops of each piece of cutlery, every bowl and box. She remembered gathering cedar roots, pounding them for hours and weaving each basket. Then she decided to fill as many baskets as the duffles could hold and leave the rest.

Swanamia faced Burrard Inlet—she could not bear to look back. Her son winced. Khahtsahlano sat straight up. Several of the women suppressed a gasp as they looked back to see that Snauq's longhouses were on fire. The men who set the fires were cheering. Plumes of smoke affirmed that the settlers who kept coming in droves had crowded the Squamish out. This is an immigrant country. Over the next ten days the men stumbled about the Squamish reserve on the north shore, building homes and suppressing a terrible urge to return to Snauq to see the charred remains. Swanamia watched as the men in her house fought for an acceptable response. Some private part of her knew they wanted to grieve, but there is no ceremony to grieve the loss of a village. She had no reference post for this new world where the interests of the immigrants took precedence over the interests of Indigenous residents. She had no way to understand that the new people's right to declare us non-citizens unless we disenfranchised our right to be Squamish was inviolable. The burning of Snauq touched off a history of disentitlement and prohibition that was incomprehensible and impossible for Swanamia to manage.

We tried, though. From Snauq to Whidbey Island and Vancouver Island, from Port Angeles to Seattle, the Squamish along with the Lummi of Washington State operated a ferry system until the Black Ball ferry lines bought it out in the 1930s.

Khahtsahlano's head cocked to one side and he gave his wife a look that said, "No problem, we will think of something," as the barge carried them out to sea. We were reserved and declared immigrants, children in the eyes of the law, wards of the government to be treated the same as the infirm or the insane. Khahtsahlano determined to fight this insult. It consumed his life. We could not gain citizenship or manage our own affairs unless we relinquished who we were: Squamish, Tsleil Watuth, Musqueam, Cree, or whatever nation we came from. Some of us did disenfranchise. But most of us stayed, stubbornly clinging to our original identity, fighting to participate in the new social order as Squamish.

Khahtsahlano struggled to find ways for us to participate. In 1905, he and a group of stalwart men marched all over the province of British Columbia to create the first modern organization of Aboriginal people. The Allied Tribes mastered colonial law despite prohibition and land rights to secure and protect their position in this country. He familiarized himself with the colonial relations that Britain had with other countries. He was a serious rememberer who paid attention to the oracy of his past, the changing present, and the possibility of a future story. He stands there in this old photo just a little bent, his eyes exhibiting an endless sadness, handsomely dressed in the finest clothes Swanamia had made for him. A deep hope lingers underneath the sadness, softening the melancholy. In the photograph marking their departure, his son stands in front of him, straight-backed, shoulders squared with that little frown of sweet trepidation on his face, the same frown my sister wears when she is afraid and trying to find her courage. Khahtsahlano and his son faced the future with the same grim determination that the Squamish Nation Band Council now deploys.

The wine grabbed reality, slopped it back and forth across the swaying room that blurred, and my wanders through Snauq were over for another day.

The hallways intervene again; I head for my office, cubby really. I am a TA bucking for my master's degree. This is a prestigious institution with a prestigious MA program in Indigenous government. I am not a star student, nor a profound teaching assistant. Not much about me seems memorable. I pursue course after course. I comply day after day with research requirements, course requirements, marking requirements, and the odd seminar requirement, but nothing that I do, say, or write seems relevant. I feel absurdly obedient. The result of all this study seems oddly mundane. Did Khahtsahlano ever feel mundane as he trudged about speaking to one family head, then another, talking up the Allied Tribes with Andy Paull? Not likely; at the time he consciously opposed colonial authority. He too studied this new world but with a singular purpose in mind: recreating freedom in the context that I was to inherit. Maybe, while he spoke to his little sweetheart, enumerating each significant non-existent landmark, vegetable patch, berry field, elk warren, duck pond, and fish habitat that had been destroyed by the newcomers, he felt this way. To what end did he tell an eight-year-old of a past bounty that can never again be regained?

Opening the envelope begins to take on the sensation of treasonous behaviour. I set it aside and wonder about the coursework I chose during my school years. I am Squamish, descended from Squamish chieftains— no, that is only partly true. I am descended from chieftains and I have plenty of Squamish relatives, but I married a Sto:loh, so really I am Sto:loh. Identity can be so confusing. For a long time the Tsleil Watuth spoke mainly Squamish—somehow they were considered part of the Squamish Band, despite the fact that they never did amalgamate. It turns out they spoke "Downriver Halkomelem" before the first smallpox killed them, and later many began speaking Squamish. Some have gone back to speaking Halkomelem while others still speak Squamish. I am not sure who we really are collectively and I wonder why I did not choose to study this territory, its history, and the identity changes that this history has wrought on us all. The office closes in on me. The walls crawl toward me, slow and easy, crowding me; I want to run, to reach for another bottle of wine, but this here is the university and I must prepare for class—and there is no wine here, no false relief. I have only my wit, my will, and my sober nightmare. I look up: the same picture of Khahtsahlano and his son that adorns my office wall hangs in my living room at home. I must be obsessed with him. Why have I not noticed this obsession before?

I love this photo of him. I fell in love with the jackets of the two men, so much so that I learned to weave. I wanted to replicate that jacket. Khahtsahlano's jacket was among the first to be made from sheep's wool. His father's was made of dog and mountain goat hair. Coast Salish women bred a beautiful dog with long and curly hair for this purpose. Every summer the mountain goats left their hillside homes to shed their fur on the lowlands of what is now to be the Sea to Sky Highway. They rubbed their bodies against long thorns, and all the women had to do was collect it, spin the dog and goat together, and weave the clothes. The settlers shot dogs and goats until our dogs were extinct and the goats were an endangered species. The object: force the Natives to purchase Hudson's Bay sheep's wool blankets. The northerners switched to the black and red Hudson's Bay blankets, but we carried on with our weaving, using sheep's wool for a time; then when cash was scarce we shopped at local second-hand shops or we went without. Swanamia put a lot of love into those jackets. She took the time to trim them with fur, feathers, shells, and fringe. She loved those two men. Some of the women took to knitting the Cowichan sweaters so popular among non-Indigenous people, but I could not choose knitting over weaving. I fell in love with the zigzag weft, the lightning strikes of those jackets, and for a time got lost in the process of weaving until my back gave out.

The injury inspired me to return to school to attend this university and to leave North Van. I took this old archive photo—photocopy, really—with me. Every now and then I speak to Khahtsahlano, promise him I will return.

My class tutorial is about current events. I must read the letter—keep abreast of new events—and prepare to teach. I detach, open, and read the notice of the agreement. I am informed that this information is a courtesy; being Sto:loh, I have no real claim to the agreement, but because ancestry is so important, all descendants of False Creek are hereby informed . . .

I look at the students and remember: this memory is for Chief George, Chief Khahtsahlano, and my Ta'ah, who never stopped dreaming of Snauq.

Song rolled out as the women picked berries near what is now John Hendry Park. In between songs they told old stories, many risqué and hilarious. Laughter punctuated the air; beside them were the biggest trees in the world, sixteen feet in diameter and averaging four hundred feet in height. Other women at Snauq tended the drying racks and smoke shacks in the village. Inside them clams, sturgeons, oolichans, sockeye, spring salmon were being cured for winter stock. Men from Squamish, Musqueam, and Tsleil Watuth joined the men at Snauq to hunt and trap ducks, geese, grouse, deer, and elk. Elk is the prettiest of all red meats. You have to see it roasted and thinly sliced to appreciate its beauty and the taste—the taste is extraordinary. The camas fields bloomed bounteous at Snauq, and every spring the women culled the white ones in favour of the blue and hoed them. Children clutched at their long woven skirts. There is no difference between a white camas and a blue, except that the blue flowers are so much more gorgeous. It is the kind of blue that adorns the sky when it teases just before a good rain. Khahtsahlano's father, Khahtsahlanogh, remembered those trees. On days when he carved out a new spoon, box, or bowl, he would stare sadly at the empty forest and resent the new houses in its place. Chief George, sweet and gentle Chief George—Chipkaym—chose Snauq for its proximity to the mills and because he was no stranger to the place.

By 1907, the end of Chief George's life, the trees had fallen, the villagers at Lumberman's Arch were dead, and the settlers had transformed the Snauq supermarket into a garbage dump. The newcomers were so strange. On the one hand, they erected sawmills that in disciplined and orderly fashion transformed trees into boards for the world market quickly, efficiently, and impressively. On the other hand, they threw things away in massive quantities. The Squamish came to watch. Many like Paddy George bought teams of horses and culled timber from the backwoods like the white man—well, not exactly like them; Paddy could not bring himself to kill the young ones. "Space logging," they call it now. But still some managed to eke out a living. Despite all the prohibition laws they found some freedom in the context they inherited.

"The settlers were a dry riverbed possessing a thirst that was never slaked." A film of tears filled Khahtsahlano's eyes and his voice softened as he spoke. "After the trees came down, houses went up, more mills, hotels, shantytowns until we were vastly outnumbered and pressured to leave. B.C. was so white then. So many places were forbidden to Indians, dogs, Blacks, Jews, and Chinamans." At one time Khahtsahlano could remember the names of the men that came, first a hundred, then a thousand; after that he stopped wanting to know who they were. "They were a strange lot—most of the men never brought womans to this place. The Yaletown men were CPR men, drifters, and squatters on the north shore of the creek. They helped drain one third of it, so that the railroad—the CPR—could build a station, but they didn't bring womans," he said as he stared longingly across the inlet at his beloved Snauq.

The students lean on their desks, barely awake. Almost half of them are First Nations. I call myself to attention: I have totally lost my professional distance from the subject; my discipline, my pretension to objectivity writhes on the floor in front of me and I realize we are not the same people any more. I am not in a longhouse. I am not a speaker. I am a TA in a western institution. Suddenly the fluorescent lights offend, the dry perfect room temperature insults, and the very space mocks. A wave of pain passes through me, and I nearly lunge forward fighting it. Get a grip. This is what you wanted. Get a grip. This is what you slogged through tons of insulting documents for: Superintendent of Indian Affairs, Melville . . . alternatives to solve the Indian problem, assassination, enslavement . . . disease, integration, boarding school, removal . . . I am staggering under my own weight. My eyes bulge, my muscles pulse, my saliva trickles out the side of my mouth. I am not like Khahtsahlano. I am not like Ta'ah. I was brought up in the same tradition of change, of love of transformation, of appreciation for what is new, but I was not there when Snauq was a garden. Now it is a series of bridge ramparts, an emptied False Creek, emptied of Squamish people and occupied by industry, apartment dwellings, the Granville Island tourist centre, and the Science centre. I was not there when Squamish men formed unions like white men, built mills like white men, worked like white men, and finally— unlike white men—were outlawed from full participation. I can't bear all this reality. I am soft like George but without whatever sweet thread of hope wove its way through his body to form some steely fabric.

I awake surrounded by my students, their tears drip onto my cheeks. Oh my Gawd, they love me.

"It's OK, I just fainted."

"You were saying you were not like Khahtsahlano, like Ta'ah. Who are they?" The room opens up; the walls stop threatening. I know how Moses must have felt when he watched the sea part, the relief palpable, measurable, sweet, and welcome.

"That's just it. I thought I knew who I was. I know the dates. I know the events, but I don't know who they were, and I can't know who I am without knowing who they were, and I can't say goodbye to Snauq and I need to say goodbye. Oh Gawd, help me."

"Well, I am not real sure that clears things up," Terese responds, her blond hair hanging close to my face. Some of the students look like they want to laugh: a couple of First Nations students go ahead and chuckle.

"Snauq is a village we just forfeited any claim to, and I must say goodbye."

"Doesn't that require some sort of ceremony?" Hilda asks. She is Nu'chalnuth, and although they are a different nation from mine, the ceremonial requirements are close.

"Yes," I answer.

"This is a cultural class—shouldn't we go with you?"

They lift me so tenderly I feel like a saint. This is the beginning of something. I need to know what is ending so that I can appreciate and identify with the beginning. Their apathetic stares have been replaced by a deep concern. Their apathy must have been a mask, a mask of professionalism, a mask covering fear, a mask to hide whatever dangers lurk in learning about the horrors of colonialism. The students must face themselves. I am their teacher. The goal of every adult among us is to face ourselves—our greatest enemy. I am responsible as their teacher to help them do that, but I am ill equipped. Still, Hilda is right. This is a cultural class and they ought to be there when I say goodbye. In some incomprehensible way it feels as though their presence would somehow ease the forfeiture and make it right.

I reconjure the stretch of trees to the west and south of Snauq for the class, the wind whispering songs of future to the residents. The Oblates arrived singing Gregorian chants of false promise. The millwrights arrived singing chants of profit and we bit, hook, line, and sinker. How could we anticipate that we would be excluded if our success exceeded the success of the white man? How could we know that they came homeless, poor, unsafe, and unprotected? Yaletowners accepted their designation as "squatters." This struck the Squamish at first as incredible. Chief George had no way of understanding squatting. It took some time for the younger men like Khahtsahlano to explain to Chief George the concept of "ownership" of the white man, the laws governing ownership, the business of property. Sometimes he resorted to English because the language did not suffice. "B.C. is Indian land, but the government regarded Snauq citizens as squatters until a reserve was established." Andy Paull explained the law, its hypocrisy, and its strangeness to old Chief George. "Not all white man were granted land and not all were granted the same amounts. But those who did purchase or receive land grants were white. The minimum land grant to white men during pre-emption was three hundred acres; for us, it was a maximum of ten acres per family."

"What has this got to do with Snauq and, more important, with this class?" someone asks. I have been speaking aloud.

"There is so much more to history than meets the eye. We need to know what happened, and what happened has nothing to do with the dates, the events, and the gentlemen involved, it has to do with impact." A sole student, eyes lifted slightly skyward, lips pursed innocent and inviting, strokes my arm.

They all pull their seats forward. "We need to finish this story." They nod, as if for the first time they seem to know what's going on. Even the white students nod, affirming that they too understand.

As I get ready to head for the ferry terminal, it dawns on me that no one in this country has to deal with ancestry in quite the way we must. The new immigrants of today come from independent countries, some wealthy, some poor, but all but a few have risen from under the yoke of colonialism. They have nations as origins. Their home countries belong to the United Nations or NATO or other such international organizations. We do not, and this court case indicates we never will. The United Nations is debating an "Indigenous right to self-government" declaration, but Indigenous people will never be able to acquire the place other nations hold. Canadians do not have to face that they are still classically colonized, that because settlement is a *fait accompli*, we can only negotiate the best real estate deal possible. Indigenous people must face this, while the eyes of our ancestors, who fought against colonial conquest and lost, glare down upon us.

"This is an immigrant nation," Prime Minister Chrétien said after the twin towers of the World Trade Center in New York were felled. "We will continue to be an immigrant nation." How do we deal with this, the non-immigrants who for more than a century were rendered foreigners, prohibited from participation? The money for Snauq will be put in trust. To access it, we must submit a plan of how we intend to spend it. The Squamish Nation gets to pick the trustees but, like our ancestors, we must have trustees independent of the nation. Our money is still one step removed from our control.

This story is somehow connected to another story, more important than the one going on now. Surrender or dig up the hatchet. The Squamish Nation has chosen surrender. Which way will my journey take me? Do I dare remember Snauq as a Squamish, Musqueam, Tsleil Watuth supermarket? Do I dare desire the restoration of the grand trees to the left and in the rear of Snauq? Do I dare say goodbye?

The ferry lunges from the berth. Students surround me. We are on a mission. We travel to Snauq, False Creek, and Vancouver to say goodbye. In one sense I have no choice; in another, I chose the people who made the deal. In our own cultural sensibility there is no choice. There are fifteen thousand non-Indigenous people living at Snauq, and we have never granted ourselves the right to remove people from their homes. We must say goodbye.

In this goodbye we will remember Snauq before the draining of False Creek. We will honour the dead: the stanchions of fir, spruce, and cedar and the gardens of Snauq. We will dream of the new False Creek, the dry lands, the new parks, and the acres of grass and houses. We will accept what Granville Island has become and honour Patty Rivard, the First Nations woman who was the first to forge a successful business in the heart of it. We will struggle to appreciate the little ferries that cross the creek. We will salute Chief George—Chipkaym—and Khahtsahlanogh, who embraced the vision of this burgeoning new nation. I will pray for my personal inability to fully commit to that vision.

The wind catches the tobacco as it floats to the water, lifts it, and as we watch it float, a lone Chinese woman crosses in front and smiles.

I smile too. Li Ka Shing, a multibillionaire, rose as the owner and developer of False Creek. He is Chinese, and he didn't live here when he bought it. I don't know if he lives here now, but for whatever reason I love the sound of his name. "Everything begins with song," Ta'ah says. His name is a song. It rolls off the tongue, sweetens the palate before the sound hits the air. It is such an irony that the first "non-citizen immigrant residents" should now possess the power to determine the destiny of our beloved Snauq. I know it shouldn't, but somehow it makes me happy, like knowing that Black Indians now people the Long Island Reservation in New York State.

The Chinese were subjected to a head tax for decades. Until sixty years ago they were banned from living outside Chinatown, though I met Garrick Chu's mother, who grew up at the Musqueam Reserve. Their economic activity was restricted to laundry businesses and tea houses. Once white men burned Chinatown to the ground. For decades Chinese men could not bring their families from China to Canada. Periodic riots in the previous century killed some of them and terrorized all of them. Underneath some parts of Chinatown they built underground tunnels to hide in as protection against marauding white citizens, who were never punished for killing Chinese. Like the Squamish, they endured quietly until assuming citizenship in 1948. For one of them to become the owner of this choice piece of real estate is sweet irony. "It was sold for a song by Premier Vander Zalm," the court records read. That too is a piece of painful, yet poetic, justice. I want to attend the Chinese parade, celebrate Chinese New Year, not for Li Ka Shing but because one of life's ironies has given me hope. Five thousand miles from here, a group of Mi'kmaq bought land in Newfoundland and gained reservation rights. Another irony. They thought they had killed them all, and 350 years later, there they were, purchasing the land and setting up a reservation. There is hope in irony.

I am not through with Canada. I am not a partner in its construction, but neither am I its enemy. Canada has opened the door. Indigenous people are no longer "immigrants" to be disenfranchised, forbidden, prohibited, outlawed, or precluded from the protective laws of this country. But we are a long way from being participants. I am not eager to be a part of an environmentally offensive society that can preach "Thou shalt not kill" and then make war on people, plants, and animals to protect and advance financial gain. The hypocrisy marring Canada's behaviour toward us is still evident, but it struggles for maturity, and while it struggles for maturity I accord myself a place. This place is still at the bottom, as the last people to be afforded a place at the banquet table where the guests have been partaking for over five hundred years; but still there it is, the chair empty and hoping I will feel inclined to sit in it. The invitation is fraught with difficulties. Although today I must say goodbye, tomorrow I may just buy one of the townhouses slated for completion in 2010. Today I am entitled to dream. Khahtsahlano dreamed of being buried at Snauq. I dream of living there.

We move to the unfinished longhouse at the centre of Granville Island, a ragged group of students and their teacher. I break into song: Chief Dan George's prayer song. "Goodbye, Snauq," I boom out in as big a voice as I can muster. The passing crowd jerks to a split-second halt, gives us a bewildered glance, frowns, sidesteps us, and then moves on. The students laugh.

"Indians really will laugh at anything," I say as the tears stream across my face. The sun shines bright and turns the sky camas blue as we drift toward the Co-op restaurant to eat.

DREW HAYDEN TAYLOR

A Blurry Image on the
Six O'Clock News

CONTRIBUTOR'S NOTE

OKA OR, MORE CORRECTLY, Kanesatake has come to refer to a pivotal time in Canadian Aboriginal history, similar to the events of the occupation at Wounded Knee in South Dakota in 1973. As has been said so many times before, and seldom better, it was the best of times, it was the worst of times.

Personally, the occurrences at Oka filtered into my consciousness slowly and reluctantly. At that time, the summer of 1990, I was on the Wikwemikong Unceded Reserve, located on beautiful Manitoulin Island. We were in the midst of rehearsing a play I had written, a little comedy called *The Bootlegger Blues*. During the day, we would be struggling to make this little play funny and fabulous, and at night, when we weren't exhausted, we would turn on the news and find out about this bizarre occupation happening a few hundred kilometres to the east of this Georgian Bay community. Many times the necessity of theatre dragged more hours out of us than most jobs, so our following of the news was sporadic at best. But we got the gist of what was happening, and as a result, a cloud of uncertainty hung over our production. On reflection, it may not have been the best time to produce and tour a Native comedy. Or it could have been the best time.

It wasn't until the play had opened and was on the road that I began to fully understand the scope of what was happening and had happened. And from that point, my attention never left the television and radio. As both a former journalist and a constant First Nations individual, I was captivated by this standoff, proud of my Aboriginal brothers taking a stand, but understandably fearful of what could happen with so many fingers on triggers.

For five or seven years afterwards, questions about Oka were among the two most popular topics I faced when lecturing or speaking. Basically, I could count on "What is your opinion of what happened at Oka?" right behind "What did you think of *Dances with Wolves?*" Events in that once sleepy community polarized the country. And that is why I ended up writing, in *A Blurry Image on the Six O'Clock News*, from the perspective of a divorced White woman. Not my usual messenger of storytelling. But it was that polarization that affected me, and the realization that, in the midst of socio-political upheaval, some emotions remain simple and highly recognizable, regardless of race or cultural background.

History and literature share many friends and many foes. Both can be forgotten, or disregarded, or simply ignored. For some, both are just classes to take in school. But history and literature can show what humans are capable of—the good and the bad. And that's what makes life interesting.

A Blurry Image on the
Six O'Clock News

The batteries on the remote control were dying and that pissed her off the most. It wasn't the fleeting glimpses of her one-time husband amid the crowds of Native people, or the brutal tactics of the Sûreté du Québec, or the seeming ignorance of the media as to the real issues involved. It was the dying electricity of the batteries in the television remote that made her curse the world. This resulted in a three-second wait between channels. She had spent hours sitting in front of the television, trying to spot her ex-husband, a displaced Ojibway in an increasingly bitter Mohawk war. Lisa had been tantalized a few times, a familiar jean jacket two hundred yards across the barriers. His hair, once fashionably short, now seemed to be getting a little on the shaggy side. Further evidence of his conversion to what he called "the cause."

It had been just over five months since the divorce. Another mixed marriage had bitten the dust. Though, she was positive, through no fault of her own. It wasn't her fault things went the direction they did. He wasn't the man she had married six years earlier. He had . . . changed. He was no longer the Richard Spencer she had met at university. He had, for all intents and purposes, become his brother, Donnelly. Granted, she

225

had changed too. Six years of being married to a Native man—Richard always hated the term "First Nations;" it sounded too political and he didn't consider himself a political person—could do that to an urban woman. And she, Lisa Spencer, descended from Irish-Scottish immigrants, always found it ironic that her married name, given to her by her Aboriginal husband, always sounded more English than the name she was born with, Baird.

That was all a long time ago . . . many moons ago, as Richard would joke. They were younger and the world less angry, or so it seemed. A White girl marrying an Ojibway man . . . Even in the early '80s it still caused members of her family to gossip and wonder. Sure he was a handsome man, potentially successful, once he got out of university, but really, an Indian . . . "Don't they have a reputation for drinking?" She heard that more than once, more often than not from her Irish relations. She couldn't help thinking there was a little "kettle calling" there. Oddly enough though, Richard, with his fashion sense and cool haircut, could easily have passed for someone of a more Mediterranean or Middle Eastern background. But the cowboy boots always gave him away. And he wasn't much of a drinker. A couple beers occasionally, during hockey or at a party. Her uncles drank way more. Physician heal thyself, she had said to herself.

Lisa found the fact that he was Native, a noble savage, as she once heard him described in a philosophy class, quite exotic. She was in her third year of sociology, planning to head toward social work, when she met him. Richard Spencer. Medium height (though she always liked taller men), lean, comfortable in a crowd though he preferred his own company. He was somewhere in the middle of his MBA when the Fates conspired to join them together, eventually in holy matrimony. And then in divorce court.

Fourteen months of dating, seven months of engagement, and six years of marriage. That was the extent of their life together. No children, no house (they rented), and only a few RRSPs that were split amicably. Now Lisa couldn't get over how ridiculous she felt, eagerly waiting for any glimpse of her husband, somewhere behind enemy lines. It had been about five months since they had last seen each other, and approximately four months since they had spoken on the phone. He had moved into his brother's house on the reserve.

Yet this was one of the reasons they had broken up. Actually, more specifically, it was because of Richard's brother, Donnelly Spencer. Lisa remembered him as having the stereotypical long hair, living perpetually in jeans, and he drummed on that big drum he was so proud of. And he was determined to be the most fluid speaker of Ojibway in the community. In many ways, the exact opposite of Richard. But in other ways, not. Richard was extremely proud of his heritage, though not enough to be annoying, and it eventually rubbed off on Lisa. She found the stories of his childhood on the reserve, the tales told to him over campfires by his grandfather, charming and necessary to the preservation of the culture. She even did her part by buying dream catchers and that ubiquitous headdress made out of safety pins that dangled from practically every car in the village.

But all that had changed. A foreign entity known as a Toyota Corolla had altered the life they knew and shared. The Corolla wasn't theirs. It didn't belong to anybody they knew. They still had never laid eyes on it. It just came out of the darkness one wintry night, like a vengeful spirit, and took the life of Donnelly Spencer, big brother of Richard Spencer, brother-in-law of Lisa Spencer.

Richard took it hard. Almost too hard, which puzzled Lisa. Richard and Donnelly had always been fairly close, no different than a billion other brothers living on this planet. One of Lisa's own sisters had died when she was a teenager, the victim of some unfortunately exotic blood disorder, leaving Lisa with only her memory. Lisa remembered being upset, crying herself to sleep on many a night, but time passed and the memory, while still treasured, lessened until it took on the official title of "fond remembrance." She also had three other siblings to lean on when necessary, the big family a leftover from their Catholic origins.

Lisa had gotten along with Donnelly, although she always suspected he never fully accepted his sister-in-law into the family. Just somewhere, behind the warm greetings and Christmas hugs, she always felt there was a hint, a subtle regret that Richard hadn't taken the time to find himself a Native woman to carry on the future of the Ojibway nation. At least the Otter Lake First Nation's portion of it. To be fair, Donnelly was always glad to see her, and she him, for he had a way with a story, and she liked that. The innate sociologist in her, no doubt. His tales of conferences, pow-wows, gatherings, and political meetings were legendary. If there was a way of making a first ministers' meeting on Aboriginal issues interesting and even exciting, Donnelly was the man.

Once, trying to be one of the gang, Lisa accepted an offer to participate in a sweat lodge being held at Donnelly's cabin. She gamely put up with the semi-nudity among strangers—"Just like going to the steam room at the Y," she told herself. Even the feel of cedar bits between her toes was distracting. In the end, it was the claustrophobia that got to her. Up until this adventure, she had never thought she was claustrophobic. In fact, she preferred small, economical cars. But the closeness of the walls, the sound of people only inches away, the darkness, and of course the stifling heat were more than she could take. Barely twenty minutes into the sweat, she found herself crawling out, embarrassed and naked, for she had left her towel on the floor of the sweat lodge. Richard had tried to placate her, saying he'd never been in a sweat lodge himself, but it did little good. Donnelly had reached out to her and she had failed to hold on.

Now Donnelly was dead. Dead and buried. And Richard was no longer Richard. He had started to change. It started soon after the funeral. Lisa knew something was wrong, but Richard was one of those kind with whom, when they couldn't exactly say what was wrong, there was no point in talking about it. But Lisa knew something was up. Richard started taking interests in things that had never caught his attention before. He vowed to take up drumming. He even signed up for a class in conversational Ojibway at the friendship centre but ended up lasting only a few weeks when he found out it was a different dialect from the one on his reserve. He started taking more interest in politics and issues, stuff that he had shrugged off before by saying, "Ah, I bet Donnelly will have something to say about that."

Lisa tried to support Richard with his new interests, once buying him an Indian Motorcycle sweatshirt. He laughed and hugged her when he saw it. He put it on immediately. She told him he should take off his tie first.

"It's a little big on me. It would have fit Donnelly perfectly. Don't you think?"

She thought it fit him perfectly, but she didn't want to contradict him. He talked more about Donnelly after his death than when he was alive. And Richard's sense of disconnectedness grew and grew. He still did his work—his job at the bank didn't suffer, he was too much of a professional for that—but he became distant. Lisa thought it was a phase, and she tried to connect with him, drawing on the loss of her sister as a bonding issue. It didn't work. He just smiled politely and changed the subject.

She put up with it as long as she could. The first anniversary of Donnelly's unfortunate death came and went, and by then Richard was thinking of quitting his job at the bank and using "his powers for good, not evil," as he put it. Maybe he'd get a job working with the Assembly of First Nations or some Native business organization, and if worse came to worst, there was always the Department of Indian Affairs—"It's better to be in the tent peeing out than outside peeing in," he said. When you know how to control and manage money, it's not that difficult to find a job.

"Maybe . . . we should consider moving back to the reserve . . ."

This was new. When they had become engaged, she had asked him if he ever wanted to move back to Otter Lake. She was a city girl and the thought made her uncomfortable. But it was a non-issue. Emphatically Richard said, "No. You can't get good Vietnamese soup back home. Too much sweet grass, not enough lemon grass."

She laughed but he was serious. "Lisa, you've never lived with all the relatives I have. All knowing what you're doing. Who you're friends with. What you've bought. I like the anonymity of living in town." And that's what they did. They rented a two-bedroom apartment an hour from the reserve in a nearby town and settled down to a warm domestic life. And during their entire married life, he had never mentioned a possible change of heart. Until now. He was becoming so different. Deep down inside she knew . . .

There he was!! On television. Or a little piece of him. Somewhere several hundred miles due east, near a little French-Canadian town, beside a Mohawk community, stood an Ojibway personal banking officer. Lisa saw him, from a distance, smoking as he talked with a warrior standing beside a structure officials had called the treatment centre. He was smoking again. He had picked it up in university to handle the stress of getting his MBA, and within two years of marriage, she had managed to convince him, as she liked to put it, to give it up. It was the only time, Lisa was convinced, she ever came close to the N-word: nagging. But it was a worthy cause, for both of them—second-hand smoke and all that. Especially someday if they had kids. And here he was, the whole country watching, puffing on a cigarette. Probably an Export A large . . . if she remembered correctly.

She couldn't get a good view of him, the cameraman was too far away; but one thing she was sure of—for a millisecond, a heartbeat even, she thought it was Donnelly. Lisa was almost sure of it and it took her breath away. The slouch, the hair, the head leaning to the side—all Donnelly trademarks. But even at this distance, she saw, underneath the jean jacket, the unmistakable cut of his Calvin Klein dress shirt. Evidently there were some things Richard was reluctant to leave behind in his peculiar transformation. Around him were many Aboriginal people from many different Nations, many dressed in jeans and T-shirts, others in camouflage outfits, but there was Richard, smack dab in the middle of everything, still clinging to the feel and comfort of his precious Calvin Kleins. Definitely one of the better-dressed Natives at the barricades that day.

She didn't even know why he was there. He'd never been to Oka; they'd been to Montreal a few times, sometimes for work, sometimes for the food. He didn't really have many Mohawk friends outside of work.

And as for the political nature of the standoff, again that was more Donnelly's area. Yet there he was. And there she was, watching her ex-husband possibly endanger his life.

Granted, his growing interest in all things Aboriginally political—or, as he called it, the "Indigena politica agenda"—continually took her by surprise. But, she reasoned, there was a tremendous difference between commenting on how the lowly tomato of the Americas revolutionized Italian cuisine and supporting an armed uprising a hundred or so miles from where they had shared their lives.

A quote from Richard and Donnelly's uncle suddenly came into her mind. When she was busy trying to get Richard to give up smoking, Uncle Thomas had told her to give up. "Every man picks his own poison," he said. "You'd be surprised how many people end up dyin' because of the way they live. Even them healthy White people. I saw on the news one time, about this guy who ran a dozen miles every day, even into his sixties, keeling over and dyin' of a heart attack on his own doorstep. In his shorts and running shoes. All set to run to heaven, I guess. You can't change a man's decision.

"With some people, it's drink. Others, too much of the wrong kind of food. Still others will have women—or men—stamped on their graves. Fast cars, farming accidents, being shot by cops while robbing a bank, or even just dying alone in their rooms. In one way or another, we all pick our own poison."

She pondered his reserve wisdom for a second. "Donnelly was killed in a car accident. I don't think he picked that."

Uncle Thomas smiled a sad smile. Donnelly had been one of his favourite nephews. A lot more sociable than Richard tended to be. "Donnelly sure did love walking the roads at night. Said the crickets and the frogs reminded him he was at home, like they were singing to him. He made the decision to walk on that road. At that time of night. As he did most nights. That dark jean jacket of his didn't help."

"Maybe," Lisa responded, "but Richard's smoking sure as hell isn't my poison. If I choose my own way of dying, then I want it to be from too much loving. Not cigarette smoke." Uncle Thomas laughed at that one. He had always liked her, and she him. Sadly, one of the unfortunate after-effects of a divorce is that you don't often get the opportunity to maintain the friendships with your partner's family. The memory of Uncle Thomas brought a pang to her heart. Almost as severe as seeing Richard on the television.

The news went back to the reporter on location. The weather looked the same as outside her window, a beautiful summer day. The only thing marring it was several hundred people on the verge of killing one another. The reporter was talking about the history of Oka, and how 270 years had led up to this past month. Lisa had heard it all before; surprisingly, she had become a news junkie during the crisis, which was very unlike her. An unlikely Aboriginal expert via her circumstances. She always preferred watching the entertainment items, while Richard had obvious leanings toward the business news. Perhaps she too was changing.

God knows a divorce can do that. Often it has shaped more lives then than marriage has. Though her divorce was fairly unobtrusive. When the end finally came, after too many months of being distant and moody, she finally challenged him on it. It wasn't angry. It wasn't argumentative. It was actually civil. "Sometimes I feel like I'm on a reserve in my head, and every time you ask me what's going on, it feels like you're trying to colonize me. Again." Though she tried to comprehend, Richard's statement made absolutely no sense to her. They were married. Bonded. Sharing each other's lives. There was no "mind reserves" or "intellectual colonization" involved. After that, he said little else. And from there onward, the marriage seemed to dissolve. She quit arguing with him, and he quit caring.

Lisa always attributed the changes in him to a reaction to Donnelly's death. Something else Uncle Thomas once said came to mind: "You take something important out of a person's death, it creates a vacuum. Something will rush in to fill it, good or bad. That's why people who quit smoking usually get fat. People who quit drinking sometimes find God." Lisa didn't view Richard's new-found interest in his heritage as good or bad. Just unusual. "It's just a phase," she'd tell herself.

Earlier on, Richard had tried to bring her into his rapidly changing world. He would talk with her over breakfast about Lubicon Lake, Wounded Knee, and a variety of other Native political catchphrases that any first-year Native studies student would know. He even encouraged her to take a few Native studies classes at the university. Lisa always begged off, saying she had had enough university and was now more interested in life. Once, while attending an elders' conference, Richard had suggested they attend the evening social, but she wasn't in the mood. After two days of attending workshops, she was "all Indianed out." It was said in all innocence, originating from legitimate tiredness and cultural inundation. But after that, Richard stopped trying to connect. And she noticed.

A few months later, she brought up the subject of separation. Then divorce. Richard, in the process of applying for a new job at the Aboriginal Economic Development Corporation, nodded solemnly. They both knew it was time. Within a month, they were on to their own little lives. She moved back to the city, and he moved back to the reserve. And life carried on. She hadn't dated yet; it was way too soon, and she had a new life to establish. She didn't know much about what was happening in his life. They hadn't talked in almost four months. She heard rumours from various mutual friends, and admittedly there was the odd occasional twinge of . . . something. A poet might have called it wistfulness, a cynic nostalgia, but she preferred to call it a marital hangover. She was sure it was just a matter of time before those twinges would disappear and the hangover would dissolve, like all polite hangovers.

Then it happened. The proverbial shot heard round the Aboriginal world. July 11, 1990. The day the Sûreté du Québec stormed the encampment at Oka, determined to put an end to the Mohawk presence in the area known as the Pines. The town of Oka had long planned to bulldoze this traditional burial ground, adding an extra nine holes to an existing golf course. Protesting against this desecration, the Mohawks from the Kanesatake First Nation had occupied the land for several weeks. By the time the smoke settled that morning, there would be one dead police officer, Corporal Marcel Lemay, and the world would hear about the two sleepy little communities of Oka and Kahnasatake.

Lisa had never heard of the place. Granted, her knowledge of other Native communities was limited. She'd been to a few powwows, mostly in Otter Lake and other nearby First Nations. She was once proud of the fact that she had developed a fondness for corn soup, an Otter Lake staple. It took almost two years, but before she knew it, it had become a fixture in her powwow life. She related the experience to her discovery of the Korean delicacy known as kimchee, cabbage fermented in hot chilies. Normally, when it came to food, she instantly liked or disliked something. There was no middle ground. These were the only two things she knew of that had slowly grown on her taste buds.

This place in Quebec entered her consciousness around noon on the day it happened. She was getting ready to go to her new job, a daycare centre position that her degree in sociology made her ridiculously overqualified for. But she liked children and it was something to do. She was even considering taking a few early childhood education classes to upgrade herself. During lunch hour, the kitchen staff had the radio turned on as they were making sandwiches. Lisa was pouring glasses of orange juice when she heard the news report. At first it didn't register . . . then key words gradually made it into her working mind.

"Mohawk . . . Native . . . shooting . . . death . . ." Her ears perked up and she put the pitcher of orange juice down. The rest of the staff were surprised when she loudly shushed them to hear what was being said.

"First Nations people from all over the country have pledged support for the actions of the Kanesatake Mohawks. And publicly condemned the Sûreté du Québec and the Quebec government for its actions. Native communities across the nation have vowed to send community members and supplies to aid the besieged Mohawk village."

Over the next week, she watched what was happening in that not-so-far-away place. These were not the people she had known, married, or known through marriage; in fact, traditionally, the Mohawks and Ojibways were enemies from the days of the fur trade. Now that rivalry extended only to hockey and baseball tournaments. Like the proverbial squabbling fingers, it was OK to fight among yourselves, but when a single digit was threatened, all the fingers came together as a fist. Men and women from all over the country, from a dozen different Nations, and dozens more from the States, were flooding into Quebec to aid the Mohawks.

Lisa hadn't thought of Donnelly Spencer in months but she couldn't help thinking that was where Richard's older brother would be right now, "doing his bit for the cause." Richard no doubt would be watching the news religiously. Especially with his new-found Aboriginal conviction. It was a pity Donnelly wasn't alive any more, she thought, they would be so close now. Two peas in the indigenous pod. But then again, if Donnelly hadn't died, it's probable that Richard wouldn't have changed so much. Thus becoming, as her old psychology professor often said, "a mooty moot point."

At one point, early on in the developing confrontation, she was consuming a bowl of soup, watching intently the latest details of the standoff, wondering and fearing where this might tragically lead. Then, in the background, hidden by a dozen or so other people of Native heritage, she thought she saw a familiar face. But she couldn't be sure . . . it had happened too quickly. Too quickly for her to even be sure who it was. She tried, in her head, going down the list of every Native person she knew. Most of those she knew, almost all residents of Otter Lake, would support the Mohawks, but it was unlikely that they would actually relocate and participate in this historic civil disobedience.

The last person on her mental list, of course, was her ex-husband. At one level of her consciousness it made sense, it was the natural progression of his social awareness . . . Perhaps, Lisa theorized, the road to Oka had started with his growing belief that the Cleveland Indians and the Atlanta Braves were racist organizations. But still, another part of her found the prospect of him doing such a rash thing completely unfathomable. This was definitely not the Richard she had married. But the more Lisa thought about it, the more she became convinced that that was indeed her ex, Richard, prowling somewhere in the crowds of Oka. So convinced was she that Lisa dialled a number she hadn't dialled in months. A number that had once connected her to another life. There was no answer. Frustrated, she tried another number, in the same area code and community. Richard's mother answered, somewhat surprised to hear a voice she considered gone out of their lives, but polite enough to tell Lisa the news. Lisa's fears were confirmed. Richard was indeed mingling with the Mohawks. And now her curiosity turned to concern. Yes, they were divorced and hadn't talked in months, but she had spent eight years living with and loving the man; she knew she didn't want to see him wounded or dead, the unfortunate by-product of a police sniper's rifle—he hadn't yet picked his poison. Her hands clinched and her neck started to ache. What was Richard doing there?

In the past week Lisa had done everything a concerned wife—ex-wife—could and would do in a situation like this. She had tried to contact the treatment centre, which seemed to be the central headquarters of everything that was going on. No luck. Same with the band office. It seems they were a little too busy to worry about the rantings of a Caucasian ex-wife of one lone Ojibway amid several dozen, some even said a hundred or so, Native people milling about, apparently ready to explode. All her old friends back in Otter Lake were less help. They were just as surprised at Richard's actions. And what if she was able to contact Richard: what would she say to her ex-lover?

She wasn't sure. "Stop. Don't do what you're doing. It's dangerous. Go home." All the possible statements that came to her seemed silly. Ineffectual. Even downright melodramatic. Especially considering she was no longer really part of his life. So, seemingly impotent, she was reduced to watching television. Sometimes three or four channels at a time, trying to perfect the highest channels-per-minute ratio she could devise while slowly destroying the channel changer in her hand. She even called in sick three times that week, putting her employment at the daycare centre in danger, especially considering she'd been working there for less than a month.

Did she still love him? Was that the reason she watched the television coverage so feverishly? Possibly, even probably. Lisa had never stopped loving him, she had just stopped being in love with him. A big and distinct difference, but these things happen. She'd even read it in a newspaper article. Still, would every ex-wife spend hours, days even, watching the television in the almost hopeless attempt to catch glimpses of her one-time husband? Unlikely. Maybe different forces, other then simple concern, were at work here, ones that she refused to recognize. If he walked out of Oka today and into her new apartment, would she take him back? Improbable, even unlikely. But there was definitely something about those fleeting glimpses, those fleeting and maddening images of him, somewhere on the other side of the insanity.

Maybe it was her own heritage that was making itself known. The Irish were known for their obsessive behaviour. Look at their own intense connection to the lowly potato. And summing up her life to that point, here was a woman of Irish descent eagerly watching an Aboriginal uprising on television, praying she could grab a peek of her ex-husband somewhere in the multitudes. She'd combined the two heritages and become a couch potato. Her own bizarre and dark mental comparison made her laugh out loud. Alone in her apartment. With a cold cup of tea sitting on the coffee table. Beside a second one.

Several times Lisa told herself she was being silly. Nothing she was doing was helping the situation. It was possible to go to work and get on with her life, and still care about what was happening to Richard . . . Richard who hated camping. Not showering on a daily basis. Confrontation. Again, she asked herself, what was Richard doing there?

And most recently, the Canadian army had been called in. Lisa wasn't sure if this was a good thing or not. Yet another potential match lit near the powder keg, or possibly the famed Canadian peacekeepers might actually be able to keep the peace. She had an uncle who had been in the army years ago, the famous Van Doos, in fact. The stories he had told Lisa about his service had been tales of valour, brotherhood, patriotism. Yet there was something definitely ominous about this development.

The army now encircled the whole community, severely restricting anybody and anything that wanted to cross yet another imaginary line imposed on the Native people by representatives of the government. And that imaginary circle kept getting smaller and smaller gradually choking the life out of the community, like a noose. There was a palpable tension in the air, like a bad smell; a rumour that at some point, the Mohawks and their allies would try to push that line back. After all, one spokesperson said, that's what this whole thing is about. "Being pushed beyond a reasonable limit."

According to some of the things Donnelly had told her, relations between Aboriginal people and cops were often a tempestuous affair. Years ago she thought just maybe he had been exaggerating things. And sometimes he would say things to playfully provoke her. Now she wasn't so sure. She had seen things in recent weeks that had puzzled, then scared her. Now Lisa could only imagine what the army had brought into the whole damn thing. This was Canada, these things weren't supposed to happen here! Tanks on streets, rows and rows of guns facing one another, barricades . . . She couldn't help wondering if this would help or hurt the separatist cause currently making the rounds yet again in *la belle province*. It seemed everybody was angry with everybody.

Reflex action made her leg knock over one of the cold cups of tea when the phone rang. Very few people knew her new number, other than those at work. Lisa's divorce and relocation had cost her quite a few of her and Richard's former friends, and with the new job, and the Oka crisis, she had had precious little time to carve out a new social scene. They were running some background footage on the television, stuff she'd already seen a dozen times, and Richard wasn't in any of the shots, so she answered the phone.

"Hello. Lisa speaking." She thought she could hear wind in the background. Who'd be calling her from a pay phone?

"Lisa? It's Richard."

With those three words, her present life, her past life, and the events in a far-off small community merged within the confines of her brain with a sudden thud that racked her body. It was Richard. She recognized the voice. And he had called her. Why?

She struggled to respond, again fearful of sounding silly or confused. "Richard ... Why ... What ... You phoned me ... ?!"

No luck this time.

"I called home. They said you were trying to get a hold of me. I guess you've heard that I'm at Kanesatake."

In her mind's eye she could see him standing at a phone booth, no doubt one of those damned cigarettes in his right hand, his left cradling the phone. He sounded tired but was probably as nervous as she was. A life that was once together, then torn apart, can make small talk kind of difficult. Lisa chose her next words carefully.

"Richard, what are you doing there? This is so out of character for you. You might get hurt. Or worse." She had found her phone voice again. Lisa could hear him taking a drag from the cigarette, and before he could respond, she blurted out, "And you've started smoking again. Do you want to kill yourself?" There was a pause, then a hearty, familiar staccato laugh. Then it occurred to her what she had said. It was her turn to laugh. They laughed together, for the first time in many months. And it felt good. The uncomfortable part of the past year seemed to drain away.

"No, I don't want to kill myself, but thank you for asking. They're light cigarettes. That should count for something ... " He paused, then added as an afterthought, " ... Mom." Again she laughed, the tension of the last week easing up.

"Are you OK?"

Lisa could almost see him nodding as he responded. "Haven't slept much in weeks. Between the helicopters, the loudspeakers and bullhorns, sirens ... this is a very noisy place. I'd kill for some earplugs. I've had a headache since the whole thing began. But the funny thing is the trees look so quiet and calm ... That's the contradiction in this place. Could sure use some clean clothes too, but other than that, and more frequent showers ... I'm surviving. Is that why you phoned?"

"No, I want to know why the hell you're there." Direct and to the point.

"That's a good question. Been thinking about that myself. You find you have plenty of reflecting time while looking over a barbed wire fence. And I think I've come up with a good answer." For a moment the sound of his voice was drowned out by a whoosh of sound that flooded across the phone lines. It was like a gush of white noise, making her cringe. "Richard? Richard! What was that? Are you there?"

The sound quickly receded. "Yeah, sorry, that was a chopper going overhead. Occupational hazard around here. There are choppers, APCs, tanks, you wouldn't believe the stuff that's happening here. Your tax money at work."

"Quit trying to be funny. There are guns pointed at you."

"Yeah, I noticed. It's not the Bahamas, that's for sure. I remember the days when getting our taxes in on time was my big worry. But don't fret about me. I'm exactly where I want to be, Lisa."

"This has something to do with Donnelly, doesn't it?" she asked.

Somewhere in the background, she could hear voices. Men talking. A woman nearby laughing. All that was missing was the sound of children playing and it would be like Otter Lake. But it wasn't like Otter Lake. This was Oka, and there was a dead police officer, and several hundred guns, half of them pointed in her ex-husband's direction.

"I just wanted to make sure you were OK. That's all. Divorce or no divorce, that's allowed, isn't it?" No response. "Hello, Richard . . . ?"

"Yeah, I'm here. Look, I can't talk long. There's not enough phones around here, so there's a lineup. And we think they're tapped anyways. Lisa, I'm here because I want to be here. I want to make a difference. Recently I've had trouble convincing myself that I can do that in a bank. Granted, all I'm doing here is making big pots of soup. But it's something. It makes me feel good. And I know Donnelly would have been happy."

"Yes, Donnelly would. But you're not Donnelly. You're Richard. I saw what they did to that Spudwrench guy. They beat that warrior to a pulp. I saw it on television, Richard. You're in danger. Get the hell out of there."

Richard was silent. "I know. His real name is Randy Horne and he's a good guy. He didn't deserve what happened to him. None of these people do. Most of the people here are expecting to die here, Lisa. You can feel the fear here, and the anger. I can't walk out. Yes, I'm scared. I don't think the SQ or the army know the difference between a Mohawk and an Ojibway, and I don't think they'd bother to ask. But that doesn't change anything."

Lisa was running out of arguments. Richard wasn't listening to reason. "Richard . . ."

"I don't think I ever told you this, but a long time ago, I was supposed to be called Donnelly originally. And he was supposed to be Richard. When he was three, our parents changed his name to Donnelly."

This definitely was news to Lisa, but she was still unsure how that fit into the whole picture of what was happening on television and in their lives. "No, I didn't know that. But what—?"

"My parents had decided to name him Richard after my mother's father, because he was sick and she wanted him to know, out of respect, that his name was passed down to their first-born. But, surprise, he got better, and my other grandfather started getting sick. It looked unlikely that my mother would have any more children so, boom, a decision was made to change my brother's name to Donnelly while my father's father was still alive, and then figure out what to do afterwards. But two months after he died, my mother got pregnant with me, and they decided to avoid all the paperwork and just name me Richard. Her father didn't mind, as long as somebody had his name. Quite a story, huh?"

Somewhere out there in what she considered the darkness of Richard's logic, Lisa struggled to find a light that would show her the way. But it eluded her. Instead, she grew more confused with the growing explanation.

"Donnelly would have been here. He was a better Indian than I was."

"It's not a contest," she answered harshly. She didn't like the direction this conversation was going in.

"No, it's not. It's life. And life is better than death. You're either part of the problem or part of the solution, as the saying goes."

"And being part of the solution involves making soup and having guns pointed at you? There have got to be other solutions. There are always alternatives. Don't let Donnelly kill you." She was practically yelling at the television.

Again silence and the far-off sound of a police siren. "Don't worry. He won't. He'll keep me alive. And . . . there are other reasons . . ."

His continuous vagueness was upsetting her. "What kind of other reasons can justify you walking into a war zone?! There are people who care for you, you know."

"Yes, I know. I know that very much. But I'm just way too tired to get into all this."

"You've never touched a gun in your life. You haven't even been in a fist fight since high school. There are other people who can do this! People who know how to fight for their causes. Richard . . . you know you're out of place there." Her tone softened. She really did care, it seemed, more than an ex-wife should.

Again, male voices in the background. Wind across the receiver. And finally Richard again. "Thank you. But there are things happening here that don't involve you. If you were here, you'd understand."

"Richard—" she began.

"Goodbye, Lisa." And with that, he hung up. The finality of the phone click startled her. The Richard she knew was gone. All she was left with was a dial tone, and Peter Mansbridge on the television. Without thought, she returned the phone to its base and leaned back on the couch, trying to make sense of what had just happened. There were motivations in Richard's mind that she couldn't fathom. And she didn't know what to do . . .

Part of Lisa wanted to jump in her Passat and drive into the next province, and try to shake some sense into him, though her conscious mind told her she'd have a heck of a time making it through the police barricades. Another part of her mind wondered if she really wanted to do that, or was it just an impulsive reaction: a sense that she needed to save him, like a mother protecting a son. He did, after all, jokingly refer to her as "Mom." Maybe she should just turn off the television and go to bed.

Nothing in the world, or at least her world, could change what had happened, and what was happening. And as her mother used to say, "A good night's sleep can solve a lot of problems."

Then, just as quickly as Richard's phone call had ended, she saw him once again. He was walking in the distance, toward the general direction of the camera. But somebody was with him, walking beside him. A woman. A Native woman. And he was holding hands with her.

She used the last of the energy in the battery to turn the television off.

Acknowledgements

This book is the result of the combined efforts, over two years, of an outstanding group of organizations and individuals. The *Our Story* Advisory Committee that included Paul Chartrand, University of Saskatchewan, Charlie Coffey, Royal Bank of Canada, Kim Crockatt, the Nunavut Literary Society, Dwight Dorey, Congress of Aboriginal Peoples, and Kelly Lendsay, Aboriginal Human Resources Development Council of Canada provided invaluable advice and help in selecting the participating authors.

The evolution of this book from a concept to final publication owes much to leadership and financial support of Enbridge Canada and the Canadian Studies Programme of the Department of Canadian Heritage, and the valued counsel of Bruce Westwood of Westwood Creative Artists. These organizations should be commended for their commitment to bringing Aboriginal culture and storytelling to the Canadian public in new and innovative ways.

The actual work of putting together *Our Story* fell to a tight-knit team. Alison Faulknor of the Dominion Institute was the driving force behind this project. From assembling the book's stellar advisory committee to working individually with the authors, Alison artfully guided *Our Story* to fruition. Maya Mavjee and Amy Black of Doubleday Canada enthusiastically embraced this project from the outset. Together, they provided invaluable help to the authors and gave the entire collection coherence and direction.

Finally, the authors. All of us associated with this project owe a great debt of gratitude to each of the writers who contributed to this volume. Told with skill, passion, and understanding, their stories are an important reminder of the power and confidence of contemporary Aboriginal culture and the role First Nations will continue to play in shaping Canada's past and future.

Rudyard Griffiths
The Dominion Institute

About the Contributors

TANTOO CARDINAL is a renowned actor whose many film and television credits include *Dances With Wolves*, *Black Robe*, *Legends of the Fall*, "Lakota Woman: Siege at Wounded Knee," and "Tecumseh: The Last Warrior." Among her many distinctions Tantoo Cardinal is the recipient of a National Aboriginal Achievement Award. She was born in Fort McMurray, Alberta, in 1950, and now lives in Calgary.

ADRIENNE CLARKSON has had a distinguished career in broadcasting, the arts, and the public service. A noted writer, she has contributed many articles to newspapers and magazines in Canada and is the author of three books. She served as Ontario's Agent General in Paris from 1982–1987, promoting the province's interests in France and Italy. She holds numerous honorary degrees from Canadian and foreign universities, and was appointed an Officer of the Order of Canada in 1992. Adrienne Clarkson became Canada's 26th Governor General in 1999, the first immigrant and second woman to hold this office.

Rudyard Griffiths is the founder and the executive director of the Dominion Institute—a national charity dedicated to the promotion of history and citizenship. He holds an honours Bachelor of Arts from the University of Toronto and a Masters of Philosophy from Emmanuel College, Cambridge. Rudyard Griffiths edited *The Great Questions of Canada* and *The LaFontaine-Baldwin Lectures,* and was a contributor to the Doubleday publications *Story of a Nation* and *Passages to Canada.* He writes regularly on the themes of Canadian history and identity for *The Globe and Mail,* CanWest newspapers, and *Maclean's.* He lives and works in Toronto.

Tomson Highway, born near Maria Lake, Manitoba, in 1951, now divides his time between Banyuls-sur-mer, France, and Ontario. An accomplished musician, he studied to be a concert pianist before coming to prominence as a playwright with the award-winning *The Rez Sisters* (1986) and *Dry Lips Oughta Move to Kapuskasing* (1989). His novel, *Kiss of the Fur Queen,* was published in 1998. Tomson Highway helped establish Native Earth Performing Arts, Canada's first Aboriginal theatre company.

Basil Johnston is a writer, storyteller, language teacher, and scholar. He was born in 1929 on the Parry Island Indian Reserve in Ontario. As a fluent speaker, scholar, and teacher of the Anishinaubae language he is also a sought after translator. He is the author of twenty books, including *Moose Meat and Wild Rice* (1987) and *Crazy Dave* (1999). Basil Johnston is a member of the Order of Ontario and has received a National Aboriginal Achievement Award and a Honourary Doctorate from the University of Toronto.

Thomas King's writing has been widely published to great acclaim. He is the author of numerous books including *Green Grass, Running Water* (1993), *Truth and Bright Water* (1999), and *The Truth About Stories: A Native Narrative* (2003) based on his Massey Lecture of the same title, which won the Trillium Book Award. He has twice been nominated for the Governor

General's Award. His popular CBC series, *The Dead Dog Café*, is being adapted as an animated television series. He is currently a Professor of English at the University of Guelph, Ontario.

BRIAN MARACLE is the author of *Crazywater, Native Voices on Addiction and Recovery* (1993) and *Back on the Rez* (1996). A former journalist for CBC Radio and *The Globe and Mail*, Brian Maracle now lives on the Six Nations Grand River Territory near Brantford, Ontario, where he teaches the Mohawk language to adults and is active in the Mohawk Longhouse.

LEE MARACLE was born in North Vancouver, B.C. She is the author of a number of critically acclaimed literary works including *Bobbi Lee* (1990), *Ravensong* (1995), *I Am Woman* (1996), *Bent Box* (2000), *Daughters Are Forever* (2002), and *Will's Garden* (2002). She is also the co-editor of several anthologies, including *My Home As I Remember* (1997). She is currently the Distinguished Visiting Professor of Canadian Culture at Western Washington University.

JOVETTE MARCHESSAULT, novelist, playwright, and sculptor, was born in 1938 in Montreal, Quebec. Her books include *Mother of the Grass* (1988), *White Pebbles in the Dark Forests* (1990), and *The Magnificent Voyage of Emily Carr* (1992). She is the winner of the Prix France-Québec, the Grand Prix Litéraire Journal de Montréal, and the Grand Prix Littéraire de la ville de Sherbrooke, and the Governor General's Award.

RACHEL A. QITSUALIK writes regular columns on Inuit culture for *Native Journal* and *News/North*. Her writing has appeared in numerous publications including *Indian Country Today*, *Nunatsiaq News*, Rabble.com, *Up Here Magazine*, *Aboriginal Voices*, and the *Ring of Ice* anthology. She is currently working on a personal anthology and a novel. She lives in Nunavut.

DREW HAYDEN TAYLOR is best known for his plays, including *Toronto at Dreamer's Rock/ Education is our Right*, which won the Chalmers

Canadian Play Award in 1992, *The Bootlegger Blues* (1990), which won the Canadian Authors Association Literary Award for Best Drama, and *Only Drunks and Children Tell the Truth* (1996), which won a Dora Mavor Moore Award. He is the author of *Fearless Warriors* (1998). He is also a regular contributor to numerous newspapers and magazines, a screenwriter, and documentary director.